POISON INK

Also by Christopher Golden

FOR TEENS AND YOUNG READERS

The Body of Evidence Series

Body Bags
Thief of Hearts
Soul Survivor
Meets the Eye
Head Games
Skin Deep (with Rick Hautala)
Burning Bones (with Rick Hautala)
Brain Trust (with Rick Hautala)
Last Breath (with Rick Hautala)
Throat Culture (with Rick Hautala)

The Prowlers Quartet

Prowlers
Prowlers: Laws of Nature
Prowlers: Predator and Prey
Prowlers: Wild Things

The Hollow Series
(with Ford Lytle Gilmore)

Horseman
Drowned
Mischief
Enemies

The OutCast Series
(with Thomas E. Sniegoski)

The Un-Magician
Dragon Secrets
Ghostfire
Wurm War

Force Majeure (with Thomas E. Sniegoski)

POISON INK

CHRISTOPHER
GOLDEN

Delacorte Press

Published by Delacorte Press
an imprint of Random House Children's Books
a division of Random House, Inc.
New York

Visit us on the Web! www.randomhouse.com/teens

Educators and librarians, for a variety of teaching tools, visit us at
www.randomhouse.com/teachers

Library of Congress Cataloging-in-Publication Data is available upon request.

ISBN: 978-0-385-73483-7 (trade)—ISBN: 978-0-385-90481-0 (glb)

The text of this book is set in 12-point Goudy.
Printed in the United States of America
10 9 8 7 6 5 4 3 2 1
First Edition

For my nephew, Jack Golden—
welcome to the world, little man.

ACKNOWLEDGMENTS

Huge thanks are due to my editor, Stephanie Lane, who got it right away and kept me on track. My gratitude always to Connie and the kids for providing love and home. Thanks also to Tom Sniegoski, Tim Lebbon, and Liesa Abrams, for listening, and to the Vicious Circle for much-needed nights out.

PROLOGUE

Pieces of her are broken.

Every bump or crack in the road jostles her, shooting needles of pain into her skull and back and searing her side where some of her ribs have given way. She breathes through her teeth, and her pain turns into a strange whistling.

A paramedic floats into view above her. With a warm, damp cloth, he wipes some of the blood from her face. Twenty-something, skin like mahogany wood, a ridiculously good-looking guy. She feels almost embarrassed to have him looking at her bloody, swollen face.

"You're going to be just fine, honey," he says.

His voice sounds tinny, buzzing. Somehow that goes well with the coppery taste of her own blood in her mouth.

The ambulance hits a pothole. Pain sings through her, and the shadows at the edges of her vision loom up and swallow her, dragging her down into unconsciousness.

When next she opens her eyes, the paramedic and the ambulance are gone. Her eyelids flutter open, and she sees a woman leaning over her, hair tied back, eyes grim behind wire-rimmed glasses. When the woman notices her patient is awake, she smiles.

"Hello, Samantha. I'm Dr. Morrissey. You're pretty banged up, but we're going to take care of you here. Nothing we can't fix, okay?"

Her face hurts so much that she doesn't even try to speak, only gives the slightest of nods.

"Great," Dr. Morrissey says. She turns to someone else, a nurse maybe, and rattles off instructions in a curt voice. Activity buzzes around them. Then the doctor glances back at her. "Oh, cute tattoo by the way."

"Tattoo?"

She recognizes this new voice, though the room has begun to blur around her again, the shadows gathering at the corners of her eyes.

"Oh my God," her mother says from somewhere nearby. "Where did she get a tattoo? Sammi?"

Her mom appears above her, looking down, her face contorted with worry.

"Who did this to you, honey? Who hurt you?"

The question hurts more than her broken bones. Her mother keeps talking—to her and to the doctors and nurses—and this time when the darkness creeps up on her, she welcomes it.

1

On the last Friday night of summer, Sammi Holland and the girls went downtown in search of ice cream. They planned to meet at Krueger's Flatbread for pizza beforehand, a necessary preamble to the main event: an utter debauchery of swirl-ins and sprinkles and fudge sauce at England's MicroCreamery. Afterward, the five of them would wander Washington Street, peeking in the windows of the candle shop, the art galleries, and the bohemian café on the corner, ending up at Cruel and Unusual Books. No way were they getting out of there without hitting the bookshop. Sammi could be very persuasive.

Downtown Covington didn't draw a lot of teenagers. Most of their classmates from Covington High School would be at the mall tonight. But Sammi and the girls just weren't the sort who hung out at the mall.

Unless they were going to the movies, Sammi and her

friends steered clear of the Merrimack River Walk. The long, outdoor strip mall had been built less than ten years before, complete with movie megaplex, massive bookstore, and tons of chain clothing stores. On Friday and Saturday nights, hordes of high school kids from Haverhill, Methuen, Jameson, and other nearby towns roved the sidewalks along the River Walk in gaggles, half of them talking on their cell phones or texting their friends who hadn't come along. Like the "main drag" in old movies and TV shows, the River Walk was all about seeing and being seen—half mating ritual and half dance of supremacy.

Sammi had no interest in that kind of poseur crap, and neither did the girls she hung around with. The five of them had been oddballs and loners all their lives, until they had found each other. Now they were like sisters, and all was right with the world. Or mostly right. So tonight Sammi walked along a stretch of cobblestoned sidewalk on Washington Street with Caryn Adams.

"Come on," she said, hooking her arm through Caryn's and dragging her away from the window of a closed gallery. "We're late."

Caryn fell into step beside her, grinning. "You're just lucky that place isn't open. Then we'd be really late."

"Aren't you hungry? I'm starving."

"Haven't you ever heard of the 'starving artist'?" Caryn said. "Kind of comes with the territory."

"Yeah, right. All those fashionistas who design dresses for the red carpet crowd, they're starving artists. If they're only eating carrot sticks, it isn't because they can't afford a decent meal."

"No argument. But first they had to suffer. They had to get down in the trenches and fight it out with all the other ambitious artists."

Sammi laughed. "You make it sound like war."

Caryn glanced at her, the fading summer sunshine gleaming on her caramel skin. "There are all kinds of wars."

Sammi blinked. She knew Caryn wanted a career in fashion desperately. Of all of her friends—of anyone she knew—Caryn had the most purpose and drive. But sometimes it verged on obsession.

"You must chill. Seriously. One of these days we'll watch the Oscars together and they'll ask, 'Who are you wearing?' and the answer will be 'Caryn Adams.' I know this. We all know it. But between now and then, you really have to chill. School starts on Tuesday, and tonight's supposed to be about just being together."

Caryn softened. "You're right. *That* me, the one who was getting all tense? Just sent her home. Girl is not allowed to come out tonight."

Sammi smiled. "Good."

Grinning, they turned off of Washington Street into Railroad Square. Sammi and Caryn were roughly the same height—five feet three inches—and close enough in size that they could share clothes. The spaghetti-strap top Caryn had on had come from Sammi's closet, while Sammi had pulled on a couple of tank tops, going for the layered

5

look. Caryn wore sneakers, but Sammi stuck with the strappy sandals she'd worn most of the summer.

They walked alongside the concrete wall of the elevated train platform toward the old brick factory building that housed Krueger's Flatbread. Most of Covington had been mills and factories once upon a time, like so many cities built north of Boston on the Merrimack River. In the past few years, the downtown had undergone serious renovation, the old buildings gutted and reclaimed for apartments, offices, and storefront shops. Much cooler than any mall.

"My stomach's growling," Caryn said.

"So much for the starving artist."

As they entered the parking lot, Sammi saw a trio of people standing at the bottom of the stairs leading up to Krueger's front door. Behind them, an old, beat-up BMW sat idling. The headlights were on. Summer nights had started arriving a little sooner this late in August, and while the sky was still blue, the sun had begun to sink low on the horizon. Between the train platform and the old factory buildings, the shadows were deep.

"There's T.Q.," Caryn said.

Sammi had already seen her. At five foot nine and with long, red hair, T.Q.—Simone Deveaux—was hard to miss.

"Who's with her?" she asked.

"Looks like Jill Barbieri and that Regan bitch, what's her name?"

"Crap. Isn't this why we didn't go to the mall?" Sammi said.

Jill and Regan were seniors at Covington High, both of them on the girls' basketball team and obsessed with their own wonderfulness. Some girls started out fine and were transformed by high school into divas, so that by the time they became seniors they perceived themselves as the elite. Others arrived fully formed. Born bitchy.

Without a word to one another, Sammi and Caryn sped up. T.Q. saw them coming, and the relief that swept over her face made Sammi want to throw her arms around her. T.Q. had an ethereal beauty that drew plenty of attention, but she hated every minute of it. A shy, quiet girl, she had shared her thoughts only with her journal until she had made friends with Sammi and the others last year. As a sophomore, she'd practically run the school paper, and this year she'd be editor. At Covington, the people who even knew her name called her Simone, but her friends called her T.Q.—for "tall, quiet one"—and she loved it. No one had ever been interested enough in her to give her a nick-name before.

Jill and Regan could screw with anyone else, but T.Q. was off limits.

"—want to kiss me, don't you?" Regan said as Caryn and Sammi hurried over.

T.Q. ignored the question.

"What's going on, Jill?" Caryn said, striding up to the senior girl. "I didn't think they let the five-dollar hookers work this corner anymore."

With the car running and the two girls just standing there, Sammi finally put it together. Their boyfriends must

7

be inside, picking up pizzas to go, and they'd stayed out here to harass T.Q.

"Oh, look," Jill said, "your girlfriends are here. It's a lesbian lovefest tonight."

Caryn balled up her fists and started for her. Sammi grabbed her arm and held her back. Jill and Regan both flinched. Caryn had a Jewish mother at home who would have tortured her with guilt for a year if she ever actually hit anybody, but the senior girls didn't know that. They saw an angry black girl, and their presumptions made them nervous. Jill and Regan were shallow and stupid, but Caryn seemed pleased that they'd lost their cruel grins. Her temper had gotten her into trouble before, but Sammi figured Jill and Regan had earned a tongue-lashing.

"You want to look for some girl love, check out your own locker room," Caryn said. "Never know who's eyeing you in the shower while you're soaping up."

Regan wore a look of horror.

T.Q. covered her mouth, trying not to laugh.

"I guess you'd know, though, wouldn't you?" Jill retorted with a sneer.

Sammi shook her head in pity. "I can't imagine anyone wanting to see you naked, Jill, guy or girl. Maybe that's why you've gotta ride Simone, because you know once a guy sees her, he's not giving you a second look."

Jill rolled her eyes. "Oh, please."

But Sammi could see that she'd hit a nerve. Caryn and Regan were staring at each other as if at any moment they might start rumbling around the parking lot.

The door at the top of the stairs opened and two decent-looking guys came out, one of them carrying two pizza boxes and the other with a paper bag of Krueger's takeout. Sammi didn't know his name, but she recognized the pizza boy as Jill's boyfriend, a college freshman.

"Hey," Sammi said, friendly as could be. "I know you guys."

"You do?" Pizza Boy said.

Sammi smiled. "Totally. You graduated last year. In fact, my friend Simone over here? She had a mad crush on you."

Pizza Boy glanced over at T.Q., and a wolfish smile spread across his face. He nodded once. "Really?"

The fury on Jill Barbieri's face was glorious to behold. She flushed red, and her lips pulled back like a snarling dog.

Sammi grinned, took T.Q. by the hand, and led her up the stairs, purposely brushing past the guys as she went.

"You have a nice night, now," Caryn said sweetly, and then she followed them.

As they stepped into Krueger's and the door swung shut behind them, they could hear Jill yelling at her boyfriend. The three girls turned to look at each other and started laughing.

"Can I help you?" the fortyish hostess asked with a be-mused grin.

Caryn cleared her throat. "Sorry. We're meeting some friends here. The reservation's under my name—Adams."

The hostess glanced at the podium where the map of the tables lay, then nodded for them to go in. "They're in the back, around behind the bar."

"Thank you," Sammi said.

The fans were spinning lazily on the ceiling and the air conditioner hummed. It felt chilly inside the restaurant, but fortunately Letty and Katsuko were sitting near the blazing brick oven where the flatbread pizza was cooked. Katsuko's hair shone damply, and Sammi figured she'd just come from swimming, getting ready for competition once the school year started. As they crossed to the table, Letty Alecia smiled and got up to hug each of them. Her milk chocolate eyes were bright and wide, her best feature, and she always dressed conservatively—even more so than Katsuko, whose parents were very careful about what they let her wear. Katsuko came off as arrogant sometimes, mainly because she was. Her parents had raised her with a superior air, and though she could be judgmental at times, ever since Sammi had met her she'd been doing her best to fight her inner snob.

Jill and Regan teased them all about being lesbians because they hung out with Letty. She had come out the year before. Las Reinas—the name the Puerto Rican girls at Covington High had given themselves—hadn't exactly ostracized her. They still spoke to her, still looked out for her as a girl from the neighborhood. But they didn't go out of their way to include her anymore. Letty never showed it, but Sammi felt certain that beneath her smile, she'd been hurt by Las Reinas.

Sammi had always been a floater. Not a loner; that was something completely different. A loner spent all her time by herself, grew uncomfortable in crowds, and got totally squirmy in the spotlight. Sammi had never been that. She got along with almost everyone, floating from group to group but never quite fitting in. T.Q. had coined the expression "No-Cats" to describe kids like Sammi, impossible to slot into one of the categories everyone seemed to want to put teenagers into. It wasn't just her classmates at Covington who did it. Everyone did. Teachers, parents, coaches. Everyone.

Sammi had friends among the jocks, the geeks, the potheads, the skaters, the cheerleaders, the Shop-Boys, and Las Reinas. Maybe "friends" was too strong a word. After elementary school, she had never been tight with anyone, really. It wasn't something she had become on purpose, it was just a natural evolution that started in kindergarten and steadily grew until it reached full bloom when high school began.

In her heart, she had wished things could be different but had fully expected to spend her life that way, without any close friendships. And then, during sophomore year, the group had slowly begun to coalesce. Letty had come out and Las Reinas had begun to distance themselves from her. Sammi had always gotten along well with her and had made it a point to sit with her in the cafeteria. T.Q. had done a profile in the school paper on student artists, covering Caryn's art and designs and Sammi's music—she had played one afternoon to entertain the shoppers at Cruel and Unusual Books. One day, they had all ended up at a table together for lunch.

It had just felt right.

They all had their faults, of course, but who didn't? Sammi found a kinship with the other girls that she had never realized was possible, and unlike with most groups, it wasn't because of what they had in common. They shared little beyond how different they were from most of their classmates. Their common trait was that they had nothing in common with anyone. And then they found many things they shared—thoughts and experiences and emotions, hopes and ambitions—and the bond became unbreakable.

"Sorry we're late!" Caryn said, sitting down.

"We were about to call the police," Katsuko said.

"Seriously," Letty said. "T.Q. went out to look for you, and I thought someone, like, kidnapped all three of you."

Sammi slid into a chair across from her. "Nah. Caryn just has to window-shop at the art galleries."

Despite the opening Letty had given them, no one brought up the incident in the parking lot. They all loved her too much.

"So this is it," Sammi said. "The year we rule the school."

Katsuko shot her a dubious look. "What, did we skip a year and nobody told me? We're juniors."

Sammi shrugged. "Yeah, but the seniors are all gonna be totally focused on getting into college or just getting out of high school, they're not going to be paying attention. Give them a month, maybe, and they'll abdicate power. Juniors are the top of the food chain."

"Maybe some juniors are," T.Q. said. "Something tells

me I'm not ruling anything. I don't even think I'm part of the food chain."

Letty took a sip from her glass. "Nah, Sammi's right." She smiled mischievously. "It's gonna be a hell of a year."

Saturday morning, Sammi and her mother packed up the car and drove to Kingston State Park in New Hampshire, only half an hour's drive from home. The other girls were all headed off with their families for the balance of the weekend, Katsuko all the way down to Cape Cod and the others to various spots along the coast of Maine. Labor Day weekend offered the last taste of summer, and everyone wanted to savor it. But Sammi's father had to work, so there would be no hotel rooms, no visits to relatives, no bodysurfing for her. Just a few hours at the lake with her mom.

Sammi didn't mind. Her mother had mood swings and a strict sense of propriety, and she tended to give even the most casual acquaintances the third degree, making them uneasy. In spite of all that, Linda Holland could be very cool. Sammi's friends all loved her mother, and Linda made them feel very much at home when they visited.

Until recently. Things had been tense at home over the past few months. Sammi had a feeling her father could have avoided working today if he had really wanted to, but instead, he'd wanted to avoid his wife. It made Sammi sad, so she tried not to dwell on it. She'd always been much closer to her mother than to her father, which seemed sort of inevitable, since her father wasn't around much. Her dad could be charming and funny when he wanted to be, but much of the time, it seemed like his mind was somewhere else. Her mother had told her a thousand times that it had nothing to do with her, but Sammi couldn't help thinking she'd disappointed her father somehow. Otherwise, why didn't he make more of an effort to be home with them, to act the way Sammi thought a dad was supposed to act?

Lately he'd been more distant than ever. But at least one good thing had come from that: at a time when a lot of kids she knew were doing their best to avoid their parents entirely, Sammi and her mother had become closer than ever.

Today was the perfect example. A picnic at the lake, lazing around together, a splash in the water—it had all sounded great when her mom had brought it up. Sammi knew it was just what her mother needed, especially with the escalating tension at home. So they chatted like girl-friends and drank lemonade and ate mozzarella and tomato sandwiches on focaccia bread from the cooler.

After lunch, Linda sat in her beach chair reading a novel by Michael Connelly. Sammi had brought her guitar along. She would never have lugged the acoustic to the beach, but the lakeshore—a hundred yards of sand and dirt—didn't have as much blowing grit and wind as the beach. They sat just at the edge of the shadows thrown by the row of tall trees so they could retreat into the shade if they wanted to. The lake was crowded, but not nearly as busy as the beaches would be today. Radios played, but only distantly, and none so loud that they distracted Sammi.

On the edge of her chair, she sat with her acoustic across her thighs and strummed one of her favorite old Jack Johnson songs, "Banana Pancakes." When her fingers were limber and her memory had caught up to the rhythm of the song, she sang along quietly.

"Can't you see that it's just raining? Ain't no need to go outside."

The irony made her smile.

No rain today. The sky stretched into the distance, forever blue, and the sun beat down on them. Thankfully, the humidity that had lingered through much of the summer was gone, and there was a breeze off the lake. Sammi loved the waterfall noise of the leaves rustling on the trees.

Worried about the sun, she dragged her chair into the shade, putting distance between herself and her mother. Wrapped up in her book, Mom didn't even seem to notice. Most everyone at the lake had slathered himself with sunblock and was enjoying the fry time. Sammi preferred the shade, preferred to be out of the spotlight. Her guitar brought her plenty of attention, but she did not seek it. If people wandered over, drawn by a shared love of music, they were welcome. But guys who just wanted to flirt with the cute blond girl in cutoffs and a bikini top could ogle her from a distance.

"Play something else," a voice said.

Sammi looked up. A guy stood just at the edge of the shade, dark hair and sleek, muscled body dripping from the water. He pushed a hand through his hair, shedding water, and smiled.

Cute. Very cute.

"What do you want to hear?"

He shrugged. "Whatever you feel like playing."

Good answer, Sammi thought.

Her fingers danced along the frets as she picked out the opening notes of Amanda Marshall's "Love Is My Witness." Keeping her voice low, not wanting to put on a show for the whole lake, she started to sing.

His smile brightened. Sammi felt warm, even in the shade. Even with the breeze.

Curious, a few other guys and two girls, apparently all friends, wandered over to listen. They kept back from the shade, remaining in the sun, arms thrown over one another. One of the guys twisted around, tripping his buddy, and tossed him on the ground. They laughed and started to wrestle.

Sammi couldn't help rolling her eyes. She stopped singing, but her fingers kept playing the song.

"What's your name?" Cute Boy asked.

She switched tunes, playing a bluesy little run. "My mother always told me not to talk to strangers."

"I'm Adam."

With a look of shock, she put her fingers over the strings to halt the music. "You're kidding. My name's Eve."

He blinked and for a second almost believed her. Then Sammi smiled and he knew she had been playing with him. Irritation and disappointment flashed in his eyes before he could hide them.

"Sorry. Couldn't resist," she said. Her fingers moved on

the guitar as if of their own accord, jumping through the rhythm of a song by the Shins. "I'm Sammi."

"You don't look like a Sammi."

"My parents are the only people who've called me Samantha and survived."

"Teachers?"

Sammi gave him a dark look. "Their graves litter the Merrimack Valley."

Adam grinned. Oh, she liked that grin.

"Pull up some shade, Adam."

He sat beside her on the sand and they talked while she played, running through tunes from Maia Sharp, Bonnie Raitt, the Strokes, Jason Mraz, and Keane. She sang a little, talked a little, people came by and watched, asked her questions about the music, about her playing, wondered if she ever played for money. As soon as she had a license she planned to head down to Cambridge and start doing the street corner thing. T stations were a possibility, too, but she hated the idea of being down in the subway with the trains rumbling by. On the street, with the people, that'd be nice. Bookstores and cafés, too. But she was too young to play in bars.

Adam turned out to be eighteen and had a car of his own, a junk heap that had gone from his father to his two older sisters before ending up with him. But it ran.

"You feel like hanging out tonight? We could hit a movie. Or there's this party these guys I know are having. End-of-summer bash."

A tremor went through Sammi. Guys flirted with her

all the time, but not guys like Adam. Her opinion of teenage boys had not changed, but spending an hour or two talking to him had shaken it, that was for sure. He hadn't used her music just as an introduction to talk to her. He spent as much time listening as he did talking, and it didn't seem to bother him that his friends were having chicken fights in the water and playing Frisbee on the shore, enjoying themselves without him. Adam was content to just sit there with her.

Sammi didn't answer him at first. She played "Blackbird," by the Beatles, and sang softly to the tune. Halfway through, she glanced at him. He hadn't pushed the question, hadn't asked again, but he also didn't seem to be embarrassed that she had not replied yet. No awkwardness hung between them.

"Not gonna happen tonight," she said. She caught a glimpse of his disappointment, then forged ahead. "I'm sweaty and grimy. And my mother would be pissed—or at least hurt—if I blew her off to hang out with you. Tomorrow she's taking me school shopping. Mother-daughter bonding stuff."

Adam held up a hand. "Okay. I get it."

She flipped her hair out of her face. "I'm rambling. I do that sometimes. Not often. Consider it a compliment. Point is, I'd love to hang out with you sometime. Just not this weekend."

Her cell phone was clipped to the pocket of her shorts. She took it off and tossed it to him. "Give me your number. I'll text you."

Adam caught the phone and then looked at her, tilting his head like some kind of bird. "Will you?"

"I just said I would."

That smile returned to his face and he nodded. "I hope you do."

He'd finished entering his phone number into her cell and handed it back to her. A couple of guys called to him, and when he turned, one of them whipped the Frisbee his way. Adam snatched it out of the air, then turned to glance at her.

"I should get back. See you soon?"

Sammi's fingers danced along the neck of her guitar, and she began to strum, idly running through the chords of a song of her own that she'd been toying with for a while.

"Definitely," she said.

Adam gave her one last look and then ran off. Sammi watched him play Frisbee with his friends for a while, playing without singing, without really focusing. A breeze rustled the leaves behind her, and then a strange feeling came over her, that instinctive certainty that someone was watching her. She glanced around and discovered that it was her mother. Mom had set her book aside and sat drinking a bottle of spring water she'd fetched from their cooler, watching Sammi.

Her mother smiled, arching an eyebrow that indicated both curiosity about the boy Sammi'd been talking to and a kind of silent approval. Mother and daughter shared a grin.

Sammi's cell phone rang. For half a second, she

wondered if Adam had pulled her number when he looked at the phone, if he might be calling her already, just to be charming. But as she looked up, she could see him up to his waist in the lake, whipping the Frisbee to one of the girls they had come with.

The cell's screen showed *Deveaux, S.* as the caller.

"T.Q.," Sammi said as she answered. "What's up? Everything all right?"

"Yeah. All good. Well, today, anyway. But it's supposed to be a crappy day tomorrow, and it's going to pour tomorrow night and all day Monday. Looks like we're coming home early. I'm willing to bet Caryn and Letty do, too. So I was thinking tomorrow night we should have a sleepover. You guys can all crash at my house."

Sammi laughed. "Pajama party?"

"I don't think we'll be doing each other's nails, but yeah. We definitely should. Nothing like staying up all night gossiping to make sure we look our best on the first day of school."

"We can sleep on Monday," Sammi said. "It sounds perfect. I just saw you guys last night, but I miss you already. What about Katsuko, though? What's the weather supposed to be down at the Cape? I mean, her father's probably too stubborn to come home even if it's a monsoon."

T.Q. laughed. "Actually, I think they were supposed to come home tomorrow anyway. It was just for one night. I'll leave a message on their machine."

"Did you talk to Letty and Caryn yet?"

"I'm about to call them."

Sammi knew it was foolish, but it made her feel good to know that T.Q. had called her first. Sometimes she felt like the most ordinary one among her group of friends, as if there was nothing special about her. The one time she'd mentioned it, T.Q. had told her she had sidekick syndrome and needed to snap out of it. That had been followed by a litany of compliments. The girl was quiet, but she wrote in her journal and for the paper all day and night, so when she wanted to, she could always find the right words.

"So, you're in?" T.Q. asked. "And you'll bring your guitar?"

"Can't wait. See you tomorrow."

2

Sammi woke several times during the night to the rattling of her windows. Her curtains billowed in ghostly fashion, and she dragged her bedspread up to snuggle deeply underneath it. She dreamed of being lost in a city where everyone was a stranger to her, with nowhere to go, and with the sun about to set and ominous shadows seeming to reach out for her from every doorway and alley.

In the morning she rose and shut her windows, pausing to peer out at the heavy clouds. The overcast sky hung like a shroud above the house, and the day had an odd, dreamlike quality about it, as though it were neither night nor day.

She pulled on sweatpants and went downstairs, still rubbing sleep from her eyes. Her father sat at the kitchen table reading the Sunday *Globe*.

"Morning, sweetie," he said without looking up.

"Morning." Sammi studied her dad. He worked in computer software, the perfect executive, and he still looked entirely too neat and tidy for a day off. He had always been that way. Sundays had always been their day—the one day he paid attention to her—but even then he seemed as if he would rather have been at the office. Sammi wished she didn't love him so much. It would've been so much easier if she didn't care.

"Your mother's at the gym. I was just waiting for you to get up before I made the pancakes," he said. "You ready for breakfast?"

Pancakes were a huge part of their Sunday-morning tradition. Her father couldn't cook anything else to save his life, but he made excellent pancakes. As long as he wasn't out of town on business, Sunday morning always brought the ritual—pancakes, coffee, and the newspaper. For the past few weeks, her mother had made it a point not to be home during Sunday breakfast. Her father behaved like nothing was wrong, and Sammi wondered if he was pretending he didn't notice she'd been avoiding him or was totally clueless. Neither would have surprised her.

She wanted to yell at him, to shake him and make him see that their family was unraveling around him. Make him care. But she couldn't do that. Their Sunday mornings meant the world to her, and if they were all she'd ever really get from her father, she wanted to hold on to them tightly. She wasn't about to do anything to ruin the morning.

"Sure. I'm just gonna jump in the shower first, though."

Her father looked up from his paper. "What's the rush?"

"Mom's taking me school shopping, remember?"

He nodded, frowning. "Right. Of course. I wondered what that pain I was feeling was all about. Now I realize it was my wallet bracing itself for attack."

Sammi smiled thinly. She almost summoned up a sharp comeback, but didn't bother. Her father remembered his own rituals, and she appreciated that. But he knew school started on Tuesday and knew that Sammi and her mother went together on this day every year—their own ritual— yet he couldn't be bothered to remember. She forgave him; he had a lot on his mind. But she didn't feel like making a joke out of it.

"I'll be down in a few minutes," she said. "Banana pancakes today?"

"Your wish is my command."

She went back upstairs, peeled off her clothes, and turned on the shower. As always, music filled her mind. She sang a few lines from a Josh Ritter song, and then the notes changed in her head and she started to hum something new, a tune of her own. Thoughts drifted to what the day would bring, where she and her mother would shop, where they might go for lunch, and then to the sleepover at T.Q.'s that night.

It wasn't until she shut the water off and reached for her towel that she thought of Cute Adam. A smile blossomed on her face. When she had dried off, she went into her room, shut the door, and grabbed her cell phone, which had been charging overnight. She had a bunch of texts from the girls solidifying their plans for later and talking about how their shortened trips had been. All except Kat-suko, of course, whose parents wouldn't allow her to have a cell phone.

Wrapped in a towel, she sat on the edge of her bed and sent Adam a text.

Told u I would text. Your turn.

Sammi had just zipped her jeans, her hair still wet, when her ring tone began to play. She snatched the phone up off the bed and saw his name on the screen.

"Hello?"

"Texting takes too long. I'm an immediate gratification kind of guy," Adam said.

"Yeah? You may be calling the wrong girl, then."

"What? Wait, I didn't mean—"

"I know. It's called teasing. A lost art, I guess. You'll have to brush up on it."

"Will I?"

The question hung there. Her implication echoed in the silence.

"My father's making pancakes and my stomach's growling," she said. "Did you just call to tell me you don't like to text?"

"Pretty much."

Sammi remained silent.

"See that, with the teasing?" Adam said. "I'm a fast learner."

"Not bad for a beginner."

"Just wondering if you'd maybe want to go out and get some dinner Friday night."

"That could work. You'd have to pick me up here. I think my parents would want to get a look at you, just in case they have to give your description to the police."

Adam laughed. "Nice to know where I stand."

"Talk later?"

"Tonight?" he asked.

"I'm sleeping over a friend's house."

"You could call me."

"I might. Or you could learn to text."

"Anything's possible."

Sammi ended the call and flicked the phone shut, then brushed out her hair before it got completely crazy. Her father called up to her from downstairs that the pancakes were ready. Sammi went down to the kitchen but found she didn't have much appetite. She forced herself to eat a couple of pancakes just so her dad didn't feel unappreciated. They made father-daughter small talk over the newspaper, and once, he noted what a good mood she was in this morning. Pleased that he'd noticed even that much, Sammi mumbled something about clothes shopping but didn't mention Adam.

She had been fleetingly involved with a handful of boys, all of whom had been her friends first. Guys from school. Most of them were people she still knew. Immature, goofy boys who had hurt and disappointed her. Chances were that Cute Adam was no different. But she felt differently. Maybe it just came down to Sammi being older now, or to Adam being someone entirely new to her, a guy who had just come up to her at the lake because he liked her music.

Whatever the reason, she felt like she was entering into strange, unknown territory. More than likely, nothing would come of it. She knew the way guys were wired.

But for the moment, at least, Sammi liked it.

The floor of T.Q.'s bedroom was as padded as a cell in an insane asylum, thanks to all the sleeping bags. Caryn and Letty lay on their bellies on the bed, and the others sprawled on the floor. They had speculated about some of the classmates they hadn't seen over the summer and talked with dread about their new teachers and classes. T.Q.'s mother had gotten an assortment of Ben & Jerry's ice cream, and all the pints lay empty in a stack in the hand-painted trash can in the corner.

Sammi had played guitar, tried out her new song on the girls, and they had all enjoyed it. Letty had offered some constructive criticism, suggesting she slow it down to give it a more melancholy quality, and they all agreed that this made it better. Now they shared two large bowls of microwave popcorn, despite T.Q.'s mother worrying they might throw up after all that ice cream, and watched DVDs of the first season of HBO's *Entourage*, their favorite show. Katsuko's parents would not have approved, and that only made the show that much better.

"So, tell us more about Cute Adam," Letty said between episodes.

"Yeah. You said he's yummy. Elaborate." Caryn slid off the bed to plop down beside Sammi on the spread of sleeping bags.

Sammi shrugged. "Not much to tell. He's just a cute guy."

"A cute guy you're going out with on Friday night," Katsuko reminded her. She pushed her black hair out of her face and arched a suggestive eyebrow. "There better be more to tell, or you're sluttier than we thought."

Sammi gaped at her for a second, then leaned over and punched her on the arm. "Bitch."

They grinned at each other. From the bed, Letty reached down and gave her a little nudge. Sammi rolled her eyes.

"Okay, fine. He's . . . I don't know, you guys. He just paid attention. He seemed interested in actually talking. I had this top on, you know that green stripy one? But he wasn't spending the whole time staring at my chest."

"But some of the time, right?" Caryn asked. "I mean, otherwise it would be just weird."

Sammi shot her a look, feeling her face flush with the heat of embarrassment.

"She's not wrong," T.Q. said.

They all looked up. She talked so little, they always paid attention when she did, hoping it would encourage her. T.Q. had a mischievous smile on her face.

Sammi sighed. "Yes, he looked. Just not the way most of the guys we know look. But that was just one thing I noticed. Mostly I just liked talking to him. You guys are making way too big a deal out of this, though. We met once. I talked to him this morning for, like, two seconds. Who knows if he'll even follow through with this thing for Friday night? He'll get distracted by some other girl once school starts, and that's that."

Even as she spoke the words, she felt a twinge in her chest, and she realized how disappointed she would be if that happened. Guys did that sort of thing all the time, but it mattered with Adam. Sammi knew how stupid she was being, setting herself up to let some guy ruin her weekend by blowing her off. She just couldn't help it.

"I shouldn't even have told you guys," she said.

They all looked at her with a kind of quiet horror.

"You *better* tell us," Katsuko said. "That's not cool, Sam. We're supposed to tell each other everything."

"And I did," Sammi said. She slumped against T.Q.'s bed, lolling her head back. "Could we move on to another subject now? God, you all need to hook up with someone so we can talk about something else."

T.Q. saved her by starting the next episode of *Entourage*.

Halfway through, they all heard the low vibration coming from someone's cell and scrambled around to locate their phones. Sammi found hers and knew, even before she looked at the screen, that it would be Adam.

A text. *U havin fun?*

"Is that from him?" Caryn asked, crawling over to try and grab the phone.

Sammi kept the phone out of her reach and turned to look at them. "Adam wants to know if we're having fun."

29

"Tell him the football team just left," Katsuko said.

"And the cheerleaders," Letty added.

"You guys are terrible," T.Q. said.

Caryn laughed. "Depends on your perspective."

Yep, Sammi texted back. *Lingerie party. No boys allowed.* As she did, she read her message out loud. The girls replied with hoots and giggles.

"Tell him to take a picture of himself," Katsuko said.

It amazed Sammi how much Katsuko had opened up since they had all become friends. The girl spent most of her time either with the swim team or swimming on her own, and the rest of it studying. In the summer, she taught swimming and was a lifeguard at the Covington Swim Club, a private pool in town. But when she was with the rest of them, Katsuko seemed to come alive.

"Right now?" Sammi asked.

Caryn scowled. "No, next week. Of course right now."

Her phone vibrated. *that hrtz.*

Send me a pic of u, she sent back.

Sammi expected him to hesitate or to ask for one back, especially since she'd told him they were all in lingerie, instead of the pajamas, shorts, and sweatpants they were really wearing. A couple of minutes went by, and then the phone vibrated again.

Adam had sent his picture with a message. *do i get thmbs up?*

"Wow," Letty said as Sammi showed the picture around. "He *is* cute. What a smile."

T.Q. glanced away after checking out the photo. "Guess I have to learn to play guitar."

"He wants to know if he gets a thumbs-up from you guys," Sammi told them.

"Oh yeah," Caryn said. "He passes."

You're cute, apparently, Sammi texted him. *Personally, i don't see it.*

ouch, the message came back.

See u friday, she typed. *g2g. Night.*

Night.

Only when she had closed her phone and glanced around did she realize that the others had gone on watching *Entourage* without her. For a couple of minutes, she'd been completely focused on her exchange with Cute Adam. Now, though, when she stuffed the phone into her backpack and slid over beside Caryn, she felt a moment of tension in the room.

"You're not gonna be one of those girls, are you?" Caryn asked. Her tone seemed light, but her expression was grim.

"What are you talking about?" Sammi said.

"You know. The girls who get a guy and blow off their friends."

"Are you kidding?"

But she could see it was no joke, and as she looked around, she realized they were all waiting for an answer. Her stomach gave a little twist, and Sammi shifted away from Caryn, turning to face them all like they were some kind of jury and she the defendant. At the moment, that was how it felt.

"That's . . ." She shook her head, glanced away for a moment, and then focused on Caryn. "That really sucks that you would think that. You should know the answer to that question. Never mind that I, like, just met the guy and he'll probably turn out to be an asshole. He could be Prince freakin' Charming and I'd never do that."

Sammi looked at each of them in turn. "Being here with you guys . . . you know what it means to me. We've talked about it. Nothing's as important as that."

She ended up on Caryn again, staring at her, and eventually Caryn looked away.

"Sorry, Sam. I'm sorry. You're right. It means that much to me, too, or I wouldn't have said anything."

T.Q. piped up. "I hope he is Prince Charming, Sammi. I hope he's the greatest guy in the world."

Katsuko reached out and took Sammi's hand. "You deserve that."

"We all do," Sammi said. "Except Letty. She deserves—"

"Jessica Biel," Letty interrupted.

They all grinned. "Yes. You deserve Jessica Biel," Sammi said. "Someday, you two will find each other. It's destiny."

"Damn straight." Letty rolled on her back and threw out her arms, closing her eyes as though offering herself up. "Come to me, Jessica."

"Maybe Cute Adam is your destiny, Sam," Katsuko said.

Sammi rolled her eyes. "And in a couple of weeks, we won't remember his name. You guys know what my luck's been like. Or have we forgotten Tim? And Matt? And Bobby McCann?"

"Bobby McCann?" Caryn said, scowling. "Wasn't he from, like, fifth grade?"

"Still, it's a pattern," Sammi argued.

"That just means it's your turn," Letty assured her.

"To answer your question," T.Q. said, "yes, we've forgotten those guys. And so should you."

Sammi smiled. "Maybe."

Katsuko cried out and swung her pillow, and the girls turned their assault on Sammi, who surrendered in a fit of giggles.

Letty stood on the bed like the Queen of the Mountain, looking around at them with the pillow in her hand, ready to defend herself. Then something in her face shifted. Her milk chocolate eyes narrowed, and Sammi saw a kind of light dancing in them.

"I have the coolest idea ever," she said.

They all looked at her. Letty knelt down on the bed, and they crowded around her like schoolchildren waiting for the teacher to read a story.

"We should get a tattoo," she whispered.

"Tattoos?" Caryn started to laugh.

"No, no. Not tattoos, not like we go together and everybody picks out something different," Letty went on. "We should get *a* tattoo. The same one for all five of us, something totally unique that nobody else in the world would have."

"I don't know," T.Q. started to say.

33

But Caryn began to nod. "That's brilliant. Something that's just us, that, like, represents our friendship, so no matter what happens for the rest of our lives, we'll never forget what we all mean to each other."

"And you can design it, Caryn," Katsuko said.

Sammi laughed softly, in disbelief. She stared at Katsuko. The idea seemed crazy, but wonderful at the same time—a permanent reminder of the bond they shared. But she never would have thought Katsuko would go for it.

"I love it," T.Q. said. She reached around to touch the small of her back. "I could get it right here. That would look so cool."

"What would the design be, though?" Sammi asked.

Caryn smiled. "I could come up with something. Or I'd do a bunch and we could all choose the one we like the best."

Several seconds ticked by without another word. The only sound in the room was the television and the breathing of the five girls. They all wore smiles of mixed disbelief and excitement.

"Are we really going to do this?" T.Q. asked.

"Definitely," Sammi said.

Letty let out a whoop of joy and jumped down off the bed, hugging everyone she could reach.

But Katsuko had gone silent, and her smile had disappeared.

"I can't," she said. "It would be amazing. To share something like that with all of you, I would love it. But my parents are never going to let me get a tattoo. And I don't think anyone's going to do it for us without permission from our parents. Nowhere good, anyway, where we could be sure they'd be safe."

Caryn and Letty started to try to persuade her, but then T.Q. swore.

They stared at her. T.Q. never swore.

"My parents, too. I don't think they'll go for it." She looked up. "What about you, Sammi? You know your parents would kill you."

Sammi only nodded, heart sinking with disappointment. That would be all her parents would need right now; something else to argue about. They all seemed to have deflated.

Then Katsuko spoke up again.

"Screw it. I'm so sick of being a good girl, always having to worry about what my parents will think. This means too much to me. They'll never understand, but they don't have to. It's got nothing to do with them."

"Yeah, but you were right," Sammi said. "You have to be eighteen, I think, otherwise you have to have a parent with you. I mean, Rachael Dubrowski has a tattoo shop, but I can't see her breaking the law for us, even if she *is* dating my cousin."

Caryn shook her head. "No. There must be places where nobody will ask questions."

T.Q. slumped back onto her sleeping bag. "Places we could get the ugliest tattoo ever, where they could mess up big time, or use a needle with disease all over it. If we could even find anyone willing. These guys have to be licensed, right? If they break the rules, they get shut down."

"Damn, aren't you Little Miss Sunshine?" Letty said. "C'mon, Simone, don't be like that."

T.Q. shrugged. "Just being realistic."

"So we just go out of state," Caryn said. "New Hampshire's right up the street, girls."

For a second they all brightened. This time it was Letty who shot it down.

"Not gonna work. T.Q., you're the only one with a driver's license, but you can't drive anyone under eighteen without an adult in the car. If we got pulled over, you'd be screwed."

"We'll do it ourselves," Katsuko said, darkly serious.

They all stared at her.

"Seriously," she went on. "We take the right precautions and we'll be fine."

"No way," Sammi said. "If I'm going to have ink on my body for the rest of my life, I want it to be something beautiful. Even if it's Caryn's design, who's going to actually carve it into my flesh? Somehow I've got a feeling it's not going to be a work of art by then."

"Plus, infection," T.Q. said.

They all looked at Letty, who had gone very quiet. When she realized they were staring at her, a sly smile spread across her face.

"What?" Caryn asked.

Letty lay sideways on the bed, lounging like Cleopatra,

her grin broadening. "There's a new place in my neighborhood. The guy's got the windows blacked out and the only sign is the one that says Open in, like, blue neon. It's always on, day or night, as far as I can tell. The guy, Dante, does tattoos. My cousin Ana says his work is beautiful. Not that it makes a difference to me, but Ana also said the guy's a total smokin' hottie. I say we go by there and talk to him."

They all looked at each other, each waiting for someone else to object.

"No harm in talking," Sammi said.

Letty smiled.

Sammi felt a sudden rush of fear, as though she had just reached the top of the roller coaster and whatever happened now was completely out of her control. The pain of the needle wasn't what bothered her. But the idea of her parents' finding out troubled her deeply. They had always trusted her, and if she shattered that trust, she knew how hurt they would be. She had always been honest with them, and it frightened her to think about throwing that away.

But when Letty put her hand into the middle of the circle they had formed, and one by one the other girls followed suit, Sammi took a breath and put her hand in as well. Their bond had been made deeper just by the idea of what they were planning, and by the secrecy that would be required of all of them.

The pact had been made.

3

The buses were late on the first afternoon of school. Sammi stepped out through the metal doors and saw the mess of kids milling around on the grass and walkways in front of Covington High. The teachers were trying to keep some kind of order, as if there had been a fire drill, but with the excitement at the end of the first day, their efforts were hopeless.

Sammi peered over the tops of people's heads, searching for red hair. At her height and with that hair, T.Q. was hard to miss. She weaved her way through the hordes as they laughed and shouted to one another, but saw no sign of T.Q. anywhere.

"Hey, Holland!"

She turned to find Caryn striding toward her, dressed impeccably, as always. Sammi knew her friend could take just about any piece of clothing and make it look great—today's combination of sheer blouse over tank top and slit-leg skirt presented a perfect example—but she could never figure out how Caryn managed not to spill any food on her clothes at lunchtime. Only the first day of school, and she'd already managed to dribble Sloppy Joe sauce on her chin and tray without getting it on her clothes.

Superpowers. The only answer.

"How was the rest of your day?" Sammi asked.

"Very cool," Caryn replied with a half nod. "I could live without the bio class. Mr. Pucillo bores me out of my skull, and just the thought of the lab sessions grosses me out. Other than that, it's kinda good to be back."

"Thumbs-up from me, too," Sammi said. "I've got Intro to Psych. I think I'm gonna like that, as long as there aren't too many papers."

With a groaning of engines and a squeal of brakes, the buses began to make their appearance in the parking lot. While the first bus pulled up at the curb, Sammi glanced around.

Letty stood on the sidewalk, waiting for her bus.

"Hey," Sammi said, tapping Caryn and pointing Letty out.

They hurried over to her. Letty hefted her backpack and pushed her hair out of her face. When she looked up at them, she squinted at the sun in her eyes.

"You guys, I so cannot wait until I get my license," she said.

Sammi rolled her eyes, sharing Letty's frustration. Riding buses had been fun back in elementary school, but they were smelly and cramped and the total opposite of cool.

"Next year, we'll be carpooling," Caryn said.

"I guess Katsuko is at some swim team thing, first meeting of the year or whatever," Sammi said, "but I didn't see T.Q., either. Did you guys see her?"

Letty adjusted the strap of her backpack. "Yeah. She's at tryouts for basketball."

Sammi and Caryn stared at her in surprise.

"Seriously?" Caryn said.

Letty shrugged. "Guess she figures she's tall enough."

"That'd be cool if she makes it," Sammi said.

Caryn raised an eyebrow. "Except it'll mean we have to go to the games. But I guess we'll survive." She turned to Letty. "So, are we all set for Saturday night?"

A troubled look passed over Letty's face.

"Is that a no?" Caryn asked.

Her eyes brightened and she shook her head. "No, no. We're good."

Sammi studied her. Letty glanced away a second and then met her gaze, and Sammi saw a soft sadness in her eyes.

"What's wrong?" she asked.

More buses rumbled into the line. Together the girls started to move down the line and stopped at the third bus, which would take Letty home to her neighborhood. Caryn's and Sammi's buses were farther along the sidewalk.

"The usual stuff with my parents," Letty said, one

40

corner of her mouth lifting in a halfhearted smile. "I think they're a little worried about you all sleeping over, like, what are all these girls doing hanging out with our lesbian daughter."

Sammi glanced at Caryn. "Well, duh, lesbian orgy."

Caryn nodded, all serious. "Absolutely."

Letty let out a burst of laughter that brought stares from a lot of the guys and girls around them. "I love you guys," she said.

Solemn, Sammi crossed her arms. "That's what your parents are afraid of."

Letty gave them each a small hug and jumped onto her bus, the last one aboard before the doors closed.

As the engine rumbled and the yellow monster pulled away, the other two girls hurried along until they reached Sammi's bus.

"Wow," Caryn said. "For Letty's sake, I hope her parents don't make it too weird this weekend. Can't they just be happy their daughter has friends?"

"It's never gonna be that easy," Sammi replied. "Letty told me she feels lucky her father still speaks to her. In her culture, I guess a lot of times it doesn't work out that way."

"Not just in her culture."

"I guess. But, yeah, hopefully they won't be too high-strung that we're sleeping over."

A sly smile crept across Caryn's face. "Guess I better get to work on those tattoo designs. I want to find something that's perfect for us."

Sammi forced a smile and stepped onto her bus.

"You'll do it. I know you will," she said.

She and Caryn said their goodbyes, and then Sammi worked her way toward the back of the bus and found a seat. A couple of rowdy guys got on right after her, and the bus driver told them to be quiet and sit down, that he'd let them off in the middle of the street if they started trouble.

Caryn might have waved to her, but Sammi didn't even turn to look. For most of Monday she had worried about the whole tattoo plan, trying to figure out a way to tell her friends that she loved them but that her parents would just never understand. Today, at school, she'd managed to avoid thinking about it very much, and when they only briefly mentioned it at lunch, she'd told herself that the idea would wither and die and she wouldn't have to go through with it.

No such luck.

Butterflies darted around in her stomach. As she started to turn the problem over in her mind again, her cell phone vibrated. Flipping it open, she saw that she had a text message from Cute Adam.

How wz yur 1st day?

Smiling, she put the issue of the tattoo aside for the moment.

i survived.

anyplace special u wnna go fri nt?

surprise me.

Come Friday night, Sammi found that Adam had taken her seriously. Of all the places she might have guessed he would take her, the Peddler's Daughter wouldn't even have been on the list. Growing up in Covington, she had passed the place a hundred times, but she had never been inside. Just around the corner from both England's MicroCreamery and Krueger's Flatbread, down a side street known for its little art galleries and a dance studio, the little Irish pub sat tucked away in the cellar of another, trendier restaurant.

The rest of that shortened first week of school had passed uneventfully. Adam had arrived to pick her up at seven o'clock and spent a few minutes chatting with her parents. To Sammi's profound relief, they seemed to like him all right. Or at least, they didn't immediately lock her in her room and throw him out of the house, despite his being the first boy to ever take her out in his own car.

In the fading light, Adam led the way down the steps between buildings to the entrance and held the door for her. The moment he opened it, she heard the music. Sammi felt her heart lift and blossom with pleasure as she stepped into the pub. Brass and dark wood and dim light gave the Peddler's Daughter an authentic air, but nothing added to that ambience more than the music that came from the tiny stage at the back of the pub, where a quartet played a rising, exultant Celtic tune. The two guitars provided the beat, while the girl playing violin and an older man on flute made the song dance and reel.

"Wow," she whispered.

Adam slipped his hand into hers. Sammi let him.

"You like?" he asked.

She grinned. No other answer was necessary. Just the idea that he had put real thought into where he would take her tonight, that he had worked to surprise her, to please her, felt new and extraordinary. This wasn't a night at the movies or a stop for pizza, and it certainly wasn't a stop by some beer bash some of his friends were throwing.

"Can I help you?" the hostess asked, coming around from the dining room.

"We have a reservation," Adam said.

Sammi marveled at the idea. She had been on dates before, but this belonged in an entirely different category. Cute Adam, it appeared, had a lot more to offer than a mischievous grin and soulful eyes.

"So," she said, after the hostess had seated her and left them their menus, "how did you know about this place?"

"My father takes me here sometimes. My parents are divorced and he lives in Plaistow. He swears by the place. Says they have the best burger in the Merrimack Valley. But I remembered they had music on weekends and I thought you'd like it."

"I do. Very much."

"Mission accomplished," Adam said, seeming genuinely pleased.

They looked at one another, their eyes lingering a few beats longer than felt comfortable, and Sammi looked away. She glanced at the menu.

"How long have your parents been divorced?"

"Since I was eleven," Adam said, studying his own menu. "I know I'm supposed to be all bummed, but I can't summon up the tears. They fought so much when they were married that life is a hell of a lot easier with them apart, for all of us."

"All of us?"

"I have two older sisters, both in college."

Sammi looked up, eyebrows raised. "That explains a lot."

"How's that?"

"Guys who have older sisters just get it more than guys who don't. 'It' being girls in general. Either that, or you just learn to fake it better as a matter of survival."

Adam laughed, nodding. "Faking it, definitely. But yeah, there's a comfort level, I guess. What about you? Siblings?"

Sammi set her menu down. "Nope. Only child, parents still married. At least for the moment."

"You think that's going to change?"

She gave a tiny shrug. "I didn't say they were happily married. The house didn't need air-conditioning this summer. You have enough cold shoulders around, it gets plenty chilly."

"Sorry to hear it."

"Me too. So what about school? What's it like to be a senior?"

The conversation went on like that for a while. Adam had been held back in the first grade. Minor dyslexia had given him trouble learning to read, which explained why he was eighteen and just starting senior year in high school. He definitely had college plans, with Somerset University just north of Boston his first choice, and UNH as a serious backup.

They both had burgers. By the time they were halfway through dinner, she had decided that if he wanted to kiss her later, she would let him. That was a bit of self-deceit, however. In truth, she had known from the moment he sat down by her on the beach at Kingston Lake that she would very much like him to kiss her. Now, though, she had a feeling she would be gravely disappointed if he didn't.

Damn, she thought as they walked hand in hand around the corner to the little park outside England's, *watch your step with this one, girl*.

Adam didn't wait until the end of the night to kiss her. While they sat in that tiny park eating ice cream, he made her laugh, and then silenced that laugh with his lips. She tasted black raspberry ice cream on his tongue, and a shiver of pleasure went through her.

Not once did she mention that she would be sleeping over Letty's the next night, or the pact she and the girls had made. The subject of tattoos did not come up. Sammi had been working hard all week to avoid even thinking about it, and being with Adam helped her to forget. Kissing Adam, she could cast off all her worries.

Even that night in bed, drifting off to sleep, she felt a pleasant buzz from her date and imagined she could still feel the touch of his lips on hers.

But she did not sleep well, and her dreams were unpleasant.

*   *   *

Sammi's mother agreed to pick up Katsuko before going to Letty's on Saturday. They drove up into the Ardmore section of Covington, over the bridge from the old factory area of the city. Ever since the days when people had sweated for sixteen hours a day making shoes and clothes and glassware while their managers and executives went home to mansions across the river, people who'd grown up north of the bridge had held a grudge against those who made their homes in Ardmore. Even now, all these years later, folks who'd grown up in Covington had an edge in their voices when they talked about Ardmore.

As her mother drove up Valley View Drive, a ten-year-old development full of minimansions and perfectly groomed acre lots, Sammi knew she must be resisting the urge to comment, and appreciated the effort.

The door opened the instant they pulled into the driveway—Katsuko had apparently been waiting for them—and the girl called back into the house and shut the door quickly. She ran down to the car with her overnight bag, smiling brightly.

"Wow," Linda Holland said as Katsuko approached, "I don't think I've ever seen the girl smile."

"She smiles, Mom. She's just very serious."

Sammi might have said more, issued an indictment about how strict Katsuko's parents were, but then the door opened and Katsuko plunged into the backseat.

"Hi!"

"Sorry if we're late," Sammi's mother said.

"Not at all. I just couldn't wait to escape. I cleaned my

47

room twice today, and I think they were inspecting it to see if I had missed anything."

Sammi glanced into the backseat. "Are you kidding? Why?"

"They didn't want me to go. I didn't give them much choice, but I'm sure they were looking for a reason to change their minds."

Sammi's mom put the car in reverse. "Then we should get the heck out of here."

Katsuko beamed. But if her mother had known what had Katsuko so excited, she wouldn't have been so sympathetic. Sammi looked at her mother and saw how pleased she was to have scored points with her daughter's friend, and a fresh wave of guilt crashed over her.

Throughout the ride to Letty's house, Katsuko and Mrs. Holland made small talk about school and swimming and college and what it felt like to be a junior. Sammi barely said a word, gazing out the window, watching as they went back over the bridge and drove through the city, passing through neighborhoods in descending order of income. When she started seeing graffiti on the sides of brick buildings, and rusted chain-link fence, she knew that they were almost there. Over the years, Covington had become a true melting pot, and it had a sizable Latino population. There were Latinos in every part of the city, but Vespucci Square had been the beating, immigrant heart of Covington for a century and a half. Italians and Germans had come first, and then the Irish. Later, there had come Cubans, Puerto Ricans, Dominicans, and now a wave of Brazilians. The condition of many of the duplexes and row houses spoke of poverty, not of culture.

Which hadn't stopped Sammi's father from hesitating when she asked if she could sleep over Letty's, or her mother from telling her to be careful, not to wander off. Sammi could not even blame them. The neighborhood could be rough, especially for people who didn't live there.

All those thoughts filled her head as her mother pulled past the dingy Citgo station beside the two-family Letty and her parents shared with Teresa, her older sister, and Teresa's two babies. The walls were so thin—Letty had warned them—that she could hear the babies crying in the night. The house itself was well kept, with a fresh coat of paint and a small, immaculate yard.

But even though she knew better, Sammi couldn't help holding her breath as she got out of the car. She would not let her mother see her nervousness. Could not let anyone see it. No matter how much she knew about the origins of Vespucci Square, the reality of the local paper was inescapable. When trouble went down in Covington, whether it was drugs or prostitution or murder, it nearly always happened within half a mile of this spot.

As Katsuko said goodbye and expressed her thanks, climbing out of the car, Sammi had to take a steadying breath. What they were planning for tonight was bad enough—trouble enough—but walking the streets of Vespucci Square after dark added to the danger in a way that sent a shiver of fear through her. *This whole thing is stupid. What the hell is wrong with me?* she thought.

By then, her mother had said goodbye and begun to pull away.

Standing on the cracked and pitted sidewalk in front of Letty's duplex, she and Katsuko looked at one another.

"Are you nervous?"

A shudder of relief went through Sammi, and she uttered a nervous laugh. "Oh my God, completely. Aren't you?"

Katsuko nodded. "Oh yeah. But it feels kind of good, you know?"

Sammi smiled as though she *did* know, but her smile was a lie.

She picked up her overnight bag and followed Katsuko up the concrete steps to 46A, Letty's half of the duplex. Sammi rang the doorbell, and they heard voices and footsteps inside, then the sound of two locks being drawn back. The door swung open and Letty opened her arms to them, giddy with excitement. She wore artfully torn jeans, low around her hipbones, and a tank with spaghetti straps.

Caryn and T.Q. were behind her in the hallway. Letty ushered Sammi and Katsuko in, and the girls all started talking at once. Caryn had dressed fairly sexy, in a ribbed top and a short skirt. Katsuko and T.Q. were conservative in comparison, but Sammi wore jeans and a loose green cotton shirt. This was supposed to be girls' night. Whom were they trying to impress?

"Letty?"

They all looked around to see Mrs. Alecia silhouetted in the entrance to the kitchen at the end of the hall.

"Hello, girls," Letty's mother said.

They all greeted her, but Mrs. Alecia stayed near the kitchen, and they did not move from their spot by the door. Sammi shifted in the moment of awkward silence as the woman appraised them, obviously wondering if one of them might be her daughter's girlfriend, and if so, which one?

"Are you sure you don't want to have dinner here? I'm cooking for your father and Teresa anyway."

Letty smiled. "No thank you, Mami. We're just going to have pizza, if that's okay. It's girls' night."

Mrs. Alecia smiled wanly. "All right. Have fun, Letitia."

Letty rolled her eyes at her mother's use of the name. "We will. We're just going up to my room for a minute. Gotta show the girls something before we take off."

Mrs. Alecia vanished into the kitchen. When Letty turned to face them, Sammi saw the sadness in her eyes, but Letty covered it with another one of those giddy smiles.

"Let's dump your bags upstairs," she said to Katsuko and Sammi. Then she looked at Caryn. "Wait'll you see the designs our favorite artist has come up with."

They all exchanged conspiratorial looks and followed Letty upstairs, as if the whole thing might be some wonderful game. Sammi went last, trailing behind the others, wishing she had never agreed to play, knowing how hurt they would be if she tried to back out now.

Knowing that by morning, whatever she decided, she would have betrayed the trust of someone she loved.

4

After dark they made their way down to Valencia Avenue, a street that Sammi had ridden past with her parents many times over the years but could not recall ever having gone down. There were bakeries and dollar stores and empty storefronts with the glass postered over or whitewashed. One relic had once been a video store, but such places were nearly extinct now.

Across the street, Sammi spotted the shop with blacked-out windows, a blue neon Open sign the only indication that it was inhabited. That particular shade of deep blue ought to have seemed cold and wintry—especially on a night that had turned so unseasonably cool—but to Sammi it looked like blue fire. Just looking at it made her flush with a strange heat that might have been excitement or embarrassment, or maybe a little of both.

Her heartbeat sped up and she ran her tongue across

her lips. Frightened as she was, the sensation of doing something so taboo, so forbidden, exhilarated her. Being bad had its allure.

"Are we really going to do this?" T.Q. asked.

Sammi blinked in surprise and looked over, relieved that someone else had put voice to the question that had been on the tip of her tongue all night. When they had sat in Letty's room looking at Caryn's intricate and elegant designs, she had tried to make herself say those words a dozen times. Knowing the way the other girls would look at her, knowing that it would hurt them, she had not been able to summon the courage.

T.Q. had asked the question. Her eyes were wide, staring across the street at the black windows, at the flickering blue neon letters. Open.

"Maybe—" Sammi began.

"Damn right we're doing it," Letty said.

Katsuko laughed as she unconsciously rubbed at her hipbone, the place she intended to get her tattoo. "We didn't come down here to just forget about it now, T.Q."

A nervous, almost giddy smile blossomed on T.Q.'s face. She nodded. "All right. Let's go."

Sammi tried to open her mouth, tried to reverse time just a few seconds, long enough for her to agree with T.Q. and maybe make the others hesitate. But the moment had passed. She had missed the opportunity. Sammi wanted to do this for her friends, but her parents had enough problems without dealing with what they'd perceive as their daughter's rebellion. She had been struggling with the decision all day, but in her heart she knew that she wouldn't know for sure what she would do until the moment arrived.

Silently she said a little prayer that this Dante guy would turn them away, solving her dilemma.

T.Q. stepped off the curb and crossed the street toward the tattoo shop, and the others followed. Halfway across, Letty realized Sammi still stood on the sidewalk and glanced back at her, brows knitted, wondering what she was up to.

Taking a deep breath, Sammi hurried to catch up to them.

"You all right?" Letty asked, her voice soft with concern.

"I hate needles. And pain," Sammi said. These were not lies, nor were they the whole truth.

"It'll be fine," Letty said.

They gathered together in front of the black windows. Sammi glanced around at her friends as they all hesitated, and their faces were bathed in that peculiar blue neon glow. They looked like ghosts.

"Place gives me the creeps," she said, unable to stop herself. "What's it even called? It doesn't have a name? He could be doing anything in there."

T.Q. stared at the front door. "You heard what Letty said. He doesn't ask any questions. You break the rules, that's not the kind of thing you advertise."

Several seconds went by without any of them moving. Even Letty seemed reluctant now that the moment had arrived. Then Katsuko reached out to open the door. She tugged on the handle.

"It's locked," Sammi said. "Must be closed."

Letty frowned. "No way. The Open sign is always on, yeah. But I heard the guy's almost always here."

She rapped on the blacked-out-glass and metal door. "It's Saturday night. He's not gonna close on a Saturday night."

Seconds later they heard someone cough inside. The lock clicked and the door opened a few inches, pushed from within. The eyes that peered out from within were icy blue, bright and ethereal, and Sammi felt their gaze fix on her.

When the door swung wider and they got a better look at the man holding it open, butterflies fluttered in her stomach. He had shoulder-length black hair, dark stubble on his chin, and the deep olive skin of the Mediterranean. He might have been Greek or Spanish or Italian or even Egyptian; Sammi could not tell. Wherever he came by his looks, one thing was certain—he was a beautiful man.

"Well," he said with just a trace of exotic, unfamiliar accent, "what has fate brought to my doorstep this evening?"

Sammi felt herself blush. Those icy blue eyes were like nothing she'd ever seen. At the same time, she realized that though it felt as if he were looking directly at her, he had that effect on all of them. Even Letty, who didn't like guys, seemed captivated by him. And who talked that way, especially in Covington?

"Hi," Letty said, nervous. "Are you Dante?"

With a smile of delight, he regarded them all again. "I am. Which means you aren't lost."

Katsuko spoke up. "Are you open? For business?"

Dante's eyes narrowed. "For customers who aren't going to get me into trouble."

"We aren't," Letty said quickly. "My cousin told me you could help us. Ana Mattei? You know her?"

Dante considered the question a moment. "I know a lot of girls."

I'll bet you do, Sammi thought, and the warmth of her blush deepened.

"We won't get you into trouble," Caryn said, with a desperation in her voice that Sammi did not like at all. "I swear."

The tattoo artist hesitated, but something about the way those wintry blue eyes sparkled made Sammi think this was just mischief. He had already made up his mind.

"Why don't you come in and tell me what you want?" Dante said.

Sammi saw the relief in her friends' faces, but her stomach was still filled with butterflies. The threshold of the store might not actually have been the point of no return, but it certainly felt like it. She knew she should hold back, just bail on the whole thing right now. But she couldn't stand the thought of hurting the girls like that.

Letty led the way into the nameless shop, and the others followed. Sammi was the last to enter. No bells tinkled above the door, and when it closed behind her, the blacked-out windows made her feel as if they were in some bunker, far underground. Inside Dante's shop only a few lights burned. He had an artist's drafting table set up in one corner, and most of the light came from the bright lamp that shone down on the designs he had been working on.

Dante picked up a bottle of lemon-flavored water that sat open on a filing cabinet and took a sip, then turned toward them, one eyebrow raised.

"All right. We're behind closed doors, just the six of us. Talk to me."

He wore a black shirt with a V-neck. The sleeves were rolled up halfway to his elbows, and for the first time, Sammi got a good look at some of the art on his skin. Entranced, she could not help staring. What little she could see of the tattoos on his chest showed her the head of a fierce lion with golden eyes and long red scars upon its face, and the tattoo on his forearms revealed twin goddesses, one grim and cruel and one lovely and pure.

Letty had started to talk to Dante, introducing all the girls by name, but Sammi had missed much of what she said while staring at his tattoos. She wondered about him, about those blue eyes on such a man. The tattooist seemed such an exotic creature to her.

"We don't want to pick something out of a book," Katsuko said, shaking her hair back and sliding her hands into her pockets.

"It has to be something that's just for us, that only the five of us will ever have," Letty went on. She shrugged almost bashfully. "It's a best friends thing, y'know?"

Dante nodded. His smile, sort of lopsided, had a warmth and charm that gave him total command of the room.

"I think I do," he said. "Wish I'd had friends that mattered that much to me. I won't even give you the usual warnings about how difficult it is to remove tattoos and how you should really think about it so that you don't regret it later."

T.Q. had been quiet, as usual, from the moment they entered the shop. Now she seemed to come alive. "We haven't thought about much of anything else all week. In fact, Caryn—"

"Hang on," Dante said, holding up a hand. He went to his drawing table. He seemed almost to have forgotten they were there. Pushing aside his work, he placed a fresh sheet of paper on the table in front of him and picked up a pencil.

Sammi glanced at Caryn. T.Q. had tried to bring up her sketches, but Dante had interrupted. Someone should have said something to him, but for the moment they were all captivated by him. Sketching quickly, Dante drew a small circle—perhaps an inch in diameter—and then began to design around it. At first Sammi thought the sketch represented some stylized image of the sun, or a star, with rays of light coming off it in lines that curled to the left.

Then Dante picked up a pen and started inking black lines over the pencil sketch. The central circle became heavy and thick, leaving only a small, round blank in the middle, like the eye of the storm.

"It's a hurricane, or a tornado, something like that," she said.

The tattooist smiled and glanced up at her, and Sammi realized they were the first words she had spoken since coming into the shop.

"It's meant to be many things at once," Dante said, returning his attention to his work. "Kinda like friendship."

He continued inking in the little hooked fingers that extended from that central circle, marching around the circumference counterclockwise. It reminded Sammi also of Egyptian hieroglyphics they'd studied in ancient history the year before.

Dante paused and straightened up, cocked his head, and studied the design. Apparently satisfied, he discarded the pen and picked up an eraser to remove any stray traces of pencil.

"Is it some kind of eye?" Katsuko asked.

The tattooist looked up from the table, his expression unreadable, but Sammi thought the question had irked him somehow.

"It shows the power of the storm," Dante said, with a smiling nod to Sammi. "Friendship is like that, isn't it? Gathering in strength, all of its elements—each of you—working together, becoming more than you could ever be on your own. Nothing can stand in the path of the storm.

"But like I said, it's many things." With one long finger, he pointed to the ring at the center. "This is the core, the world itself, the bond you share. Circling the world is the ocean, and here are the five of you, waves on the water."

Sammi saw that he meant the curling prongs that swept up from the outer rim of the sphere, and felt foolish that she had not seen that before. There were five of those stylized waves, one representing each of them. As they watched, Dante added small dots around the waves that might have been stars in the sky above the world, or parts of the storm, whatever metaphor they wanted to use to interpret the design.

"It's beautiful," Letty breathed, staring at the drawing as the tattooist put down his pen.

There were fans blowing in the shop, a small one in this front room and at least one larger one in the back. Sammi could hear the buzz through the half-open door that led back there. Despite the fans, the shop had begun to grow uncomfortably warm. She reached back and lifted her hair off her neck.

T.Q. looked a bit flushed, but whether from the heat or embarrassment or excitement, Sammi couldn't tell.

"It is," the redhead said. "It is beautiful, and very cool of you, but we've actually got . . . Caryn, she's an artist. She designed a bunch of—"

Dante glanced at Caryn. "I'm sorry. I should've heard you out before I let inspiration run away with me. If you've already picked something out, that's fine. Can I see your designs?"

Caryn reached for her back pocket, where she'd carried the folded-up designs they had all discussed at Letty's. On the way over here they had all seemed unanimous about which design they liked best. Now, though, Caryn hesitated, then gave a small shrug.

"Yours is much better."

"But we want something just for us," Katsuko said, all business. "Unique."

Letty touched the edge of the artist's drawing table, staring at Dante's design. "This is unique. I love what Caryn did, especially the Pisces kind of thing with the fish, but this is, like, the perfect symbol for us. Don't you guys see it?"

T.Q. nodded, crossing her arms. "Yeah. I see it. I just don't want to see it on anybody else if it's supposed to be *ours*."

Dante slid off his chair and stood. He put a hand on Letty's shoulder and reached out to touch T.Q.'s arm. Both girls drew stares wherever they went, and at school were considered startlingly beautiful. According to a lot of guys Sammi knew, T.Q. seemed unapproachable to them. They mistook her shyness for disdain, as though her academic ability made her think herself their superior. In truth, guys made her nervous as hell, and whatever she saw in the mirror, Simone Deveaux did not think herself beautiful. Most guys left Letty alone simply because she was a lesbian, although some of them flirted with her harder because of it, as though that were a kind of game for them.

Next to Dante, both girls seemed only ordinary.

Letty smiled when he touched her shoulder. T.Q. flinched and shifted her weight from one foot to the other, blushing furiously.

The tattooist seemed not to notice. He looked around at the other girls, at Katsuko, then Caryn, and finally at Sammi.

"I won't pressure you. But the design exists because you came into my place looking for something special, and that inspired me. I created this for you. If you like it, I promise you I'll never tattoo it on anyone else. No one else in the world will have it. You can take the design with you when you leave."

The other girls all exchanged glances, and the reality of the reason for this visit swept over Sammi again. She could see just from their eyes and from their body language that Dante had persuaded them.

Hell, he'd persuaded Sammi, too. His design was perfect for them. She felt a tingling pleasure at the idea of having it tattooed on her skin, a silent rebellion taking place in her head. But her parents might never forgive her.

She'd never felt so torn.

Letty took a deep breath and looked around at her friends with a nervous, coquettish smile. "I'll go first."

Dante clapped his hands happily. "Excellent!"

He did not bother to check their IDs or even ask them how old they were. With a playful glint in those pale, wintry blue eyes, he led the way through the door into the back of the shop, and they all followed.

If the front of the shop existed as the artist's studio, the room they now entered was his operating room. Sammi took it all in, thinking that it looked a lot like a dentist's office. On one side of the room sat a heavy-duty reclining chair, and on the other a padded table that looked like something from a doctor's examination room. Next to both table and chair were separate sets of tools on long cables like dentist's drills, but Sammi also saw a shelf full of metal instruments. Racks of towels sat on shelves, and there were containers both for hazardous waste and for needles, as if they'd come to give blood.

The tools of the tattooist were on top of rolling cabinets whose drawers, she imagined, were filled with different inks. Sammi couldn't look too long at the instruments without feeling a little faint. She glanced away and caught Dante studying her curiously.

"Now," the tattooist said, "are you all going to have the same color, or different? And if it's the same, do you want black or something more vivid?"

His accent made the question sound exotic. The girls exchanged silent looks.

"Black is bold," Caryn said. "If it's just going to be one color, black makes a statement."

T.Q. and Katsuko nodded. Sammi gnawed her lower lip. When Letty glanced at her, she smiled, a mask she put on to hide the turmoil inside her.

"Black it is," Letty said. "Where do you want me, on the table or in the chair?"

Dante spread his hands open. "Where am I going to be working?"

Sammi arched an eyebrow, wondering how daring her friends might be, or how secretive. If she herself was going to go ahead with this, there were very few places she could imagine hiding from her parents. The tattoo might go on one of her breasts, or on her lower abdomen, low enough that even her lowest-waisted jeans would not reveal it. Either way, she would have to bare part of herself to Dante that she would hide from almost anyone else.

The thrill of the forbidden tingled through her, now joined by a rush of embarrassment.

"The base of my back," Letty said, reaching around to show exactly where. It occurred to Sammi how fortunate Letty was that her parents would be okay with the tattoo. After she'd come out as a lesbian, a small, tasteful tattoo would probably get barely a blink.

"You want your friends to step out?"

Letty shook her head. She ran her tongue over her lips, revealing a nervousness that surprised Sammi.

"All right," Dante said, as he made his way over to the table and began to spread clean towels over it. "You can leave your shirt and panties on. Lie on your stomach on the table, and we'll get started. Let me just get the design. I left it up front."

The tattooist hurried out, and the girls all exhaled as if they'd been holding one enormous breath. They smiled, a bit uncertainly, but then Letty slipped out of her skirt. She climbed onto the table and lay down on her stomach, as though she expected Dante to give her a massage.

"You know, we didn't even ask how much," Letty said.

As she spoke, Dante reentered the room with the design in one hand. "It's all one color, and the design isn't very complex. Unless one of you wants it really big, I'll charge you seventy-five apiece. Call it a group rate."

None of them replied. They had agreed to bring a hundred bucks apiece, not sure what the cost would be. Sammi thought of the things she could do with seventy-five dollars.

Dante folded Letty's shirt up to just below her bra strap, then slid down her panties a few inches to prepare the space for her tattoo.

"In some tribal cultures, tattoos used to be hand carved," Dante said as he went to the sink and washed his hands with water so hot it steamed, even with the warmth in the room. "They would cut the design in, then rub pigments or dyes, sometimes ashes, into the wounds. Some people still do it that way, believe it or not. Barbaric, I think. I'm an artist. I prefer not to use my art to serve some bizarre fetish. Cutting flesh is for surgeons."

He pulled on a pair of latex gloves. "No latex allergies? Good."

At Letty's side, he squirted a brownish liquid onto her lower back and then began to spread it with his fingers, rubbing it in, covering the entire area. "This is a combination of disinfectant and topical anesthetic. It helps dull the pain."

At the mention of pain, all the girls seemed to pause. Letty, however, seemed perfectly comfortable.

"In Japan, they sometimes use sharpened bamboo needles and create the tattoos by hand, moving slowly, inserting one needle at a time. I respect the discipline of *irezumi*, but I'm not that patient." He smiled. "Also, I don't believe art has to ignore technology. With the machine, the needles puncture the skin a hundred times a second or so."

Sammi arched her eyebrows. "And, oddly enough, that doesn't comfort me."

Dante nodded. "I see you're nervous. You don't need to be. It stings, sure, but I promise that you have been hurt more than I will hurt you tonight."

Having once tripped over a board studded with bent and half-rusted nails, Sammi still didn't feel reassured.

"Can we stop talking about the pain and the needles?" Letty called out from the table. "I'm trying to stay in my happy place here, and you're all making it very difficult."

Dante went to a small silver machine and flicked a switch. It hummed almost like a microwave, and when he turned it off and opened the door, steam billowed out.

"Every one I use will be sterile," he said. "Even so, you'll have to care for the tattoos properly afterward, to avoid infection."

The tattooist continued talking them through what he was doing, sharing odd facts about the history of tattooing and body modification, very serious about his business. Sammi watched his hands, how deftly his fingers moved, and she studied those blue eyes.

Only when he set to work on Letty's back, glancing again and again at the design he had drawn and then pressing the tattoo needle against her flesh, did Sammi have to look away. As she did, she noticed another door off to one side, between a metal cabinet and a shelf filled with plastic containers. The door had a padlock on it, and she wondered where it led. Not to the alley in back of the building. She tried to imagine the layout of the strip of shops on this block. If Dante had more space beyond that door, it must be storage or something. But if the shop was locked up, why would he need a padlock there?

Letty hissed through her teeth.

"You're all right," Dante assured her. "The closer we are to bone, the more it hurts. We're above the tailbone here."

"Be gentle with me," Letty said, as though she were the heroine of some old romance novel.

Dante did not glance up from his work. He pushed the needle down again, moving it in a circle, creating the world, the ocean, the storm of his inspiration.

"Always."

Katsuko offered herself up next. Since she was a swimmer, there were very few places she could hide the tattoo, and though she had made a lot of noise about wanting to shock her parents, when it came down to it, she became more wary. Her tattoo went on her right hip, low enough to be hidden by her pants or skirt, but high enough not to be revealed by her bathing suit. It did not take Dante long at all, because Katsuko's tattoo covered only about an inch of flesh.

T.Q. had hers done on the back of her neck, just below the hairline. It would only show if she wore her hair up. Caryn had a hard time deciding. She wanted to have Dante tattoo her belly, with her navel as the center of the design, the uninked core.

The tattooist did not like that idea. "It ruins the design. And it won't match your friends', which I thought was the point."

Caryn looked irked; then Letty spoke up.

"You don't want it there anyway." Letty reached around, gingerly, to touch the bandage Dante had put over her tattoo. "We'll all be old ladies with saggy bellies someday. Even if you're still thin, it'll look awful there."

Caryn decided on her shoulder blade.

As the time had gone by and the hour had become later, Sammi had watched in fascination as her friends were inked—branded. When Dante turned those ice blue eyes on Sammi, she took a step back, bumping into a shelf full of art books, overflow from the design studio in the front.

The girls stared at her.

Dante narrowed his eyes.

Katsuko was the first to understand the expression on her face. "Sammi, you can't. We all agreed. There's no bailing on us now."

Then they all got it, and she saw it in their eyes. Disappointment. Anger. Betrayal. All along she had planned to go through with it, despite knowing how her parents would react if they found out. But now that the moment had arrived, she couldn't bring herself to let Dante touch her with that needle.

"I'm sorry, you guys. I thought I brought the money, but I think it's in my bag back at Letty's."

T.Q. smiled, looking relieved. "Don't scare us like that. The four of us have enough left over to spot you."

Sammi trembled, caught in the lie. In the back of her mind she could hear her parents, could practically see them standing in the corner like ghosts, staring at her with angry, disdainful expressions. It had come down to a choice: disappoint and betray the expectations of her friends or those of her parents.

"You guys, I'm sorry," she said, feeling her face flush and her eyes begin to moisten.

"Sammi," Letty said, shaking her head, not understanding. "You were on board with this."

"What?" Katsuko said. "This doesn't mean anything to you?"

"My parents—" Sammi started.

Katsuko shook her head, hurt and angry. "Come on, Sam. You know what *my* parents will do if they find out. If it meant enough to you, that wouldn't matter."

Sammi looked to Caryn for support but found none. "You're ruining the whole thing, Sammi," she said, her disappointment etched on her face. "Ruining it all. Now, instead of looking at these tattoos and thinking about how much we all wanted them, and why, we're gonna think about how you *didn't* want yours."

Letty sighed. "There are five waves in Dante's design, Sammi."

Dante's beautiful features had turned ugly. From the look he gave Sammi, it was as though she had insulted him, had ruined his inspiration instead of theirs.

She opened her mouth but nothing came out. Sammi shook her head, reached up to wipe away tears, and then turned from them, unable to look for another moment at the hurt on the faces of her friends. She ran into the front room and pushed open the door, stepping out onto the street and letting the black-painted door close behind her.

Once there, in the blue glow of neon from the Open sign, she felt exposed and endangered. This neighborhood wasn't the kind of place where a girl ought to be walking alone—and she knew she was alone. She thought about taking off, going into a shop to hide from her friends. Her skin prickled with goose bumps and her face burned with embarrassment and tears.

They'd be coming out any second.

She pulled out her cell phone and flipped it open, even started to call her mother. It was still before midnight. Her mother wouldn't mind. She had always said if Sammi ever got into any trouble to call, that she would come and get her daughter. But Sammi knew that whatever her mother said about "no questions asked," eventually she would have to explain what she had been doing down in this neighborhood, and why she and her friends had been arguing.

The door opened and the girls came out.

Sammi didn't even look up at them. T.Q. put a hand on her shoulder, a quiet reminder that as mad as they might be at her right now, they still loved her. In almost total silence, they walked back to Letty's house. What little discussion took place had to do with who was going to sleep where. Once they arrived, they spread out on their sleeping bags on the floor of Letty's room and watched television for a while, the room full of awkwardness and hurt feelings. They were disappointed and angry and confused, and Sammi could not blame them. She felt like a coward, and despised herself for it.

In the dark, lying on top of her sleeping bag because it was too warm to slip inside, she could not take it anymore.

"You guys, I'm so sorry," she said, her voice hitching with emotion. Sammi had never let anyone down this badly in her life, and she vowed never to do it again. "I'll go see Dante tomorrow night. I'll get it taken care of. I just . . . I freaked out. But I don't want to ruin this. I want to show you what it means to me to have you all as my friends."

Letty sat up in bed. In the light that filtered through the curtains from the streetlight outside, her hopeful expression broke Sammi's heart.

"Do you mean it? You promise?"

They were all sitting up, watching her now.

"I swear," Sammi said. "I feel like such a loser."

"You are," Caryn said. "But we love you anyway."

She reached over to grab her jeans where they lay on a chair and plucked a folded piece of paper from her pocket. At first Sammi thought it was the designs that Caryn had done for them, but as she unfolded it in the gloom of the bedroom, she saw that it was Dante's design, the tattoo they had inspired him to create. He had said he would give

5

On Sunday morning, Caryn's mother came to pick up her daughter just after ten o'clock. When Mrs. Adams offered Sammi a ride home, she did not hesitate at all. Her own mother wasn't supposed to pick her up until lunchtime, but she did not want to spend another two hours fumbling awkwardly around the girls who were her best friends in the world. They had all tried to be nice and behave as if they weren't upset with her about the way she'd let them down the night before, but Sammi knew there was only one way to fix what she'd done.

The damn tattoo.

Now she rode in the back of Mrs. Adams's SUV with Dante's design folded in her back pocket. Rain pattered on the windshield, and the wipers had a rhythmic, hypnotic quality that kept drawing her eyes. Caryn talked to her a little—small bursts of conversation accompanied by halfhearted smiles—but it all felt forced. Even if the girls forgave her, Sammi knew that wouldn't erase their hurt.

She stared out the window, just watching the rain, and pulled her hands inside the sleeves of her Covington High sweatshirt. With the rain had come a chill.

Mrs. Adams pulled into Sammi's driveway and threw the car into park, then turned around in the seat to give her a smile. "Home safe and sound."

Grabbing her bag, Sammi popped open the door. "Bye, Caryn. See you tomorrow."

Caryn lifted her hand in a wave. "See you later."

Sammi forced a smile. "Thanks, Mrs. Adams. I'm sure my mom'll be happy not to have to make the trip."

"Anytime, sweetie. You know that."

As the car pulled away, Sammi ran to her front door with her overnight bag over her head, fishing her keys out of her pocket. When she entered the house, her mother sat on the living room floor with the Sunday paper spread out around her. Linda Holland looked up and smiled.

"Hey. What are you doing home? I thought I was supposed to come and get you."

Sammi stepped out of her sneakers and left them on the mat inside the door. Her house enveloped her with welcoming arms. The smell of coffee brewing seemed to ease some of the tension from her shoulders. For the first time since agreeing to get that stupid tattoo in the first place, she felt safe. "Caryn had to go home early and Mrs. Adams offered, so I figured I'd save you having to get out of your pajamas," Sammi said. And this time when she grinned, it felt real, as though she'd woken up from a bad dream and found her mother at the edge of her bed, telling her everything would be all right.

Her mom glanced down at the cotton pajamas she wore and the white socks on her slender feet. She didn't sleep in the whole outfit, but on weekend mornings she pulled PJ's on the instant she woke up and didn't shower and change until she went to the gym. Most Sundays for the past few months, that had been uncharacteristically early. Sammi had missed the Sunday-morning ritual with her father today, but she took it as a hopeful sign that her mother hadn't rushed off this morning.

"You're just jealous of my jammies."

Sammi went into the living room and plopped onto the couch, pulling her legs up under her. "True. Very cozy. Anything interesting in the paper?"

"More every day," her mother said. "All the things you think are boring when you're sixteen—stuff you can't imagine ever being anything but boring—becomes strangely fascinating when you get older."

"Sorry. Can't see it."

"It sneaks up on you."

"On you, maybe."

Her mother gave her a familiar look that suggested the wisdom of the ancients and then looked back down at the paper.

"You want to go to the movies later?"

"If we can go at dinnertime. I've got some stuff to do today. Library stuff. I think I'm gonna meet Caryn there,"

Sammi told her mother. It surprised her how easily the lie rolled off her tongue.

"Where's Dad?" she asked.

"At the gym. The Patriots game is on later. He's getting his workout in before he sets up camp in front of the TV."

Sammi rolled her eyes. She didn't mind football, but the season felt like it started earlier every year. And when the Patriots played, the living room became her father's man cave.

"Fantastic. You enjoy that."

Her mother stuck out her tongue. Sammi laughed and hopped up from the couch. Maybe her parents had made amends. The way their relationship had been fraying lately, she hardly dared hope. Overnight bag in hand, she trotted up the stairs, all too aware of the folded paper in her back pocket.

She'd promised the girls she would go back to Dante's today. In the back of her mind she could still hear the whir of the tattoo needle, smell the ink, see Katsuko flinch as the little design—that tiny world with its five ocean waves—was scarred into her flesh.

In her bedroom, she tossed her bag on the floor at the end of her bed and pulled off her sweatshirt. Sammi hadn't bothered taking a shower at Letty's house, just wanting to get home. But before she could shower, she had more pressing business. Moving back to her door, she peered out and looked down the stairs. When she saw no sign that her mother had abandoned the newspaper, she darted across the hall into her parents' room. The taller of the two bureaus belonged to her mother, who always kept her address book beside the small jewelry box on top.

Sammi slipped out her cell phone. Flipping through the pages of the address book, she found the number she wanted and keyed it into the phone but did not press the green button that would send the call through. The address book went back to its place on the bureau and Sammi hurried back to her own bedroom, closing the door behind her.

Staring a moment at the number she had punched in, she hit the button. Her face felt warm, and she glanced anxiously at her door, hating secrecy. A song started to play on the line, and at first she thought it would be voice mail. Then she realized it was just a ringback tone, some thrash metal thing that pounded into her skull so that she had to hold the phone away from her ear.

"Hello?"

"Zak? Oh, wow. I didn't think you were going to answer. Hey, it's Sammi."

"Samalamadingdong! What's up? Hey, wait, is something wrong?"

"No, no, everybody's good. I just . . . need some help."

Zak hesitated. When he spoke again, the lightness had gone from his tone. "You know I'll always help if I can, Sam. We're family. Talk to me."

Sammi wanted to shout. She felt so trapped between obligations to her parents and her friends that it was as if she were all alone in the world. Cute Adam might be sweet, but they'd just met and she didn't want to scare him off with any weirdness. Zak would never know how much it meant to her, just to have someone to rely on.

Though she didn't see him often—he was in college and five years older than she was—Zak was the only one of her relatives aside from her parents who had ever taken much interest in her. The whole family thought him bizarre, but he had always been a sweet guy, so they indulged him.

While working toward his degree at New England Community College, Zak made a living handcrafting leather, everything from decorative masks to jackets, vests, and chaps for people who loved their motorcycles a little too much. He set up a booth at Renaissance fairs and that sort of thing. Sammi had always thought him wonderful, loved how he went through the world as an artisan, doing what he loved. If he had been a musician, he'd have been some kind of troubadour. And Zak had always encouraged her music.

Sammi wasn't alone. She reached into her back pocket and unfolded the paper, staring at Dante's design.

"You still going out with Rachael Dubrowski?"

"Yeah, of course. What's this about, Sammi?"

Rachael was two years older than Zak, but they'd had a thing going on for years. Sammi had gone to school with her younger sister, Anna, since the first grade.

"Rachael still has that tattoo shop downtown, right?"

how'd ur sleepover go?

The text from Cute Adam came through a little after nine o'clock that night. Sammi had just come back from

78

the movies with her mother—Dad still celebrating a Patriots win—and when she got to her bedroom, it was a relief not to have to keep worrying about her shirt riding up to reveal the upper edge of the bandage on her lower abdomen.

kinda weird, she texted back. *long story*.

what @ ur date fri. nite? how'd that go?

Sammi smiled and burrowed down under her covers. The windows were open and the curtains billowed in the breeze. The rain had stopped and the night air smelled amazing.

pretty good, i think. he's cute. smart. different.

u think u'll c him again next wknd?

if he asks.

huh. got a feeling he will.

A warmth spread across her chest. She had only just met Adam, but she liked him. A lot. He was all the things she'd said, and clever, too. A little goofy, but she liked that, too.

i hope so, she texted. A risk, but she felt daring. *g2g2bed. talk tmrw?*

definitely. sweet dreams.

nite.

Sweet dreams. After last night, Sammi wouldn't have thought it possible, but maybe she would have sweet dreams tonight after all.

The old school bus shuddered, engine groaning loudly. Sammi sat in back, next to a window, with a freshman girl next to her who didn't say a word. She rested her forehead on the glass and looked out at the houses passing by, the thrumming of the bus making her skull vibrate. Her stomach felt tight as a fist; she hadn't been able to eat anything at all this morning. A glass of orange juice had been all she could manage, and that only because her mother insisted.

The rain had cleared overnight, but the gray skies remained. The whole world had a muted, washed-out look, and Sammi had looked in the mirror this morning and thought similar things about herself. A gray girl on a gray day.

A knocking sound came from somewhere under the bus and for a second she held her breath, wondering if the old beast would just seize up and drop its engine right there on the road. All of these old school buses rattled and moaned and belched out thick exhaust. Either they weren't street legal and no one cared, or the laws were more lenient on bright yellow tanks.

And why am I so focused on buses?

To avoid thinking about other things. Sammi knew that. In the eighth grade a bunch of other kids had told her that Kevin Mitchell wanted to ask her out. Every day for a week she had dreaded the prospect of running into him in the hall, both afraid that he would ask her out and worried that he wouldn't. In the end, Kevin had taken her for pizza once, only to make them both realize they had nothing in common.

That week of dreadful anticipation had faded in her memory, but this morning it came rushing back. She felt that way again for the first time since.

The bus managed to lumber into the Covington High parking lot. Backpack slung over her shoulder, Sammi stepped off the bus last and joined the throng flowing into the school, trying to ignore the way her pulse throbbed in her temples. Tony Gregson, a hockey star who had been in her advanced English classes all through school, said hello as he passed. Sammi mustered a smile and kept it plastered on her face as she made her way up the stairs to the second floor corridor where her locker was located.

Weaving in and out of the crowd, the hall deafening with chatter, she spotted T.Q. ahead and hurried to catch up.

"Hey," she said, falling into step beside her.

T.Q. smiled. "Hey." Then her smile faltered—the memory of Sammi's betrayal rushing back—and a kind of sadness came over her face. "What'd you end up doing yesterday? Did you hook up with Cute Adam again?"

Sammi made sure her smile-mask did not slip. She arched an eyebrow. "Duh. What did I *say* I was going to do yesterday?"

"You went? You really did?" T.Q.'s face lit up with excitement and gratitude. Sammi had tainted everything on Saturday night, but it could be all right again, and it was obvious T.Q. wanted that as much as she did.

Sammi felt sick.

"I said I would."

Lowering her voice to a conspiratorial tone, T.Q. asked, "Where'd you get it?"

They had slowed down, and now the flow of students

passed around them, mostly freshmen and sophomores worried about getting to class on time. The juniors and seniors were never in quite as much of a hurry. Sammi glanced around guiltily, as if she were about to make some surreptitious drug deal.

With a meaningful look at T.Q., she patted her lower abdomen, just inside her right hip.

"Sweet. How big did you do it?" As she spoke, T.Q. idly touched the back of her neck where her hair hid her own tattoo.

Sammi led the way to her locker, worked the combination, and pulled it open. Shielded by the door and T.Q., she tugged down the front of her jeans to show the inch-wide tattoo. Her heart thundered in her chest, and her throat went dry.

T.Q. made a small squeal of delight and hugged her. "This is great. The girls are gonna be completely psyched."

They shared the same homeroom, so after a stop at T.Q.'s locker they managed to beat the bell into the room. T.Q. seemed unusually talkative, impatient to learn if she had made the basketball team—the list would be posted by noon—and Sammi found some of her anxiety going away. Things were going to be all right now.

Between periods she saw Letty and Katsuko in the hall, but when she stopped to talk they were distant and made a lame excuse about needing to get to trigonometry early to talk to the teacher. Left standing by herself in the corridor, Sammi took a deep breath and brushed it off. It wasn't as though she could have just flashed her tattoo there in the hallway, drawing all kinds of attention.

After third period, she threw herself into the tide of people moving down the central stairwell to the cafeteria in the basement. A couple of Las Reinas nodded in greeting, going up the steps against the flow. Her all-time favorite teacher, Mr. Geary, who taught history and had always encouraged her music, stood by the main doors directing traffic and making sure nobody decided to use the prelunch chaos to make a break for it and blow off the rest of the day.

The cafeteria was at the back of the school, its own wing, with three sets of metal doors propped wide open. The smell of today's mystery meat made her stomach growl, and she remembered that she'd skipped breakfast. Her front right pocket bulged with the presence of her phone, and she hoped she'd have a few minutes before the girls showed up at lunch so she could text Adam. She needed a little reinforcement at the moment from someone outside her circle.

Letty stood between two sets of cafeteria doors, waiting for her. They spotted each other at the same time, and a happy smile blossomed on Letty's face.

"Hey, chica."

Sammi went up to her, nervous and wondering if Letty would notice. "Hey. I guess you talked to T.Q."

"I did," Letty said, falling into step with her. She bumped Sammi in the shoulder as they went down the five steps into the cafeteria. "I'd kiss you, but I'm not up for a scandal this week."

"Nothing wrong with a little scandal," Sammi said. "Besides, if the boys think I swing both ways, you know how much they love that."

"Yep. The boys love lesbians. And they never seem to understand why that does nothing for us. What's so hard to fathom about gay girls? Not really interested in entertaining guys."

They got into the lunch line and picked up trays, already craning their necks to see what the glass cases revealed. They would choose the least repulsive meal, just to have sustenance.

"That's why we hang around with you," Sammi teased. "Gorgeous lesbian man-bait. You draw them in and the rest of us can snare them."

Letty's eyes flashed. "Glad to know I'm useful for something."

Sammi rolled her eyes.

The lunch ladies said hello, familiar by now with most of the upperclassmen, and Sammi chose a chicken parmigiana sandwich. Letty went with steamed vegetables and rice, rarely trusting the meat from the cafeteria.

"That's it," she said as they filled water glasses, "I've got my life's work ahead of me. I'm goin' to culinary school and come back here and teach these ladies how to cook. Or I'm gonna have a show on a cooking channel and have every school in the country sign up and force the lunch ladies of America to watch it every day."

Sammi nodded her approval. "It's a commendable mission."

By the time they walked back to the table, Caryn and T.Q. were in line. Katsuko had somehow gotten there early and already had a table waiting for them in the far corner where they always sat, in whatever combination shared a lunch period. Their schedules were such that Monday and Tuesday were the only days they were all together during lunch this semester, and those days were always cause for celebration.

Letty sat down beside Katsuko. Sammi slid her tray onto the table across from them.

Katsuko gave her a sly smile. "I hear you bit the bullet."

"I couldn't let you guys down."

"What about your parents?"

Sammi shrugged. "I'm with you. We'll just have to make sure they never see it. It's in an intimate location. I won't be flashing it around."

"Except to Cute Adam," Letty said, leaning back in her chair as though offering herself up. "Oh baby, I've got something to show you. Take a real close look. Closer. Closer. Cloooo-ser."

Katsuko snorted a little when she laughed and then covered her mouth in embarrassment, as if the sound had come from there.

"Oh, please," Sammi protested, grinning. "I only just met him. He hasn't been promoted to tattoo inspector yet."

T.Q. and Caryn joined them, sliding into seats on either side of Sammi.

"So, did you show them yet?" T.Q. asked.

Sammi rolled her eyes. "I'm not yanking my pants down in the middle of the cafeteria."

"What's stopping you?" Letty asked.

Caryn nudged her. "Come on. Let's see."

Sammi hesitated, but thought this might be perfect. Any nervousness, any blushing, they'd just chalk up to embarrassment. The table was in the corner anyway. She stood up quickly and refused to draw attention to herself by glancing around.

"Is anyone watching?" she asked in a whisper.

"No, you're good," T.Q. said.

The other girls' attention was riveted on her hands as she slipped her fingers into the waist of her jeans. No way would she unbutton or unzip them. Instead, she sucked in her belly and just tugged them down in the front, far enough to let them see the top half of the tattoo.

"Good for you, girl," she heard Caryn say.

Letty gave a low wolf whistle and a silent golf clap. But Katsuko's smile fell and she frowned deeply, staring at the tattoo.

"It's different," she said.

Oh shit, Sammi thought. Her skin prickled with warmth and her heart raced.

"What do you mean? It's the same design," she said.

Now all of them were looking more closely. She wanted to pull her jeans up and sit down but had to prove herself.

Caryn shook her head. "No, she's right. The hole in the center is smaller and the waves dip more at the top."

Sammi glanced around self-consciously. Some people were staring, and she made a show of reacting to being observed, covering her tattoo and returning to her seat.

"It's not a big deal," she said. "It's the same design. You can't expect him to do it exactly alike every time, like a machine or something."

T.Q. had a crestfallen expression on her face. Sammi couldn't look at her.

"Ours are all the same," Katsuko said, pushing her curtain of black hair away from her eyes. "Identical. Did you really go back to Dante?"

Here it is, Sammi thought. *Cards on the table.* How could she lie outright, to their faces? If they suspected a lie, all they had to do was have Letty drop by Dante's and ask.

"Not exactly," she began. "But what difference does it—"

"It's not real," Letty said sharply. Her mouth had turned into a thin line of anger and her eyes narrowed.

The others all seemed confused.

"Define 'real,' Katsuko said.

Letty sniffed in disgust. "She won't show it to us again, or you could see for yourself. I didn't even notice until you said it wasn't the same, but Sammi just had this done yesterday? Where's the swelling? Where's the redness? Mine's still healing, still going down, but hers looks fine. It's gotta be henna, or airbrushed. In a week or two, it'll be gone."

On Saturday night, they'd been hurt and disappointed. Now Katsuko and Caryn only shook their heads and glared at her, mouths twisted in disgust and anger.

"Sammi?" T.Q. asked, gentle as ever. "Tell them they're wrong."

That moment was the worst; T.Q. still believing in her, still hoping. Sammi could only hang her head.

Letty stood first, the legs of her chair squeaking on the linoleum as she slid back, rose, and picked up her tray. One by one, the others got up as well. Sammi wished they would yell at her, so that maybe she could try to explain why she had done it. But they walked away, moving to another table, and left her in the corner alone.

All eyes in the cafeteria must have been on her, but Sammi did not turn to look. She kept her back to everyone, pushing her food around with a fork. She'd lost her appetite again.

6

The rest of the day Sammi walked the halls of Covington High in a constant state of humiliation. In sixth grade she'd had a recurring dream about showing up late for school, completely naked. As she moved from class to class, from locker to bus line, she felt that dreamlike hyperreality envelop her. Every glance or whisper troubled her. No matter how she told herself they weren't talking about her, that a lot of people hadn't even noticed the way her friends had abandoned her and it simply wasn't interesting enough gossip for the rest of the school to care, still she felt exposed.

Her skin prickled with pins and needles all day, her cheeks burning with embarrassment. Worse yet, a stone had somehow exchanged places with her heart. Cold, hard stone. It made Sammi walk more slowly, made it hard for her to lift her chin, made it hard to breathe and to swallow.

In her entire life, she'd never felt so lonely. Without the

girls, Sammi floated at sea, cast adrift. She might as well have been the only one in school who spoke English, for all the good the rest of them would do her.

She had other friends, and she kept telling herself that. But they weren't her real friends, not close. Not intimate. For the first time, she hated being a floater. In all the school there was no one to whom she could turn for reassurance, for a safe harbor. Before her final class of the day, she huddled in a stall in the girls' room and sent Adam a text message.

today's a disaster. can u talk later?

Sammi waited as long as she could, even past the bell to begin class, but Adam did not reply. When she hurried into psychology late, enduring the wrathful gaze of Mr. Sullivan— the knitting of those bushy eyebrows—she had to bite her lip to stop herself from crying.

Which pissed her off.

By the time psych ended and Sammi threaded through the crowded halls to her locker, some of the hurt and humiliation had turned to anger. When she saw Katsuko coming in the opposite direction, she stared into her eyes for a second and then looked away. They brushed past one another, shoulders coming into contact.

"Bitch," Katsuko muttered.

Sammi flinched. The word cut deeply, but instead of blood, the wound filled with anger. She gritted her teeth and willed her heart to go cold against the girls—against her friends. If they were going to take things that far, then to hell with them.

She jammed her books into her backpack and slammed her locker. As she left the school, she kept her eyes fixed firmly in front of her. Sammi refused to look at anything except what was straight ahead. She raised her eyes just long enough to mark the location of her bus and then headed in that direction. Out of the corner of her eye, she caught sight of T.Q.'s hair—as always, the girl was impossible to miss.

Katsuko had always tended to be arrogant and Caryn had her temper, but if any of them would give her the benefit of the doubt, it would be T.Q. For a second she hesitated, wishing she could just put an end to the emotions that had wound her up so tightly. But then Sammi pushed on, getting in line for her bus. She had tried to deceive them, had lied to all of them, but they had to know why. At least they could have given her a chance to explain.

So much for sisters, she thought, stepping up onto the bus.

Once in her seat she pulled out her cell phone to find no messages. Adam hadn't replied to her text yet, and why should he? They'd just met. Now she regretted having sent it at all. Sammi had never been one of those girls who thrived on drama, who stoked it up like a fire. But if she started unloading all of this crap on Cute Adam, he'd start seeing her that way for sure.

Mistake.

As the bus started to rumble away from the sidewalk, she rested her forehead on the back of the seat in front of her. Some of the tension and anger that had coiled up in her all afternoon seeped away, and she felt her muscles relaxing.

"Sammi?"

Frowning, she looked up. On the seat in front of her, a sophomore kid named Eli Burns had turned on his knees to face her.

"The thing, at lunch? Totally harsh," he said. The pity in his eyes made her fists tighten. Eli shrugged. "Just thought someone should say it. Whatever it was about, they were total bitches."

The chunk of ice that she had willed her heart into becoming did not melt, nor did she flush with either embarrassment or rage. Instead, she felt the color drain from her face and just stared blankly at him.

Eli blinked, cocked an eyebrow, and turned around in his seat. "Oookay. Maybe it isn't them."

Sammi felt like slapping him on the back of the head. Instead, she sat rigid in her seat and waited as the bus made its rounds, bristling at the delay every time the vehicle groaned to a stop to disgorge some freshman or sophomore. Most of the juniors who did not yet have their driver's licenses managed to catch a ride with someone who did. Sammi and the girls had talked about it—had agreed that they would all ride the bus and ignore the snide looks it brought them—but this afternoon she would rather have walked home.

The sky remained gray, threatening more rain, but not a drop fell.

Eli might have been looking at her when she got up to

get off the bus. Sammi kept her eyes front, pretending to be the only person on board. She moved along the aisle, then went down the steps and dropped to the curb three blocks from her house. Ahead of her were two freshman girls who'd gotten off before her. The bus rolled away, belching dark gray exhaust, and Sammi held her breath until the breeze had carried away the cloud of fumes.

If she'd wanted to, she could have caught up to the freshman girls. But she'd never bothered with them before, and today wouldn't change that. She hung back until they had turned down Winchester Road, then hooked her thumbs through the straps of her backpack and picked up her pace.

Her house should have seemed welcoming to her, but on that gray day, and with no one home, it had an ominous stillness that gave her no comfort. Sammi took out her keys and let herself in, then let her backpack slide to the floor. She left the door open, letting the September breeze in through the screen on the storm door.

The empty house sighed as if grateful for her presence.

Sammi stepped out of her shoes and went up the stairs to her room. As she lay down on her bed, she flipped open her cell phone. Texting Adam had been a mistake. They'd been out exactly once. Putting her troubles on him would probably scare him off fast.

He still hadn't texted her back.

"Smart move, Holland," she whispered. Her thumb hovered over the phone's keypad. She wanted to call Caryn, or Letty, to put all of this behind them, but a wave of bitterness swept over her. No way would she call. Sammi had already apologized, and they had totally overreacted.

No, it was their turn.

For a second she fought the temptation to call Cute Adam, just to have someone to talk to, but then she would be verging into stalker-girl territory.

Snapping the phone shut, she tossed it on the bed and got up, walking to her computer. Sammi logged onto her online journal, and her friends list popped up, revealing that Caryn had already gotten home and gone online.

She clicked to open an instant message box and began to type.

Hey. I know you don't want to talk to me right now, and that's fine. But I've already apologized. What else do you want from me? You know how things are with my parents. You're all supposed to be my friends, but you can't even TRY to understand?

Tempted to delete it without sending, she got up and walked away from the computer. Outside, at last, a light drizzle sprinkled against the windows. The storm had been holding its breath all day, and now it exhaled.

If her mother had been home, maybe they could have talked it out together. But she wouldn't be home from the bank until five-thirty.

Sammi strode back to the computer and clicked Send.

Her phone trilled. She jumped a little in the chair, then went to answer it. The incoming call was from Adam, and just seeing his name gave her some comfort. A friendly, sympathetic voice would be so welcome right now.

"Hello?"

"You all right?" She could hear the concern in his voice, but also a kind of wary curiosity.

"I'm okay. Mondays, y'know? Kinda butting heads with my friends, but I'll survive. How did *your* Monday go?" She spoke too fast, the words running together, and anyone who knew her would understand how upset she was. But Adam didn't know her. He probably thought she was just psycho.

Way to go, Sam.

"Kind of disappointing," he said. "My clever plan for world domination failed."

Sammi laughed, maybe a little too much. "So what next, evil overlord? What's Plan B?"

"No Plan B. I met this girl, see. She's a musician. Beautiful music, beautiful girl. Makes me think maybe it's time to leave world domination schemes to my flunkies, stop and smell the roses, blah blah blah. Want to hang out Saturday night?"

I so do, she thought. But she took a breath. Looking eager was never a good idea.

"Well, if it means preventing world conquest by a tyrannical madman, it would be selfish of me to say no."

Adam gave a quiet laugh. "Throwing yourself to the lions. Admirable."

Her computer binked. Sammi glanced over and saw that Caryn had replied to her IM. The ice she had summoned up earlier re-formed around her heart, but the spark of hope burned there, too.

"Hey. Can we talk later? I've got some stuff."

"Sure. If you have a chance. If not, we'll catch up to-morrow."

"Thanks. Bye."

"Bye."

Sammi closed her phone. Catching up tomorrow might be better. Now that she'd managed to dig herself out of the pitiful text she'd sent Adam earlier, no way would she lay all of her drama on him. When she knew him better, maybe. But right now all she wanted to show him of herself was the girl he'd had so much fun with at dinner the other night.

Sliding the phone into the clip on her belt, she went back to her chair, but never got to sit down. She put her hands on the back, staring down at the instant message window that stood open on her screen.

You're all righteous now? Caryn had written. *Our bodies are branded with a mark that—for the rest of our lives—is going to remind us what a traitorous bitch you are. You didn't ruin a moment. You put a stain on us that'll be there every day in the mirror. That's forever. Don't even think about talking to me again.*

Sammi stared at the words, trying to make sense of the rage and regret that filled her, to put it into words. Something blinked on the right of the screen, and she focused on her friends list. The others were all there now. BrownEyedGirl93 was Letty. T.Q. used her real name, SimoneD. Katsuko hated when people called her Kat, but used KatScratch for her screen name.

StylishCarA had vanished.

Caryn had not just logged off. She had blocked Sammi from her friends list.

And now, as Sammi watched, one by one the others all defriended her as well, blinking out. BrownEyedGirl93. SimoneD. KatScratch. They were all gone, leaving behind the names of a few people at school and several she knew only from the Internet, people who might be on her friends list but didn't really belong.

The girls had deleted Sammi from their lives.

At half past five, Sammi's mother came home. Sammi heard the door shut and called down to her, but didn't get up immediately. She was in the middle of changing a string on her guitar. Homework left zipped away in her backpack, she'd spent the afternoon playing angry songs that made her feel self-righteous—Alanis Morissette, Fiona Apple, and even "What I Am," an ancient tune by Edie Brickell and New Bohemians. Anything that she could sing well while pissed off worked just fine.

Once she'd replaced the string, she fiddled with the guitar for a few minutes, making sure it was in tune. Trying to shake off her mood before seeing her mother, she picked out the first few notes of "Summer Girl," a song of her own she'd been working on that followed a single girl's emotional arc over the course of four seasons, from autumn to summer. She had another that needed work—"Invisible"— but it involved school and friendship, and she wouldn't strum a note of that one today.

Sammi sang the first verse and chorus of "Summer Girl" before she realized that the house seemed awfully quiet. Her mother had come in but had not yet come upstairs to say hello to her. No cabinets were banging, no pots and pans, so Mom hadn't started on dinner, and she didn't hear voices, so Mom wasn't on the phone.

Curious, she stood up, propped her guitar on the stand in the corner, and went downstairs. Several windows were open, and the curtains rustled lazily with a cool breeze, heavy with the moisture of the damp day. Television voices droned from the living room, and Sammi followed them.

Her mother lay on her side on the couch, a pillow under her head and her eyes closed. On the cooking channel, a skinny British girl flashing tons of cleavage mixed some kind of concoction in a bowl, smiling and chatting away as though talking to her best friend—her audience.

Sammi stepped into the room and her mother opened her eyes. She didn't seem to have been sleeping, and her attempt at a smile looked as though it pained her.

"You okay?" Sammi asked.

"I've had better days."

"Me too."

Her mother frowned and sat up. For the first time, Sammi noticed the uneven line of her mascara, as though she might have been crying but done her best to eliminate the evidence.

"What's wrong?" she asked.

Sammi shook her head. "Nothing important. Teenager

stuff. It'll pass." Lies. All lies. "What about you? Something bad happen at work?"

A wry smile touched her mother's lips and she shook her head. "No. Work's fine. Listen, I really don't feel like cooking tonight, and I'm in even less of a mood to go out. Any objection to just ordering pizza?"

Sammi tried searching her eyes, but her mother glanced away. A selfish voice inside her began to whine. Her mom had been the one person she'd hoped to talk to about her falling-out with the girls, but now she had her own burdens, whatever they were. It didn't seem fair.

But at sixteen, Sammi had already learned that life wasn't fair. It was selfish to think only of herself when her mom was obviously hurting, too.

"Pizza's fine. Are you hungry now? I could order it."

"Thanks, sweetie. Mushroom and pepper sound good?"

"It's pizza. Pretty much any pizza makes me happy. What about Dad, though? Should I get half pepperoni, do you think?"

Her mother winced. Then she smiled as though catching herself doing something foolish. "He won't be home for dinner." She sighed, shaking her head with a soft laugh of disbelief. "We'll have to see if he makes it home for breakfast."

Sammi's stomach lurched. "What's that mean? Did you guys have a fight?"

With great deliberateness, her mother focused on her, as though for the first time, her gaze kind but forlorn.

"He's thinking about leaving, your father. He's trying to decide if he wants to leave, and I'm trying to decide how long to wait before I take the choice away from him."

Sammi's mouth hung open in a little "o" of surprise. There had been many days when the tension in the house made her hide away in her room, but she had never let herself believe it could come to this. Her parents could be cold to each other, navigating around the house to avoid having to speak, but that wasn't all the time. She'd heard them fight about money, but mostly the conflicts revolved around the amount of time her father spent at the office, the nights he came home late.

But this? Had he been cheating on her, or had they just gotten sick of each other? Sammi stared at her mother, eyes narrowed, trying to make sense of this new information, something that would not have seemed possible to her only minutes before.

"You guys . . . you fight all the time, but you make up. He'll come home."

Her mother grimaced, swallowing hard, and lifted a hand to cover her mouth. Her eyes glistened wetly, but she did not cry.

"Maybe. Maybe not. I don't know which would be worse."

"I do," Sammi said quickly. She wanted to stomp her foot and cry, to try to force her mother to realize that only one outcome made any sense at all. They had to stay together. They were her parents, and they belonged here in the house with her. The way it should be. Her father might not be the most attentive dad in the world, but she couldn't imagine never having Sunday morning pancakes with him again.

"I'm sorry, Sammi. I shouldn't have said anything."

"No. You should. I'm sixteen, Mom, not some kid. I just . . . it's so hard for me to imagine."

"Well, don't try imagining it right now. Let's think about happier things and not worry about what we can't control. Your father and I aren't going to do anything crazy, not without talking things over. I'm sure of that much. You go and order the pizza. Is your homework done?"

"Not yet."

"Why don't you take care of that, and after dinner we'll watch a movie. Something funny."

Sammi nodded, wondering if there existed a movie in the world funny enough to lighten her heart tonight. The shadows of the day's events hung over her, made her feel a little queasy. It seemed surreal, not having her friends to call right now, not having them to talk her through what was going on with her parents. But they weren't her friends anymore. And so much for talking to her mother about the tattoos and the way the girls had turned their backs on her. Linda Holland had enough troubles of her own.

Sammi gnawed her lower lip, holding back all the things she wanted to say. Her guitar waited upstairs. All her confusion could be put into the music, exorcised like a demon.

But first she would keep her mother company for a little while. Sammi went into the kitchen to get the phone.

She called the Aegean, the local pizza place they liked the best, and then went back into the living room.

Homework could wait. She sat down next to her mother on the couch and they leaned into one another, huddling together the way they always had when Sammi had been very little. Mom handed her the remote control and she started surfing channels, not paying much attention, just looking for something to make them smile.

7

When Sammi stepped off the bus Tuesday morning, it felt like the first day at a new school. The gloomy weather of the past few days had at last abated, and the blue sky stretched forever in all directions. September always seemed a tug-of-war between summer and fall. Autumn would win in time, but on that morning summer had the advantage. Sammi wore cotton pants that zipped at the hip and a loose, short-sleeved burgundy shirt over a white tank, and she felt much too warm.

She'd been lucky in her life. Her family had always lived in Covington. Maybe that would change if they split up—*God, how can I even be thinking like that?*—but other than kindergarten, she'd never had to start a school without at least having some kids around that she knew. Still, she understood what that experience must be like, everybody studying the new kid out of the corner of his eye, checking her out, watching to see if she had two heads or a weird accent, waiting for her to define herself for them.

Today felt like that.

She crossed the quad in front of the school through a sea of familiar faces, but most of them glanced away quickly. No one spoke to her. Several people whose groups she'd floated in and out of over the years smiled or nodded to her, but no one came over to talk. Had she done that to herself? Alienated them? Or were they just keeping clear so they wouldn't be infected by the humiliation she'd suffered in the caf the day before?

Sammi threw her backpack over one shoulder and held her head high. The notes of her song "Summer Girl" were playing in her head, and she sang a few lines softly to herself and hummed a little as she made her way into the school. The corridors rang with voices and slamming lockers, and she found odd comfort in the familiarity. The rest of the world might be falling down around her—her parents' marriage, her friendships—but at least she could rely on the routine of high school.

She didn't look for the girls, but she watched out for them warily. It would take time for her to adjust to the way they'd defriended her, but the more she thought about it, the more confident Sammi felt that she'd been wronged. Should she have been honest with them right up front? Yeah. But trying not to hurt anyone's feelings shouldn't be grounds for just cutting someone off.

Whoever they were, they obviously weren't the girls she'd thought they were. It hurt. God, it hurt. But she'd survive this. And she cruised the corridors that morning cautiously anticipating the moment of first contact. Sammi needed that, needed to know she had the strength to ignore them. She had no doubt that they wouldn't be speaking to her—their bumping her from their IM friends lists had made that clear. But she had no interest in trying to talk to them, either.

She'd miss what they had all shared, but she had always been a floater. She would adjust.

"Morning, Sammi," a voice said.

She turned around to find Kyrie McIntosh falling into step beside her. "What's happening?"

Sammi smiled. "Nada. Getting back into the rhythm, y'know?"

The dark-haired sophomore had a retro-goth look that suited her. Short and petite, Kyrie seemed much younger than her age until you looked into her eyes and saw the intelligence and wisdom there. She was part of the theater crowd.

"I know. Nice not being a freshman anymore. Feels like I can exhale."

"What show are you guys doing this fall?" Sammi asked.

Kyrie rolled her eyes. "It's a big debate. I'm fighting for *Sweeney Todd*, but the dweebs want to do *High School Musical*."

Sammi shuddered in sympathy. "Good luck."

"Thanks. And if I win the debate, you better audition."

Kyrie was always telling her to audition. Sammi's response never wavered. She always just said, "We'll see."

But not today. "I might just do that."

They reached a T-junction and split up. Kyrie waved and said goodbye and Sammi made a beeline for her locker. She half-expected to find rude graffiti scratched on the door or painted in lipstick. The way the girls had been behaving, it wouldn't have surprised her. But it didn't appear that anyone had disturbed her locker. In some ways that was worse. They'd forgotten about her, just like that.

Maybe that's best.

She slid her backpack to the floor between her feet and spun through her combination, then popped open her locker. As she dug out her books, Sammi glanced up and saw Ken Nguyen coming down the corridor with a couple of the other guys on the basketball team.

"Hey, Ken."

He glanced her way and smiled, then broke off from the other players to join her at her locker.

"Sammi, what's goin' on? I haven't seen you once since school started."

The towering senior's laid-back manner set her at ease. She slid her backpack into her locker. "Since June, really. I don't think we've seen each other since school got out in the spring."

Ken nodded. "Yeah. True. You look great, by the way. Being a junior agrees with you."

Sammi arched an eyebrow. "Was that some kind of line?"

He laughed. "Maybe a little. Doesn't make it untrue."

"Dude, you are so going to have to work harder than

that. I don't just mean with me, but in general. You could do with lessons."

"Are you suggesting I'm not smooth?"

"Chunky peanut butter. Extra chunky. Especially from a guy I've known since, what, fourth grade?"

Ken hung his head in mock shame. "I'm deeply wounded."

Sammi laughed and shut her locker, holding her books in the crook of one arm. "Somehow I think you'll survive. When's your first game?"

"This Friday. You gonna come cheer us on?"

"I was never much of a cheerleader. The uniforms are creepy fetish objects for drooling, unshaven pervs desperately in need of a bath."

Ken shrugged. "All guys love girls in cheerleader uniforms."

She shook her head. "Still, creepy."

"I just figured you'd come, with Simone on the girls' team and all."

Sammi blinked. "She made the team?"

"Didn't you know?"

Innocent enough, the question still erased the smile from her face. Sammi glanced away a moment and then gave him an apologetic look.

"We're sort of not talking at the moment."

Scratching the back of his head, searching for something to say, Ken settled for the obvious. "I'm sorry to hear that."

"It happens. I'm glad she made it, though."

Relieved to be back on comfortable terrain—basketball—he nodded. "Yeah. She surprised everyone. Sure, she's tall. A lot of people think that automatically means you can play hoops. But that's just stupid. Tall people are just as clumsy as anyone else. But Simone's way more athletic than I ever would've thought. I mean, she edits the school paper."

Sammi arched an eyebrow. "So nerds can't play sports."

"Not usually, no." Ken smiled as if to say that might sound prejudiced, but it was also true. "Plus, she's . . ."

"You can say it. She's gorgeous."

"Hey, you said it. But it's no lie. She's, like, the last person I'd expect to be able to play that well."

"And now she's your perfect woman."

He paled a little. "I didn't say that."

Sammi gave an apologetic shrug. "Sorry, Kenny. I can't talk you up to her. Like I said, we're kinda not talking at the moment. But go for it. Maybe you guys can play some one on one."

"Now you're talking."

She held up a hand. "Enough. And, I'm just saying, gross."

The morning bell rang and they walked together until Sammi had to split off from him and go into her homeroom. Ken called out to someone and ran to catch up, and then Sammi stepped into the room, steeling herself to see T.Q. Her smile vanished and she put on a mask of stillness and calm.

But T.Q. wasn't in the room, and by the time the bell

rang for the students to make their way to their first classes of the day, she still had not shown up.

Only when Sammi walked into her fourth-period English class and saw that Letty and Katsuko were not in their usual seats at the back of the room—were, in fact, not there at all—did she realize that none of them had shown up for school. All day she had been on edge, anticipating that first encounter, but it wasn't coming.

When the bell rang signaling the end of fourth period, she flooded out into the corridor with the rest of the class. Her locker was on the other side of the school, and the growling of her stomach helped her decide not to bother switching her books around for trig until after lunch.

On the west wing stairs, she looked out the window and saw them. All four of them were there, talking and laughing. They'd come to school after all, just hadn't bothered to come inside. Sammi froze on the stairs, the flow of students moving around her, some of them muttering in annoyance. She ignored them.

Caryn leaned against a tree, smoking a cigarette. Letty leaned her head back and pursed her lips sexily, then blew out a cloud of smoke before tossing her cigarette to the dirt and grinding it under her heel. She tossed her head toward the school. The bell had rung, and it looked as if they were finally coming inside. Maybe they were hungry.

Sammi stared. Her friends didn't smoke. They never had. It seemed a small thing, yet at the same time huge, as if she'd woken up in some freakish alternate dimension. She shook her head, trying to make sense of it.

As if she'd seen the motion, Letty glanced up at the window.

She probably could have bolted, moved away before Letty could have gotten a good look and seen it was her. Instead Sammi frowned and kept staring. They were maybe twenty feet below the window, in a small cluster of towering old-growth trees. Even from that distance, Sammi felt mesmerized by Letty's milk chocolate eyes and what she saw there. No sadness. No resentment. No amusement. Just cold hate.

Sammi shivered.

Letty did not open her mouth, but the other three turned then, as one. Slowly and without a word, they looked up at her. Not one of them made a gesture, nor did their expressions flicker. They stared until Sammi backed away from the window, shaking her head, and started down the stairs again.

She felt as if she might throw up.

Was it really so awful, what she'd done? Did she deserve this?

"Bitches," she muttered, shaking it off. No more. Sammi had had enough of letting them make her feel that way. And how weird was that smoking thing?

From the smell wafting out of the caf, she figured either pizza or meatball subs for the more aromatic course. It might be just salad for her today. Carrying her books under one arm, she went down the steps and into the throng.

The entire time she spent in line, she kept glancing at

the doors, wondering when the girls would come in. On Wednesdays through Fridays they were separated, but today they all shared this lunch period with her.

With her salad and a small bowl of chocolate pudding, a beautifully balanced meal, she searched for a seat, for someone she knew, and was relieved when Anna Dubrowski waved her over. Sammi slid into a seat across from her and said hello to the group she was with. She knew most of them, guys and girls who were all pretty good students and who seemed to revolve around Anna.

But she paid little attention to the conversation, always watching the doors.

When the bell rang to end the period, the girls still had not shown up. She wondered where the hell they were if they hadn't come into the school yet. And then she worried that the whole year would be like this, her so focused on them that she ignored the people around her.

"You okay?" Anna asked as she took her tray up to be cleaned.

"Just a little spaced, sorry."

"That thing yesterday? With your friends?" Anna said.

Sammi felt grateful not to have to explain. She nodded.

"Don't let them get to you. We're all just marking time here," Anna told her with a smile. "After graduation, all this is going to be like a four-year dream."

"Or a nightmare," Sammi said.

"Or that."

"Oddly enough, that makes me feel better."

* * *

The day seemed to last forever. When Sammi walked into her last class—twentieth-century American history—she faltered at the sight of Letty seated in the back row. The Puerto Rican kids in Covington tended to hang out together: strength in numbers. Letty had explained it to Sammi once upon a time, said it wasn't a matter of prejudice, but of shared experience. They might become friends with others, but their parents all knew one another and they had grown up sharing the culture of their neighborhoods. And if anything went badly, they circled the wagons and shut out the rest of the world.

Other groups did the same thing, defined not by heritage but by loyalties nearly as strong. Football players and cheerleaders, theater and band geeks. They backed each other up.

Letty sat in the far corner at the back of the room, bathed in afternoon sunlight. At the desk beside her, Rafe Navedo sprawled in his chair, leaning toward her with a wolfish, suggestive smile on his handsome face. Rafe had thick, curly black hair almost to his shoulders and killer eyes, the type of guy who knew precisely how good-looking he was and made the most of it.

He whispered something to Letty, and she giggled quietly, flirtatiously.

Sammi felt as if she'd seen a ghost. Once upon a time, back when she'd spent all of her time hanging out with Las Reinas and guys like Rafe and Eddie Ocasio, Letty had kissed her share of boys. She'd flirted and put on the mask of hard-edged sexuality that Las Reinas all seemed to project, mostly as a way to tell the boys what they couldn't have. But once Letty had come out, once they knew she was gay, they'd cast her adrift. They were still loyal to her, and she to them, but Letty had felt a rough static between herself and the community of kids she'd grown up with. She had confessed once to Sammi and the other girls that if Las Reinas ever circled the wagons, she feared she'd be left on the outside.

At the time, Katsuko had assured her that they had their own wagons. The phrase had become a kind of shorthand to them for the way they promised always to look out for each other.

But the girls had circled the wagons, and it was Sammi who'd been left on the outside.

Sammi moved down the aisle near the door, toward the back of the room and an open seat in the second to last row. When she glanced back toward the far corner she caught Letty staring at her. The moment they locked eyes, Letty leaned toward Rafe and whispered something in his ear. Rafe glanced over at Sammi and made a small laugh, almost like a bark, before turning to Letty and lolling theatrically upon her shoulder. The two of them snickered together while Sammi slid into her chair.

"Surprised you decided to honor us with your presence," Sammi said, voice low, the sting of their laughter too much for her not to respond.

"I had a doctor's appointment. Not that it's any of your business."

Right. Four doctor's appointments? Sammi might have spoken the thought aloud, but the shock of Letty actually speaking to her kept her silent. Long seconds ticked past as she tried to decide how to respond. Curiosity got the better of her. She had to know what the girls were up to.

Sammi started to say her friend's name. She didn't get past the first syllable. The death glare that Letty shot her stopped her cold. *If looks could kill*, Sammi thought.

Even Rafe seemed shaken by that look. He laid a comforting hand on Letty's thigh. With a string of hissed Spanish curses, Letty dug her nails into the back of Rafe's hand. He swore and pulled his hand back, and Sammi saw the red streaks where blood welled up in fresh scratches.

"Crazy bitch. What's the matter with you?"

Letty's upper lip curled in disgust and she stood, moving toward the middle of the room, where a single seat still stood unoccupied. Rafe started to get up to follow. *Back off*, Sammi thought. For the first time, she started to think of Letty as dangerous.

A rustling at the front of the room drew her attention, kids opening their notebooks as Mr. Geary walked into the room. Maybe fifty years old, he had an earthy quality that Sammi liked. She imagined that once upon a time he'd been a genuine hippie. His hair always seemed in need of a cut and he wore a shaggy beard. But his eyes were kind and a little sad. She'd had him for history first semester last year as well, and had never learned so much in one class, mostly because his lectures were so memorable.

"Good afternoon, my friends," Mr. Geary said as he settled his books on the desk. He pulled out a purple folder,

and from within, a stack of papers that looked all too familiar. "We're going to do a little research together today."

He held up the papers. "This is a test."

The groan of the entire class echoed off the walls and
could probably be heard in the hallway and outside the
windows, where the warm, glorious afternoon had already
begun to slip away.

"Before you drink the purple Kool-Aid and go toes up
in the aisles, I assure you that your performance on this test
will not be counted toward your grade."

An exhale. A sigh of relief.

"That wouldn't be at all fair. It's a surprise, after all, and
only a week into the school year. What can you have learned
when you haven't even started paying attention yet?"

Mr. Geary laughed at his own joke and reached up to
stroke his beard.

"No, this is merely a test to see how much you know. I'll
study the results tonight, and then I'll have a better idea
where to focus our efforts this semester. So, no pressure. Just
do your best."

He went along the front row of desks handing a small
stack of tests to each student, who then began to pass them
back.

"If you have any questions, I'm at my desk, preparing
some notes for tomorrow's class. I'll also be working up the
assignment for your first paper, so try not to be disruptive,
please, or an eight-page paper might turn into eighteen
pages."

Some of them laughed politely at the joke. Enough so that Mr. Geary smiled, nodded, and went to sit down. He shifted some books around on the desk and then he was gone. As she took the tests from the guy in front of her and passed the rest back, Sammi thought this was when Mr. Geary was at his happiest, just lost in his books and research.

Sammi wrote her name on top of the test and gave it a quick once-over before answering any questions. Most of it was multiple choice, but there were fill-in-the-blanks as well. Those would probably tell a lot more about what the class knew than anything else. The multiple-choice stuff would be easy, so she skipped down and started with the blanks.

Soon she found herself calmer than she'd been in days, at least without her guitar. Music could soothe her, slip her sideways into a calmer place where her troubles seemed far away. Without the pressure of a grade looming over her, the test provided the same escape.

When she had finished the fill-in-the-blank questions, she paused before moving back up to the multiple choice. As she did, she glanced up the aisle at Letty, and the muscles in her back and neck tightened anew. Her grip on the pencil hurt her fingers. She longed for the weekend, for two full days without having to see the girls who'd turned their backs on her. Maybe then she could really uncoil the wires of tension that seemed to twist around her.

For a moment she closed her eyes. Sammi took a deep breath to clear her head, opened her eyes, and studied the first multiple-choice question. But something about her glance at Letty stuck in the back of her head and, slowly, drew her attention back up the aisle.

She studied the back of Letty's head. From this angle, she could see the right side of her face as the other girl studied the test in front of her. While Sammi watched, Letty frowned at the paper, glanced up at Mr. Geary, and then leaned over and looked at the test of the girl beside her. Andrea Cooper gave her a sneer, shielded her test with her arm.

"Quit it," Andrea whispered.

Mr. Geary looked up, but by then both girls had looked down at their tests. Frowning, he went back to taking notes.

Letty reached out and tapped Andrea's arm.

The look she gave the girl made Sammi shudder, and it wasn't even directed at her. That glance held the dark promise of violence, and it was one that Sammi had never seen on Letty before. Las Reinas were legendary for the way they would punish other girls in the parking lot after school, but Letty had never been like that.

Not before today.

Andrea moved her arm and pretended not to see Letty copying off her test—a test whose grade meant nothing.

Sammi shivered in disgust and went back to her own work, but in the back of her mind, one question had started to loom much larger than all of the others for her, and it wasn't multiple choice.

Could she really have been so wrong about the girls

she'd chosen as her friends? She'd thought they had so much in common, that they believed in the same things, and that there were a lot of things none of them would ever stoop to. In just a few hours, that faith had not merely been shaken, it had been torn down brick by brick.

When the bell rang to end class, it seemed to wake Mr. Geary out of a trance. He looked up as though he'd been napping instead of taking notes.

"All right, everyone. Bring your tests to my desk on the way out. Make sure your names are at the top. Have a good night, and I'll see you all tomorrow."

They filed past the desk to deliver the tests and then streamed out into the corridor. Sammi's mind was already rushing ahead to homeroom. She would check out, get her things from her locker, and get on the bus. The ride home would seem like an eternity today. All she wanted was to get home, to have time to relax with her guitar or just flop in front of the TV before her mother came home from work.

And then she remembered her father, and she knew that instead of relaxing, she would be spending the afternoon wondering if her father would be home for dinner tonight. He had been there this morning when she woke up, so that was a good sign. Maybe the fight her parents were having would blow over and her father would apologize for what he'd said.

Sammi hoped so. She had nowhere else to go. Nowhere she could exhale.

As she left the class and headed for homeroom, she saw

Caryn leaning against a row of lockers. Her nostrils flared when she spotted Sammi, but then her expression changed. Caryn looked past her. Sammi turned to see Letty coming along behind her . . . and Rafe following after, trouble brewing in his eyes.

"Hold up, Letty. Something you oughta say to me."

With a condescending smile, Letty rolled her eyes and kept walking, a bounce in her step as if she'd just gotten a compliment. She carried her books against her chest like some wholesome 1950s schoolgirl.

Rafe grabbed her arm.

Letty froze and turned to look at him, fire in her eyes. "*Canto de cabrón. No me jodas más.*"

"*¡Marimacha!* What is your problem?" Rafe snarled. Sammi could tell he was furious, but he was looking around, uncomfortable with so many people watching them.

Letty tried to pull her arm away but he held on tighter. She went to slap him and he grabbed her wrist, trapping her free hand.

She laughed then, mischief glittering in her eyes. "*Careculo,*" she said.

Rafe's anger turned to confusion. "Are you on crack? The hell's wrong with—"

He didn't get to finish.

Caryn went by so fast, Sammi almost didn't realize who it was. Rafe looked up, blinking in surprise at the black girl in the stylish skirt rushing at him. He didn't even have time to defend himself.

"Let her go!" Caryn shouted, her hands balled into fists.

She hit Rafe so hard that the sound echoed down the corridor. He staggered two steps backward. As he reached a hand back toward the lockers to steady himself, Caryn shot a kick at his balls.

Rafe went down on the floor, curled into fetal position, sucking and wheezing air into his lungs as if he were having an asthma attack.

Letty stood over him, looking down with open amusement. She shook her head. *"Careculo,"* she said.

Then she giggled and started away, with Caryn falling in beside her. They laughed together, linking arms. Peering down the corridor beyond them, Sammi could see T.Q. coming toward them.

She looked at Rafe. For a moment she considered trying to help him, but then she remembered the way he had snickered at whatever nasty crap Letty had said about her when she'd walked into history class and figured he could deal on his own.

"What's going on here?"

At the voice, she turned and saw Mr. Geary staring at Rafe. In a kind of wonder and bafflement, the teacher looked around for an answer, but the students in the hall started scurrying away.

"Samantha?" Mr. Geary said, turning those sad eyes upon her. "What's going on?"

She clutched her books against her.

"I wish I knew," Sammi said.

Then she turned and headed for homeroom, the strangest day of her life finally come to an end.

8

On Wednesday, they didn't come to school at all.

The day seemed oddly still. Not a trace of cloud appeared in the sky, yet its blue was a pale, pitiful color, without any vividness. No wind blew. When Sammi walked the corridors of Covington High, the voices of the other students and the other sounds of the school seemed strangely muted. She moved through the halls as though in a dream. On Tuesday, she had been comforted by the friends who'd been cool to her, talked to her at her locker, invited her to sit with them at lunch.

Today she just felt alone.

The night before, Sammi had not slept well. Falling asleep had been easy enough, but she'd tossed and turned and woken at five, unable to drift off again. While she'd been getting dressed and eating breakfast, her parents had been like ghosts passing each other in the halls and in the kitchen. They seemed locked in a kind of détente, a tenuous peace that existed mainly because they had stopped talking. Sammi had walked past their room on the way to the shower and caught a glimpse through the door of an old bedspread and a pillow made up on the carpet. Her father had spent the night on the floor.

The way the girls had blown her off had hurt her badly, but somehow knowing they weren't even there felt worse. When she thought about their behavior the day before—cutting class and smoking, Letty going psycho bitch on Andrea Cooper, and Caryn beating on Rafe—it made her shiver. Plenty of kids cut class or smoked, but not these girls, not her friends. At first Sammi had wondered if she had just never seen the real them. They had all had their faults, and she knew she had her own. But had this kind of nastiness been there in them all along, and she'd just never realized it?

No. Impossible. She had rolled it over and over in her mind, and she knew that wasn't the case. They were different. They'd changed, and she knew exactly when it had happened.

It's me, she thought as she hurried to her locker after fourth period.

It's my fault. I spoiled it all. I'm the trigger.

Sammi knew it made no sense, but couldn't deny the timing. She had ruined the friendship they had all shared, and as a result, all four of them had undergone major attitude adjustments. And not for the better. Hell, they weren't even in school today, and no way did they all have legitimate excuses. They must have left their houses this morning so their parents would think they were going to school and met up somewhere later. Sammi didn't even want to think about what kind of trouble they might be getting into at the moment.

Yet, at the same time, she couldn't help wishing she could be with them. Letty, T.Q., Caryn, and Katsuko might be able to just throw a switch and suddenly hate her, but Sammi didn't have that cold a heart. As much as it hurt her the way they'd defriended her, she missed them.

The flow of hallway traffic carried her toward her locker. She moved toward the wall on the left side of the corridor, slipping past a couple of basketball boys who nodded to her as she passed. Her locker was just ahead, right after the entrance to the girls' bathroom.

Hands grabbed her arms and pressed against her back, driving her to the left. Before Sammi could say a word, they crashed her into the bathroom door. It banged open, and they pushed her inside. She staggered, barely able to keep herself from tripping over her own feet, and then they shoved her and she couldn't stop herself. Arms pinwheeling, she went down hard on the tile, her books flying from her hands and sliding across the floor.

"What the hell is wrong with—?" she began.

Her words cut off when she looked up to see the three girls standing beyond the sinks and stalls, silhouetted by the light coming through the windows. The tall girl in the middle had long, curly brown hair with red highlights. Sammi knew her, but not well. Her name was Marisol, and when Teri Gomes had graduated the year before, she'd become leader of Las Reinas. They all listened to her.

The other two were faces she knew, but Sammi couldn't remember their names.

She climbed slowly to her feet, turning to see the two girls standing by the bathroom door—the two who had shoved her into the bathroom from the hall. Jesenia and Cori. A twinge of sadness touched her. She knew these two well; they had always been friendly to her.

"Cori—"

"Don't talk to her. Talk to me," Marisol said.

The words, and the hard edge of her voice, made the fog of surprise clear from Sammi's mind. She understood, now. Trouble had found her. She turned to face Marisol.

"Okay, then you tell me. What's your problem?"

Marisol blinked, and her eyes grew stormy. "You might wanna rethink your tone with me, girl."

Sammi held up both hands. "Look, you guys know me. Or some of you, anyway. Cori and Jesenia, they know me. Some of your other friends, too. All I'm saying is, if you wanted to talk to me, you didn't have to drag me in here."

Marisol smiled, eyes twinkling with malice. "Who says we wanted to *talk* to you?"

Sammi's breath caught in her throat as she felt fear blossom in her chest. She glanced back at Jesenia and Cori, who both looked away. All Sammi could do was shake her head and stare at Marisol.

"What the hell's this about?"

Marisol leaned back against the windowsill. The sunlight

washed through the opaque glass and blurred around her, so she seemed like some kind of ghost or angel.

"Your friends didn't show up for school today. You could take a lesson from them, Sammi. None of 'em are here. Really, we wanted Caryn Adams in here with us today, and Letty, too. But since they're not here, we might as well start with you."

Sammi shook her head. "Caryn? Why do you . . ."

Her words trailed off. She squeezed her eyes shut, one hand coming up to touch her forehead as she realized what had brought this trouble down on her today.

"This is about Rafe, isn't it?"

One of the girls with Marisol swore under her breath. The words were a harsh whisper, and Sammi couldn't make them out, but their intent was clear.

"There you go," Marisol said. "Now at least you'll know why this happened to you."

She nodded, and the two girls on either side of her moved away from the window. At the bathroom door, Jesenia took a couple of steps toward Sammi as well. Desperate, Sammi glanced at the stalls, hoping someone might be in there, but then it struck her that they would not be that stupid. They'd have cleared the room first. This would not be the first time Las Reinas had given a little payback in this bathroom.

Cori braced herself against the door to prevent any intrusion.

Sammi focused on Marisol. Again she shook her head.

"You've got it all wrong. I saw what happened, but I

wasn't involved. Rafe grabbed Letty and then Caryn hit him. It's got nothing to do with me."

Marisol almost looked sympathetic, but she didn't say a word.

Sammi put her hands up to protect herself, and one of the girls slapped her. The other grabbed her hair, then her throat, and slammed her against the frame between two toilet stalls.

Sammi got pissed. She shoved out one hand, grabbed the girl by the face, and pushed her away. The girl stumbled, but still had a fistful of her hair, and Sammi cried out in pain as she was dragged forward. By instinct she grabbed the girl's wrist and shoved her thumb into the pressure point there, forcing her to let go.

Jesenia grabbed her arm. Sammi tried to hit her, but Jesenia grabbed the other arm as well, and they faced off.

"What are you doing?" she said, staring into Jesenia's eyes. "We were friends?"

Jesenia shook her head. "I like you, Sam. Doesn't make us friends."

Sammi's nostrils flared as she fought a terrible nausea that churned in her belly. It would have been easy to think of this as just the latest in a series of betrayals, but that wasn't true. This wasn't about Jesenia or Marisol, and it wasn't about Sammi Holland.

"Just listen to me for a second!" she snapped, and she shook Jesenia off and backed up, nearly against the stalls again. Sammi looked desperately around at Las Reinas, her breath coming hard, her whole body coiled and ready to fight or run, knowing how it would end if she had to do either.

"They're not my friends anymore," Sammi said, and she winced at the pain of speaking the words aloud. She bit her lower lip and felt tears welling in her eyes, and that only made her angrier. "They blew me off, okay? You got a problem with them, take it to them. They don't want anything to do with me anymore, and the feeling's totally mutual."

Marisol blinked, and for the first time Sammi saw hesitation in her eyes.

This time, when Sammi looked at Cori, standing by the door, the girl did not look away.

"Cori, maybe we're not friends, but you know me. Ask around today. Anyone who was at lunch with us on Monday saw them get up and leave me sitting there. They're treating me like something nasty they stepped in. Caryn and Letty embarrassed the hell out of Rafe. I don't know why you're looking for payback instead of him, but I don't care. It's got nothing to do with me."

Sammi felt a chill spider-walk up her spine as she put down her hands and locked eyes with Marisol. "If you're gonna do something to me, I can't stop you. But if you're doing it to get at Letty and Caryn, they're just gonna laugh. They won't lose any sleep over it."

Her cheek stung where she'd been slapped and her scalp burned from having her hair yanked, but telling these girls the truth about the way her friends had humiliated and abandoned her was much worse.

Marisol glanced over at Cori.

"It'd be easy to check. But for what it's worth, I believe her," Cori said. "Sammi's not stupid. She knows there isn't anywhere to run."

With Cori distracted, the door swung open six inches before she tried to stop it. The girl coming into the bathroom looked annoyed and shoved it open.

"Do you mind?" she said, pushing past Cori.

Then she saw the other Reinas and her gaze darted to Sammi, the one person in the room who didn't belong, and she paused.

"Sorry," she said, unsure now. "I didn't mean to interrupt."

Marisol shook her head. "Nah. You're not interrupting anything. We all got classes to go to, right, Sammi?"

Sammi stared at her without answering.

"Better pick up your books," Jesenia said. "That was a bad spill you took."

Cori helped her pick up the books even as the other Reinas departed. Sammi kept silent until the newcomer—a sophomore girl she vaguely recognized—went into a toilet stall. Then she looked at Cori.

"Thanks," she said, her voice low.

Glancing away, Cori shrugged one shoulder. "Sorry. Just the way things are."

"I don't get it, though," Sammi whispered. "Why—"

"Rafe's gotta act like it didn't mean anything. If he did anything himself, he'd look even worse. But Marisol can't let it go. It's an insult to all of us."

Sammi thought about Las Reinas and the way they

always stuck together—not just them, but the Puerto Rican boys, too. In the cafeteria, they always sat in clusters, the same way some of the black students and the Dominicans did. They weren't gangs; she'd realized that a long time ago. But they shared culture and heritage and often neighborhoods as well. These were the kids they'd grown up with. But they were no strangers to violence, so sometimes in order to get their point across, they got reacquainted with it.

"I still don't get it, but it's not my problem."

"No," Cori agreed. "You got other problems. You're all on your own now, huh?"

Lips pressed grimly together, Sammi nodded.

"Sometimes that's better," Cori told her, handing her the last of her books.

The toilet flushed. Sammi looked in the mirror at the red mark on her face from where she'd been slapped. She set her books on a ledge by the window and washed her hands. When Cori left, she said nothing, and when the girl came out of the stall—looking as if she might want to ask what had happened—Sammi kept her gaze straight ahead.

She grabbed her books and left the bathroom just as the bell rang for class. It seemed incredible to her that the confrontation with Las Reinas had taken only a few minutes. Now, though, she had to dump her books in her locker and get the notebook for her next class.

When she opened her locker, she found that her hands were trembling.

More than anything, she hated the temptation she felt to call Caryn and warn her that trouble was on the way.

Sammi wanted to protect them, if she could. No matter what they'd done to her. Crazy as she knew it was, she realized that she felt responsible for everything that was happening. They were being totally irrational, but if she'd just gotten the tattoo, none of this would have happened.

But she thought again about the way they'd defriended her and their bizarre behavior the day before. Caryn and Letty had brought trouble on themselves. They were just going to have to deal with it.

The Merrimack River Walk usually had mobs of people strolling back and forth, streaming in and out of stores. That night shoppers were scarce. The crowds of teenagers that would have thronged the area in front of the movie theater and the Starbucks on Friday or Saturday night had other things to do on Wednesdays.

Sammi didn't mind. In fact, she preferred it that way. She had never spent much time at the River Walk, shopping at Old Navy and Borders and Abercrombie. Even tonight she would normally have been at home, but both of her parents were there. In a million years she would never have imagined wishing her father would take a business trip, but the way things were going in her house she wanted him to be anywhere but home. When her mother had come home from the bank, Sammi had felt as if she had to hold her breath. At any moment, it seemed, the place might explode.

She had called Adam, not patient enough to text.

Now she stood leaning against a lamppost near a small

tree set into the concrete sidewalk as she watched the parking lot for his car. The sky had started to darken, but night had not fallen quite yet when the Borders sign flickered to life. When a fortyish couple went past her and opened the door, she could smell fresh coffee brewing inside and craved a mochaccino. But she wasn't moving from this spot.

When Adam drove past her, searching for a parking space, he waved to her. That simple act lightened her mood incredibly and she waved back.

He parked the car, and she watched as he crossed the lot toward her, admiring him. His unruly hair made him appear to have just rolled out of bed, but she liked that about him. Adam wore a short-sleeved, open-collared shirt, and black jeans with black shoes to match.

"You look nice," she said as he stepped up onto the sidewalk.

"You too," Adam said.

Sammi had taken her time getting dressed. She knew girls who wore nothing but flip-flops, but that look just seemed sloppy to her. She'd put on a pair of tank tops—one black and one burgundy—and dark jeans with her sandals. She'd spent time on her hair and makeup, too. The more time she'd spent getting ready, the less time she had to be with her mother. And when her father had come home, she'd met him in the driveway and asked for a ride to the River Walk. He'd complied without complaint. Neither of her parents had balked when she'd told them she was going out. Maybe they understood.

"So, where do you want to eat? Bertucci's?" Adam asked.

"Sounds good. But can we just walk a little first?"

"Sure."

He took her hand—which Sammi liked very much—and they wandered along the River Walk, looking in store windows. Bertucci's was behind them, but that was all right because Sammi wanted to drag Adam into the bookstore before dinner.

"So, I guess I kind of showed my hand, huh?" Sammi said. "Calling you today, I mean. Just saw you on Friday night, and now I'm, like, dragging you out to dinner. Blew my cover."

Adam laughed. "You're cute when you babble."

"Which is good, considering how often it happens."

"Yeah, it's just, what are you talking about?"

Sammi felt her face flush with heat and knew her cheeks must be turning red. "Well, I had the whole aloof thing going, kind of. Now I didn't even wait till the weekend to see you. Kind of putting my cards on the table, right? Embarrassing."

Adam squeezed her hand. "I'm glad you called. And I'm not very good at card games. Or any other kind of games, really."

She smiled and started to reply.

He kissed her into silence.

Sammi held him close. Adam traced his fingers along the sides of her face, and they lingered in the midst of that kiss so long that when at last they separated, she had to catch her breath. All her tension and fear and sadness had evaporated for the moment.

With a look of pure mischief, Adam took her hand, and they walked on as though nothing had happened.

"So, you want to tell me what's got you so worked up?" he asked after a minute.

She laughed softly. "I'd think that'd be pretty obvious."

When she glanced at him, she saw that his expression had turned serious.

"You know what I mean. I'm glad you called. But my ego isn't so big that I couldn't tell it was more about getting out of the house than hanging out with me."

Sammi shot him a sharp look. "That's not true."

"What, about my ego?"

In spite of herself, she smiled.

"Talk to me, Sammi."

She didn't look at him. Now that she had Adam there, Sammi found that what she really wanted was for him to make her forget her troubles, not to talk them out. But he had made the trip down to meet her and he deserved an answer.

"Let's turn around. I want to hit the bookstore before dinner."

Adam obliged her but kept casting expectant looks in her direction.

"You just met me," Sammi said. "I don't want to scare you off."

"Sammi . . ."

"Okay. All right." She took a deep breath. "You were right. I needed to get out of there. Turns out my parents are trying to figure out if they want to still be married to each other."

Adam shook his head. "Man, that's rough. I'm sorry."

"Me too. And maybe they'll stay together, and maybe they won't. But either way, I don't want to be there right now. They're working so hard to ignore each other that they don't really notice me."

"And your friends? You still on the outs with them?"

Sammi swallowed. The situation with her parents truly was bothering her, but she'd brought it up to avoid having to talk about the wreckage of her relationship with all four of her best friends.

She nodded. "Yeah. I can't really talk to them."

"So I'm your basic distraction, someone to take your mind off of your troubles?"

Horrified, Sammi looked at him. "No, why would you say that?"

"No?" he asked, raising one eyebrow.

Confused, she shrugged. "I don't . . . Maybe? A little? But you make it sound so cold, and it's not like that."

"I don't know. I kind of like the idea of being your distraction."

They passed by Abercrombie, and he studied the window displays. Sammi tugged on his hand to get his attention.

"Was that supposed to be romantic, or just sexual innuendo?"

"Both."

Sammi rolled her eyes. "Boys."

Some guys she knew would have bristled at being called a boy. Adam only grinned and walked on beside her. She had been concerned that he would push her to talk more about the situation with her parents, but he seemed content to let her decide how much, if any, she wanted to discuss. They'd only seen each other in person three times, but they'd texted and talked often enough that it seemed much more than that. She liked him, a lot. Liked being with him.

And he was a very cute distraction.

They wandered into the bookstore, where Sammi perused the mystery shelves and Adam led her through the science fiction section. She told him about Cruel and Unusual Books in Covington, and he confessed he'd never been through the front door. She much preferred it to any of the big stores. The chains had a better selection, but the people at Cruel and Unusual knew her, and knew what she liked. Sammi liked the intimacy of the place.

"Coffee?" Adam asked.

"We haven't had dinner yet."

"Is there some kind of rule nobody told me about?"

Sammi pushed him toward the café in the front corner of the store. "Mochaccino, then. Dessert before dinner."

While they were in line at the café, Sammi glanced

past Adam and was stunned to see Caryn and Katsuko come into the store. If he hadn't been looking up at the menu board at that moment, he could not have failed to notice the way she stiffened at the sight of them.

Sammi stood beside Adam, standing in his shadow, hiding from them. As they ordered she kept stealing glimpses at them as they moved through the music and DVD section. The machine that whipped her mochaccino whined like a dentist's drill.

Adam said something, but the words didn't filter into her head.

"Sounds good," she said, with no idea what she'd agreed to.

He received his coffee and went over to the small sidebar to pour cream and sugar into the cup. When they handed Sammi her mochaccino, she went and stood behind him.

Over Adam's shoulder, she watched as Katsuko and Caryn browsed a shelf of TV series boxed sets on DVD. The expensive ones were all locked away in a glass case, but this stuff was right out in the open. As Sammi looked on, the two girls turned toward one another, maybe to shield their actions from the view of cameras. But Sammi could see between them. Katsuko stripped the plastic from the DVD box, opened it, popped out all four discs, and handed them to Caryn, who pushed them down the front of her pants.

Katsuko stuffed the plastic wrapping into the box and closed it, putting it back on the shelf. Whatever antitheft devices the store used, they'd be in the box or the wrapping.

They left the store, chatting casually, as though they hadn't just committed a crime.

Sammi burned her tongue on the mochaccino and barely noticed.

9

On Thursday morning, Sammi walked through the corridors of Covington High holding her breath. Every slam of a locker and raised voice made her blink or flinch. Her house had become colder and more silent than ever, but despite the noise and the usual frantic pace in the halls at school, it felt somehow the same to her. At home she always felt as if she was in the midst of a truce, and war might erupt at any moment. And that morning as school bells rang to move her from one class to the next, she kept watch for Marisol and the other Reinas with one eye, and Letty and the girls with the other.

Whatever mystery ailment they'd used as an excuse to skip school on Wednesday, they had obviously recovered from it. Sammi ran into T.Q. and Katsuko before homeroom and saw Letty in history class, and passed Caryn in the cafeteria. They pretended not to even notice her. Part of her exhaled in relief that they did not approach her, but still it hurt. People were nice to her. Sammi had gone back to floating from group to group, smiling and trying to fit in, but for the first time in her life she hated being a floater. She could never have predicted how lost she felt. She missed being a part of something, even if she no longer knew exactly what that something had been.

And those were the questions that haunted her through much of that morning. Who *were* these girls? Had they always been so cruel and malicious at heart, and she'd just never noticed it because they had accepted her before? Now that they had banished her from their lives, was she simply seeing their real faces for the first time?

The idea made her want to puke.

After lunch she stood at her locker, staring at the books piled inside and just drifting, wondering how it had all come to this. The metal felt cool under her touch. She tuned out the voices around her. Whatever happened with Las Reinas and the girls, Sammi decided she didn't want to witness it. The hell with that idea. Maybe Letty and Caryn had earned an ass-kicking—maybe it would even be the shock they needed to stop acting like such bitches—but she didn't want any part of it. Sammi had let her friends down, but their reaction had been totally out of proportion.

She tried to tell herself she never wanted anything to do with them again. Only a total loser would go crawling back, even if they'd ever take her back. So why couldn't she hate them?

Lost in thought, just staring into her locker, she didn't

notice Ken Nguyen come up beside her until he tapped her on the arm and repeated her name. Sammi blinked and looked at him.

"Hey. Are you feeling all right?"

"Sorry. Just drifting. What's up?"

Ken shrugged. "Well, first off, the bell rang. Didn't look like you heard it."

"I'm totally spaced today, but wow. I didn't think I was that far gone. Gonna have to go to bed early tonight."

Sammi knew she didn't sound at all convincing, that Ken had to realize she was blowing off his concern. She only hoped he realized that she appreciated it, even if she wasn't going to talk about her troubles.

"Maybe you should take a nap in psych."

She smiled. "I don't think that would go over very well."

"Ah, you're fine. You have my permission."

Sammi laughed softly. "Well, I'm sure that makes it okay, then."

But even as she allowed her mood to lighten, she saw Ken's smile falter. He glanced down.

"So, did you hear about your friend Simone?"

Her stomach gave a sick little twist. "What about her?"

"She's saying Coach Kelleher assaulted her. Sexually, I mean."

Her mouth dropped open and she stared up at him. "Are you kidding? Oh my God. He raped her?"

Ken glanced around, obviously nervous that someone would overhear him—a basketball player—gossiping about the accusations against his coach. "Not quite. She's basically saying he seduced her or whatever. How he's supposed to have gotten her alone, I have no idea, but that's what she's claiming."

Ice raced through Sammi's veins. She studied Ken. "You don't believe her?"

"I sure as hell don't want to," he said, and she could see in his eyes the way the news was tearing at him. "I mean, you have an image of somebody, y'know? Coach is . . . well, he's Coach. I can't imagine him doing something like that, but I guess you never really know what's going on inside somebody else's head."

Sammi thought about the girls and shook her head. "You really don't. But think about it. T.Q.? Seriously? I've got some issues with her right now, but there's no way she would make something like that up."

A flurry of thoughts went through her mind. After the way her friends had behaved lately, the one who'd surprised her the most was T.Q. Caryn had always needed a little anger management, and Katsuko could be so damn superior. But T.Q. had always been so quiet and gentle and kind. Maybe this was the piece of the puzzle Sammi'd been missing. Of them all, T.Q. was the most inexperienced with boys. The girl was totally naïve.

Or she had been.

"God, I've got to talk to her. I can't imagine how she must feel."

Ken dropped his gaze a moment and sighed, looking up at her. "I know you're probably right. I guess I've just been hoping it would turn out to be bullshit. Not that it would matter. It's probably already too late for Coach. The school suspended him this morning, while they investigate, apparently. But once word gets out that he's been accused, the damage is done."

He touched her arm again. "I'll see you later, Sam. I've gotta get to class."

"Me too."

As she pulled out her books for Intro to Psych, Ken went off along the hall and left her to ruminate on the news. She'd already been feeling anxious and a little nauseated, but now it grew much worse. The thought of what T.Q. had gone through sickened her. Despite the trouble between them, she knew she had to reach out to her friend.

All through psych class Sammi felt like she was in a fog. The teacher's voice droned into gibberish like all the adults in the Charlie Brown holiday specials. By the time the bell rang, she'd retained nothing from the class except the assignment the teacher had given for the next class—which wasn't until Monday, thankfully.

The rest of her day consisted of a study hall and then math, which allowed her to put some strategy to use. Why bother doing her trig homework at home when she could do it right before class? That strategy had worked in the past, but somehow she had a feeling it would be very difficult to focus today.

And that was before she heard Letty's voice in the stairwell.

The stairs were packed between classes, flowing in both directions. Sammi reached the second floor and turned to keep going up to the third, where she'd have study hall in Ms. Ostergaard's room. But as she started up the stairs she heard that familiar, flirtatious laugh, and looked up to see Letty and Katsuko standing next to the window on the landing between the second and third floors.

"Come on, Josh, stick around. Free show," Letty said to a skinny sophomore passing by.

The kid blushed deeply, head hanging in humiliation. Sammi recognized him right off as a boy who'd had an enormous crush on Letty the previous year, and who'd been teased mercilessly by his friends when they learned she was gay. From the look of it, Sammi had to assume the taunting had started earlier, maybe in the third floor hallway. But now Letty and Katsuko had stepped aside on the landing to let Josh pass.

Letty wore a belly shirt and a daringly short skirt with striped stockings that came up to her thighs, drawing even more attention to the inches of bare leg between the top of the stocking and the hem of her skirt. Katsuko had probably come to school that day with a shirt underneath the gray vest she wore, but if so, she had shed the garment. Her pants rode so low that her hips barely kept them from falling down, and if she wore underwear, it must have been so tiny it didn't show. On top, all she had on was the vest, which left little to the imagination.

Sammi froze on the steps and stared at them in disbelief. She wasn't a prude. In fact, Letty and Katsuko had

143

both given *her* a hard time more than once about the way she dressed. But the line between attention whore and just plain whore could be perilously thin, and to her mind it was all about how you presented yourself.

"What the hell?" she whispered.

Someone jostled her and she dropped her books. Sammi swore and knelt to pick them up as the flow of traffic on the stairs parted and swept around her.

"Come on, Josh," Letty pleaded as the red-faced sophomore continued down the stairs. "I know you want some. You know you want some."

Sammi bristled with disgust. When she had snatched up her books, she saw that Josh had continued down the stairs without reaction.

"Hey, Josh!" Katsuko shouted.

All conversation on the stairs stopped. People slowed down. There must have been thirty or forty kids who turned to look, and that included Josh. He paused with his hand on the railing and sighed with frustration, then turned to look.

"You're just not her type," Katsuko said, with a lascivious grin.

Her hand slid out, and she pushed her fingers through Letty's hair. Letty reached for Katsuko and caressed her face. Grinning, laughing, uttering little mews of pleasure, they pulled one another into a deep kiss, full of slippery tongues and roving hands.

Shock stole Sammi's breath away. She blinked in astonishment. Everyone in the stairwell looked on in fascination.

Some of the guys began to mutter appreciation. Even a couple of the girls began to hoot encouragement. A few turned up their noses in disgust at this display and started moving up or down the stairs again.

The kiss ended with the girls flushed and breathless. It might have been for Josh's benefit—for Josh's torment—but clearly they had enjoyed themselves.

Sammi glanced at Josh as he started down the stairs again. He'd been blushing before, but now had turned ghostly pale, his humiliation complete.

The traffic on the stairs started to move again.

When Sammi passed Letty and Katsuko on the landing, they were still hanging on each other, snickering softly and sighing with amusement, as though it had been the funniest thing they'd ever seen. They stole glances at one another that said they were tempted to start in again. Sammi had never had a problem with Letty's sexuality, and if Letty and Katsuko wanted to be together, she would have been happier for them than anyone. But if their romance came in the form of someone else's torture, that was just sick.

"You two are just evil," Sammi said as she passed.

Katsuko and Letty looked at each other and burst out laughing.

Sammi imagined she could still hear them all the way to study hall.

For that entire period, she accomplished nothing. Sammi sat in Ms. Ostergaard's room as if she had gone catatonic, doodling in a notebook or staring out the window, trying and failing to make sense of it all. When the bell rang and she shuffled off to trigonometry, she had not even opened the book, never mind done the homework. She barely noticed the teacher's displeasure and paid little attention.

For the first time, all her guilt had vanished. Whatever had happened to her friends, it had nothing to do with her. But she worried about them now. What kind of trauma would cause people to change so dramatically? Sammi wondered if they'd all started using drugs, but could not imagine where they would have come into possession of something that could screw them up so completely.

Haunted, she managed somehow to scribble down the night's assignment and then followed the peal of the school bell out into the hallway. It echoed out there, coming from everywhere and nowhere all at once.

As she hefted her backpack and fell into the current of students leaving school, her cell phone vibrated in her pocket. Sammi pulled it out and was relieved to see she had a text message from Anna Dubrowski.

Hey. If u aren't doing anything 2mrw nite, want to come to the b-ball game with us?

For the first time that day, Sammi felt three-dimensional. The whole world had seemed gray to her, like some kind of ghost world or the landscape of a dream. Now Anna's invitation woke her up, reminded her that there was more to life than Las Reinas and her freakish friends.

Love to, she texted back. *Time?*

7:30. We'll save u a seat.

Sammi managed a smile as she went down the central

staircase to the main exit. After last night, the last thing she wanted to do was dump more of her stress on Cute Adam—especially if she hoped to keep him around. But having an excuse to get out of her house Friday night gave her a happy feeling.

Lost in her own thoughts, she nearly collided with T.Q. as she went out the front door. The girl glanced at her, and Sammi was surprised to see no emotion at all on T.Q.'s face. The redhead didn't look happy to see her, but neither did she scowl or sneer the way Letty and the others had all been doing this week. That lack of emotion gave her the courage to speak up.

"Hey," she said, going down the stairs beside T.Q. "You okay?"

"Why wouldn't I be?"

Sammi lowered her voice. "I heard about that thing with the coach."

They reached the bottom of the steps. T.Q. paused and gave her a look that said Sammi must be the stupidest girl on the face of the Earth. Then she smiled, and her eyes twinkled with mischief, as though she'd just told the world's greatest joke.

T.Q. leaned in and whispered in Sammi's ear. "He said I was too young for him. But I persuaded him to reconsider. He loved every minute of it, but after, he started feeling all guilty. Told me he'd been stupid, risking his family and his job like that. He begged me to understand. But I'm just not that understanding."

She stood up again, glancing around for her bus. "It

taught him a lesson, though. You can't be halfway corrupt. If he hadn't given in the first time, or if he hadn't blown me off afterward, he'd be just fine right now. Instead, the bastard got what he deserved," T.Q. said, and then she walked away, leaving Sammi staring after her.

"Oh my God," Sammi whispered.

Then someone cursed her out for blocking the bottom of the stairs, forcing her to start walking. Somehow she found the right bus and climbed on. She sat in the first empty seat and hugged her backpack to her chest, so lost in thought that she nearly missed her stop.

Her life truly had become a nightmare. Her friends had been cool and funny and sweet; they'd been decent human beings. Now they were the nastiest bitches she had ever seen. It all seemed so impossible, but she could not deny what her own eyes and ears told her.

Everything had been poisoned, and the poison was spreading.

Later she would realize how naïve she'd been, but by Friday afternoon—when Las Reinas had still made no attempt at violent payback against Letty and Caryn—Sammi let herself exhale. Either Rafe had interceded and gotten Marisol to back off, or Letty had somehow made amends.

Of greater concern to Sammi was the situation with T.Q. She'd struggled with the decision, but in the end she knew she wouldn't report what T.Q. had said to her. Maybe Coach Kelleher had been seduced into sleeping with her, but the end result was the same—he'd had sex with a girl who was underage, a student. Manipulated or not, that was just wrong. If he lost his job, it was no more than he deserved.

T.Q. deserved to pay for what she'd done, too. She'd set the coach up and ruined his life with a kind of cold calculation that Sammi would never have imagined the girl capable of. But what could she do? If Sammi went to the principal, it would be her word against T.Q.'s, and chances were good she wouldn't even be disciplined. The coach had crossed the line, and no matter what Sammi said, the adult world would never see T.Q. as responsible.

But they hadn't seen her face, or heard the glee in her voice. It made Sammi shudder just to think about it.

As Friday afternoon wore on, she thought she might feel like hiding, just burying herself under her covers and hibernating there for the weekend. But she had managed to avoid all but the most tangential contact with the girls on Friday, and once the final bell rang, she felt a tremendous weight lifted off her shoulders.

Tomorrow night she'd see Adam.

Tonight she'd go with Anna Dubrowski to the basketball game. It would be nice to spend a little time around a bunch of guys and girls who were normal. Maybe her cousin Zak would bring Anna's sister Rachael, if they could be convinced to hang around with high school kids for a night.

On the way out to her bus, Sammi kept her eyes on the

ground. Whatever the girls might be up to today, she didn't feel like bearing witness to it. No more. For the first time all week, she rode home without closing her eyes.

The day had started with clouds, but now the sky had cleared to a brilliant, crystal blue. As she walked from the corner where the bus dropped her off, a crisp, cool breeze made her shiver, yet she did not mind at all. She had a lightweight brown leather jacket to wear tonight. Sammi had never minded the autumn, even when it came early. In many ways it was her favorite season, beautiful and contemplative.

At home she dumped her book bag, forgetting about the research she had to start for a history paper, and went for her guitar. For more than an hour she sat in her room and played, alternately rocking out and slowing the music down for something sweet. "Summer Girl" sounded perfect, now, but she decided that as much as she loved the song, it might be time for "Autumn Girl" instead.

The thought ignited her imagination. She could do a quartet of songs, Sammi Holland's own "Four Seasons." Almost instantly a new melody came to her and she hummed a little, searching with her fingers along the frets for the notes to make it come to life. A smile touched her lips as she played, purging herself of all the ugliness of the past week.

By the time she had the basics of the tune worked out and looked up from her guitar, the clock read 4:27. Sammi blinked, staring at it. Some of her good feeling fled instantly as she thought about seeing her parents. Her father wouldn't be home until at least seven o'clock, but her mother would be coming through the door in an hour.

She tossed aside her guitar pick and unfolded herself from the plush chair she'd been lounging in to prop her instrument on the stand in the corner of the bedroom. Sammi peeled off the shirt she'd worn to school and stepped out of her pants. With her cell phone in hand she went across the hall to the bathroom and turned on the shower. The hiss of the water against the tiles soothed her.

Flipping open her cell, she called Anna Dubrowski.

"Sammi? What's up? Don't tell me you're bailing."

"The opposite, actually. I feel like getting out of here. Any interest in meeting up early? We could go to the Sampan first."

"Totally," Anna said. "I was just talking to Rachael and Zak about hooking up first. My parents aren't going to be home anyway. Rachael's driving. We were talking about pizza, but I'd much rather have Chinese. The Sampan sounds perfect. I'm sure I can convince them. Want us to swing by and get you first?"

Steam started to rise behind the opaque glass door of the shower. "What time, do you think? I'd kinda like to be out of here before my mother comes home from work. That way I can just leave her a note and not get an argument about it."

"Let me call Rachael and I'll call you right back."

"Thanks."

She closed the phone and set it on the shelf next to the sink, then removed her bra and underwear and slipped into

151

the shower. The hot water prickled her skin and sluiced down her body. It felt incredible, and she could have stayed under the stream for an hour. Instead she quickly washed her body and face, careful not to get her hair wet because she didn't have time to blow it dry. Her legs needed shaving, but she hadn't planned on wearing a skirt tonight anyway.

Once out of the shower she brushed her hair and then tied it back into a ponytail with a rubber band. With a facecloth she wiped condensation off the mirror and started putting on eyeliner.

Her cell phone rang. She snatched it up and flipped it open. On reflex, she checked to see who was calling and then was glad she had. The screen said *Mom*. Sammi let the call go into her voice mail. Before she could put the phone down her ring tone played again, but this time it was Anna.

"Hey," she answered.

"Hey. Rachael says she'll swing by and get you first. Fifteen minutes?"

"I'll be ready."

Eyeliner would have to do. Naked, Sammi peeked out into the hall to make sure no one had come home unexpectedly and then rushed across to her bedroom clutching her cell phone. She tossed it on the bed and quickly dressed in rust-colored jeans, a green long-sleeved top, and sandals. From her jewelry box stash she peeled off three twenty-dollar bills, and then she dug her leather jacket out of her closet.

As she waited at the front door, she double-checked her ponytail in the mirror and decided it would be just fine for tonight. All she carried was her phone, her keys, and her cash. Running her tongue over her teeth, she wished she had brushed them again but figured she could pick up some Altoids or something.

When she heard a car pulling up out front, she realized she hadn't written her mother a note. She ran back into the kitchen and grabbed a pencil, then scribbled on the pad they left by the phone. *Gone out with the girls for Chinese and b-ball game at school. I won't be late. Love, Sammi.*

The girls. It wasn't a lie, really. Why bother explaining that it wasn't the same girls her mother would assume? It would only be another thing for her mother to have to think about, and another thing for her father not to pay any attention to. Something for them to blame each other for.

10

Sammi locked the door behind her and hurried across the lawn to Rachael's little Kia. As she dropped into the seat and pulled her door shut, she glanced at the dashboard clock and saw it was quarter past five.

"The great escape," Rachael said with an impish grin, pulling away from the curb. Rachael was no more than four-ten, and with her curly brown hair she looked way too young to be behind the wheel of a car, but at twenty-three she was seven years older than Sammi.

"Thanks for the rescue," Sammi said.

"My pleasure. And all good. With you along, there's no way Zak can deny us Chinese food."

Her boyfriend, Sammi's cousin Zak, was a lanky six feet tall and wore round, rimless glasses instead of bothering to get contacts.

"He doesn't like Chinese?"

Rachael grinned. "He did until we started going out. Thing is, I love it, so we have it all the time. But don't feel sorry for him. He'll survive. And if he behaves, he knows he'll get rewarded."

"Chinese food for sex. Sounds tawdry."

Rachael glanced at her, grinning. "Let's hope so."

"Eew. My cousin, hello?"

Rachael snickered.

Rachael had a flirty attitude and a gutter mouth, but it was so obviously all in good fun that she didn't seem anything but sweet. Her playful personality was the polar opposite of Letty and Katsuko's behavior in the stairwell the other day.

They picked up Zak and then Anna. Rachael got out of the car and spent a few minutes talking to her mother. Sammi wondered what it would feel like when she no longer lived at her parents' house, when she would drop by and be visiting instead of going home.

They headed off to the Sampan. Halfway through their meal she caught herself in the midst of a laugh and realized she was having a really good time.

"Hey," she said to Anna during a quiet moment when Zak and Rachael were distracting each other with a kiss. "Thanks for asking me to come tonight. It's like my whole life's been ready to explode this week, and this is the first time I feel like the fuse isn't burning."

Anna smiled. "Nice image. You should write songs or something."

"I'm serious."

155

"It's cool. I'm glad you came."

A thought crossed Sammi's mind as she took another forkful of kung pao chicken—she'd never understood the urge some people felt to use chopsticks.

"Do you even like basketball?" she asked Anna.

Zak laughed, and he and Rachael both looked over at them, their expressions making it clear Sammi had just said something utterly ridiculous.

"My little sister doesn't even know how many points you get for a basket," Rachael said.

Anna brushed the words out of the air with a hand. "Please. Does it matter? I'm here to ogle boys, not keep score."

"So you don't care who wins?" Sammi asked.

"Not the tiniest bit."

"Excellent," Sammi said. "Neither do I."

"That's better," Zak said. "Then we have a good time either way."

Full of Chinese food and tea, they rode over to the school and parked in the lot across the street. The smaller lot—beside the doors to the gym—would be reserved for the visiting team's bus and school personnel only.

As it turned out, their attitude about winning and losing served them well. As the second quarter drew to a close, the Jameson Mustangs were beating the Covington Cavaliers 32–23, and the home team had gotten their score up that high only because of a trio of three-pointers Ken Nguyen had shot.

Sammi didn't care. She watched the cheerleaders half

the time, trying to understand the subculture the way an anthropologist might study some lost Amazon tribe. The game, she discovered, really was more a social event than an athletic one. People tapped her on the shoulder to say hello, waved from across the court, or stopped her on her way to the water fountain. More than a few seemed to be making an extra effort to be friendly to her, and she winced inwardly at the idea that their kindness came out of pity. Sammi decided it didn't really matter. None of these people was an intimate friend, but at least they were happy to see her, glad she was at the game.

It felt good. Even better, she'd seen no sign of her former friends. Sammi doubted Caryn, Katsuko, or Letty had ever been to a basketball game. A football game, maybe. Homecoming weekend. And some of Katsuko's swim meets, of course. But that would be the extent of their school spirit as far as supporting the sports teams.

As the last seconds of the first half ticked down, Rachael leaned between Sammi and Anna.

"We're gonna take a walk. See you guys in a bit."

Rachael took Zak by the hand and they walked down out of the stands. Anna raised a suggestive eyebrow, and Sammi chuckled. Then the air horn blew for halftime and a flood of people came down off the stands to go to the bathroom or get snacks from the table set up in the corridor outside the gym.

Sammi and Anna stayed put.

"So, tell me more about this guy Adam," Anna said.

"Cute Adam," Sammi corrected. She had talked about

him over dinner, and now she found herself telling Anna the story about how they'd met at Kingston Lake.

"You're like the Pied Piper," Anna said. "Next time we get together, you should bring your guitar and play a song that'll bring a cute guy over for *me*."

Pleased to hear Anna talking about them hanging out more in the future, Sammi was about to promise to try to work her musical magic to lure as many cute guys as possible. But Anna had stopped paying attention. Her brow furrowed with worry. Sammi twisted around on her seat to see what had alarmed her and saw Rachael pushing past people to get to them. Her expression spoke of fear and danger and serious trouble.

"Sammi!" Rachael called, gesturing for them to come down from the stands.

But they were already moving. When they reached the basketball court, Rachael reached for Sammi and started to drag her toward the gym doors. Anna followed along in their wake.

"What's going on? What's wrong?" Sammi asked.

"Just come on. Maybe you can do something."

Sammi pulled her arm away. "Do something about what?"

Rachael glanced nervously around and then leaned in so that only they could hear her. "These girls—Zak says they're your friends—they're fighting in the parking lot. There's a lot of blood."

For a second, Sammi froze. It had to be T.Q., Letty,

Katsuko, and Caryn. She didn't know if she could do any-thing to help, or if she even wanted to help. But then she shook it off. If nothing else, for all of their sakes, she had to try to get them to stop before the police came. She'd never be able to look any of their parents in the face if they got ar-rested and she hadn't at least *tried*.

"Shit," she whispered.

Sammi broke into a run. Rachael and Anna hurried to catch up. She slammed through the gym doors and out into the parking lot. To the right there were lights above the cars where some of the teachers had parked. To the left was the empty bus that had brought the Jameson High team. From beyond that, in a dark area lit only by the moon, came the sound of someone crying and a grunting noise, followed by the slap of fists upon flesh. Someone swore loudly, voice shrill and enraged.

Her shoes clacked on the pavement as Sammi ran around the side of the bus. She stumbled to a halt and stared in horror at the scene unfolding there.

Rachael had been right. There was a lot of blood.

In the moonlight, she could see it painting faces and arms and gleaming where it had been smeared on the side of the bus.

Las Reinas had finally gone after payback, but from the very first glance it was clear things hadn't worked out the way they had planned. Caryn had Marisol on the ground. The girl all of Las Reinas looked up to started to rise, and Caryn hit her in the side of the face so hard that Sammi heard something crack, echoing like a gunshot all the way across the parking lot. Marisol tried to crawl away, and Caryn kicked her in the ribs.

A couple of Reinas staggered away—one with a hand over her face and another holding her arm against her chest like it was broken. They headed for the back of the school, where paths would lead out to the main road and escape.

Katsuko straddled a girl on the pavement, punching her repeatedly. A Reina named Teresa grabbed her by the hair and tried to haul her off. Katsuko went with the momentum, thrust herself up and twisted around, reached out her hands and clawed Teresa's face and neck. The girl screamed and shot a fist into the side of Katsuko's head. The swimmer barely flinched as she grabbed Teresa, pulled her in close, and started to punch and then knee her in the gut and chest, driving her to the ground.

T.Q. threw Jesenia up against the bus, pressing her face against the metal, smearing blood from a gash on the girl's cheek and from what had to be a broken nose onto the yellow paint.

Shouting, Zak grabbed T.Q. by the shoulders and pulled her away. T.Q. yanked away from his grasp, turned, and launched a vicious kick at his balls that made him cry out and fall to his knees, then curl into a fetal ball on the pavement. Zak started hyperventilating, air whistling through his teeth.

Rachael ran to him. T.Q. ignored her.

Sammi stood and stared, saw it all unfolding at once.

When she could breathe again, she turned to Anna, whose eyes were wide with horror.

"Get back inside. Find coaches, teachers, whatever. Call the police."

Anna ran.

Sammi heard another cry, a wail for mercy, and from the darkness near the front end of the bus came a figure bent at the waist, staggering in pain. The girl looked up, searching for some escape, and in the moonlight Sammi recognized Cori.

Then Letty went after her.

Letty didn't run. She had done enough damage that she knew Cori wouldn't be going anywhere fast. Instead, Letty strode after her, fists clenched with grim purpose. Blood spattered her grinning face, but Sammi did not think the blood was Letty's own.

She caught up to Cori and launched a savage kick at the base of the girl's back that knocked her to the pavement, sliding on her palms, scraping them raw.

Then Letty started kicking. She caught Cori in the head, in the ribs, in the arms the girl lifted to defend herself, and her grin never wavered.

But she never said a word.

Underneath all the horror and revulsion, her former friends' silence filled Sammi with fear. Las Reinas cried out in pain, they cursed, but Letty and the girls said nothing.

Cori covered herself as best she could with her arms. Tears streamed down her face. Letty kept kicking.

Sammi began to scream.

"Stop it! God, Letty, just stop!" she cried.

Her awful paralysis broke at last and she rushed across the parking lot. Caryn looked up and gave her a dark, warning glance. Katsuko reached out to try to catch her, but Sammi darted past, bolting toward Letty.

Sammi had never had a fight. She had never thrown a punch. As she ran at Letty, she could think of only one way to stop her from hurting Cori any further. At full speed, she slammed into Letty from behind, wrapping her arms around her and driving her to the ground. Letty twisted in the air and they hit the pavement side by side, rolling.

"You little bitch," Letty said, seething. She reached behind her, trying to pry herself loose, but Sammi held on as tightly as she could.

Letty bucked and Sammi started to lose her grip. They were roughly the same size, but Letty was so much stronger. She began to shake Sammi off, shrugging herself free. Sammi struggled to hold on, her arms slipping down around Letty's waist. The girl's shirt rode up, baring a stretch of her lower back. Her skin glistened in the moonlight, goose bumps rising in the chilly September night.

Pistoning her legs against the ground, Letty tore herself loose.

"No!" Sammi shouted, and reached out, hooking her fingers into the rear waistband of Letty's pants.

Then she froze.

In the golden glow of the moon, she stared at the tattoo Dante had drawn on Letty's lower back. Dread spider-walked down her spine, and her skin prickled all over.

The core of the tattoo remained just as Dante had originally designed it, just as it had been that night when he had engraved it in the flesh of her friends. But the five waves that came up from the heavy black circle at the center were no longer waves at all. They were black lines curling like vines in all directions, radiating out from that circle like veins from a heart. Like poison, they were spreading.

"Let go!" Letty snarled, twisting around to glare at her.

Sammi looked into her eyes and saw nothing familiar. It felt as though she were staring into the eyes of a stranger.

With a grunt of effort, Letty pulled away from her again. Sammi tried to grab hold, but too late this time. They were both still sprawled on the pavement when Letty drew up one leg and kicked her in the face, one hard heel striking Sammi's cheek. Pain shot through her, and she felt bone give way. The crack echoed in her ears.

Sammi cried out, then tried to catch her breath as she dragged herself across a few feet of pavement. Letty rose, fury etched on her face, lips twisted into a mask of hatred. Sammi tried to get up.

She staggered right into Caryn, who caught her by the arms. For a second, Sammi thought the girl might be trying to help her. But then Caryn hauled back and punched her.

Darkness gathered at the edges of Sammi's vision, and she went to her knees. Disoriented, she tried to rise again, looking around in search of some kind of help even as she attempted to back away.

Katsuko came up behind her, grabbed a fistful of her hair, and forced Sammi to the ground.

"Please," Sammi said, tasting the copper tang of her own blood in her mouth and on her lips. One side of her face had gone completely numb save for the deep pain of broken bone. Even uttering that one word was like having shattered glass in her cheek.

The pavement felt cold against her other cheek. The leather jacket she'd worn seemed to be weighing her down.

Out of the corner of her eye, Sammi saw legs moving toward her. She kicked out, trying to do damage, to hurt one of them—all of them.

T.Q. loomed over her, red hair glinting in the moonlight but falling like a curtain to hide her face in the deepest of shadows. From those shadows came a laugh that burrowed into Sammi's skin and froze her to the marrow of her bones. Insidious and intimate, her laugh seemed simultaneously loud and a whisper in Sammi's ear.

The rest of them started to laugh with that same soft malice.

T.Q. kicked her first. Sammi grunted, bones jarred by the blow.

"Please, don't do this," she said, her cheek stabbing with pain as she tried to get the words out.

They all moved in then, kicking her in the side and the legs. Every blow made her want to scream. She rolled on her side, but that was worse. Kicks struck her spine, her breasts, her belly, and she let out a roar of agony and frustration and sorrow.

Tears slid down her face. The world had become a nightmare. These were her friends.

Someone kicked her in the face, breaking her nose. Pain shot back into her eyes. Blood cascaded down over her lips and slid along her cheeks as she twisted and moved, trying to find a spot where she could best defend herself. But there was no defense.

Nearby, people were yelling. She heard Zak's voice. Rachael screamed for help. Someone stopped kicking long enough to stop them from interfering with the beating. Sammi heard adult voices and, in the distance, police sirens.

A heavy shoe struck her in the temple.

Consciousness fled into the shadows; darkness enveloped her.

The last thing she heard was the sound of their shoes slapping the pavement as the girls ran away.

Damage done.

11

Sammi had the sensation of floating, drifting in the ocean. Her skin felt cold. Somewhere in the distance she heard a steady beep and muffled voices. A squeaking wheel passed by. Someone swore, and she heard the chirp of rubber soles on linoleum.

Floating. Drifting. For a while—how long she could not have said—she heard nothing. Instead she felt herself gently swayed by the currents eddying around her. Her fingers and toes were cold but the rest of her grew strangely warm.

Arms outstretched, she floated.

Drowning . . .

With a gasp, she opened her eyes, dragging in a painful breath as though she had been suffocating a moment before. Inhaling hurt her chest. Breathing, she immediately discovered, sent small splinters of pain through her upper torso.

It felt as though her brain were wrapped in gauze. She'd been hung over before, but this was no hangover. Her eyes opened only to slits. Every muscle felt slack and a terrible film covered the inside of her mouth. On her tongue she tasted the copper tang of blood. Lips twisting in disgust, she winced with fresh pain in her nose and forehead, and only then did she feel the deep, throbbing ache in her left cheek, as though some sadistic dentist had ripped out all of the upper teeth on that side with a wrench.

Her tongue probed that spot and found that one tooth had been broken, but the others were intact.

The pressure across the bridge of her nose and in a band across her forehead increased. The sudden urge to move made her try to sit up. She became dizzy and weak and slumped back to her pillow, disoriented. Sammi took a few moments to steady her breath and let the strange fuzziness of her thoughts clear. Experimenting, she lifted her hand, thinking to investigate her face and head for bandages. But the weight of that hand distracted her. She heard something shift, felt a pinch on her wrist, and when she managed to turn her head, she saw the cast on her right hand and saw the IV that had been hooked up to her arm. Moving around had made the needle shift where it lay jutting from her forearm.

"Oh shit," she whispered.

"Sammi?"

Her mother's voice.

"Sammi, honey? Are you awake?" Linda Holland said.

Just hearing those words made Sammi want to cry with

relief. Whatever had happened to her, whatever was wrong, at least she wasn't alone. Her mother would be there to look out for her.

Carefully, she let her head loll to the right. Her mom rose from where she'd been sprawled beneath a blanket on a large, soft chair. There were dark crescents beneath her eyes and she wore her hair pulled back into a ponytail, her clothes wrinkled, her face without any makeup.

"Mom?" Sammi croaked. Her voice was a harsh rasp.

"Oh, sweetie, I was so afraid," her mother said, coming around to the other side of the bed and gripping her unbroken hand. "But I'm here. Mom's here, Sammi."

The tiniest smile touched the corners of Sammi's lips, sending a fresh jolt of pain through her face. Her mother was talking to her as if she were still a five-year-old. Normally it would have driven her crazy, but right now Sammi just wanted to be taken care of, and Mom knew how to do that better than anyone.

"What . . . ," she started, then winced in pain. She forced herself to overcome it and studied her mother closely. "What happened to me?"

The question drew curtains across Linda Holland's eyes. Whatever her mother was really feeling, Sammi understood that she had determined not to reveal too much to her daughter.

"Oh God," she whispered, her voice a dry rasp. "Is it bad?"

"No, no," her mother said, shaking her head, touching Sammi's arm. "I mean, you were pretty beaten up, sweetie.

But you're going to be just fine. You're already on the mend. The doctor says you're very tough." Her mom smiled. "Of course, I told her I'd always known that."

Sammi tried to return the smile, inviting fresh pain.

"I know it hurts, honey. They can give you something more for the pain if you want."

"No," Sammi said. "I just woke up. I'll be okay for a little bit. I don't want to zone out."

Every word hurt, but she tried to conceal her pain as best she could.

"Okay. But when the nurse comes in, she'll probably ask you again about the pain. And the . . . the police wanted to talk to you as soon as you were up to it."

The pain had begun to throb deep in her cheek and jaw. She hurt in other places as well. Bandages had been wrapped around her body just beneath her breasts and inhaling created a rhythmic ache. But her face was the worst.

At the mention of the police, however, the pain receded.

"I don't understand," Sammi said.

"How much of the attack do you remember?"

Butterflies fluttered in Sammi's chest and stomach. Flashes of violence splashed across her mind, terrible images of her old friends savagely beating Las Reinas, and then turning on her when she tried to interfere. Worst of all, she remembered the grin on Letty's blood-flecked face.

And then one last thing—something that made her catch her breath and close her eyes. Burned in her memory was the image of the tattoo on Letty's lower back, its five

169

waves turned into black tendrils of poison that had spread like vines. The tattoo had changed. And in her memory—because it could not have been in reality—she could almost see the tendrils moving, the black etching now fluid just beneath Letty's skin.

"Sammi?" her mother said, worry in her voice.

"Sorry, just thinking," she lied. "Not a lot, I guess. I remember coming out of the gym and seeing the fight going on, then trying to stop it. After that, nothing."

What? a little voice said in her head. *Why did you do that? Why lie to your mother, never mind the police?*

But Sammi knew. Deep down, she knew. If she tried to tell the story of what really happened, she would get to the point of that tattoo, and they would all just stare at her. Tattoos couldn't change by themselves. They didn't spread. And they certainly didn't move of their own accord.

"What are the police saying?"

Her mother hesitated, obviously afraid to burden her with unpleasant news.

"Mom, please. I'm going to find out eventually."

"Everyone has a different story. Your friends—"

"They're not my friends," Sammi corrected.

Her mother nodded, frowning as if to say, *Of course. Of course they're not your friends.*

"Letty, Caryn, Katsuko, and that Simone girl are claiming they were attacked and only defended themselves. Marisol Garces and her friends are saying they were assaulted and accusing the others of being on some kind of psychotic drug. Zak and the Dubrowski girls are sort of contradictory. Some people tried to say you were with your . . . with Caryn and the other girls, that you were a part of it. But the police have ruled that out because of the statements from your cousin and Rachael and Anna. Anyway, you're not in any trouble, thank God. But the rest of them are all being charged with assault."

Sammi frowned. "The rest of who?"

"All of them. The Reinas—or whatever you all call them—and Caryn and Letty and the others, too."

"Are they in jail?"

"They should be, but no. Apparently the idea of holding all of those girls didn't appeal to the judge. They're all out right now. But the investigation is . . . Hey. Are you all right?"

Sammi's eyes had begun to feel heavy, pain exhausting her, sleep creeping up to take her unaware. She forced her eyes open.

"Fine. Just sleepy."

Her mother got up. "All right. You rest. The doctor will be in soon and—"

"Wait. You didn't tell me . . . what's wrong with me?" Sammi asked, raising her cast. "What's the damage?"

Her mother's sadness permeated the room. "Nothing that won't heal, honey. Your cheekbone is broken, but Dr. Morrissey says it will heal quickly. More of a crack than a break, she said. Most people who have a broken cheekbone also end up with a broken jaw or a broken—what do you call it?—orbital bone. Your eye socket. And that requires surgery. But you won't need surgery, thank God. The swelling has gone down a lot since Friday night—"

Sammi narrowed her eyes. "What's today?"

Now the fear practically sparkled in her mother's eyes. "Sunday."

Ice spread through Sammi. "I lost a whole day?"

"You weren't in a coma or anything. The trauma did you in, and then they had you on serious painkillers all through yesterday and last night. You might not remember anything, but you were awake sometimes. You were just . . ."

Lifting a shaking hand to her forehead, Linda Holland dropped her gaze. Tears began to well in her eyes and her lip quivered.

"Mom?"

Smiling weakly, she wiped her tears away. "Sorry. I'm sorry. I was just so afraid. Seeing you like that, disoriented and all bandaged and bruised. No matter what the doctor said, I couldn't help fearing the worst. It was like I was holding my breath the whole time, and now, talking to you, I can exhale for the first time."

Sammi felt her own eyes beginning to well up. "I'm gonna be okay, Mom."

Linda Holland nodded. "I know." Then she raised her eyes and studied Sammi more closely. "So your face will heal. It's going to hurt to talk for a while, and you've got to be really careful. Percocet is going to be your friend. Yogurt and ice cream and soup, too, because solid foods are pretty much off limits for a couple of weeks. I guess chewing works against the crack in the bone closing.

"You've got two broken fingers under that cast. Three cracked ribs. And a concussion. I know it doesn't seem like it, but Dr. Morrissey says you were really very lucky. None of the ribs gave way."

Sammi closed her eyes. On the screen in her mind she saw the faces of her former friends gathering around her, smiling and sneering and even spitting at her as they kicked. She flinched at the memory of the kicks that had landed on her sides and back and breasts and skull.

"I must be bruised all over," she said, opening her eyes.

Her mother nodded. "Bruises heal, Samantha. So do bones. All that matters is that you're still here with me."

Me.

Sammi studied her for a moment, then looked around the room. Her gaze landed on the door out into the hospital corridor. Exhaustion had begun to pull at her again. The throb in her face had grown worse, and she thought that some painkillers would be very welcome at the moment. She looked at the clear bag and the long tube that led to the needle stuck into her arm. The IV drip probably had something in it besides nutrients and water, but she needed a little more.

"Where is he?" she asked.

Her mother did not need to ask whom Sammi meant.

"We've been taking turns sitting with you," her mom said. But the tone revealed so much. Sammi understood immediately that her father had visited, but not as often or for as long as her mother thought he should have.

"What aren't you telling me?"

"I really think we should talk later. You should rest some more. Get your strength back."

"Mom."

Linda Holland sighed, then nodded slowly. "Your father is moving out. He's going to stay at a Residence Inn for a while, until he figures out his next step. Right now, we're both just focused on getting you well, and soon."

Sammi stared at her, eyes burning as tears began to spill down her cheeks. Her throat seemed to close. Barely able to move without spikes of pain in her side and chest and face, she hardly shook at all as she cried.

There would be no more Sunday-morning pancakes. No more family dinners.

Hell, no more family.

"Son of a bitch," she hissed.

"I shouldn't have told you," her mother said.

"I wanted to know. Needed to. It's done now, right? All that's left now is living with it."

Her voice was filled with such bitterness that she did not even recognize it herself. Sammi winced, hearing her own pain. Those words could apply to so many things. Her betraying her friends' faith in her. The way they'd banished her from their lives. The violence that had put her into this bed, all blood and broken bones.

All of it was in the past now. All that remained for her was to live with it.

"We'll get through all of it, Sammi. I promise," her mother said, taking her unbroken hand. "And your father isn't gone from your life. We'll all get through it."

Sammi sighed. "I love you, Mom."

"I love you, too, honey."

For long minutes they sat together in silence. Sammi closed her eyes and drifted in and out of fitful sleep, the pain in her face and her ribs flaring any time she inhaled deeply or shifted on the bed.

When the nurse came in and asked how she was feeling, she told the truth. Whatever they had attached to her IV, it worked wonders. The nurse touched a machine that beeped softly beside the bed, increasing the flow. Within minutes, the pain had abated somewhat.

Her thoughts began to feel slippery, her body floating on a gentle ocean.

"I like your tattoo," her mother said.

Sammi blinked and stared blearily at her. "What?"

"Well, not at first. When I thought it was real, it scared me, like I didn't know you anymore. But then Kim, one of the nurses, told me it was a temporary one. It's cute. I don't know what possessed you to get one, but all in good fun, right?"

"Gonna sleep now," Sammi thought she said.

"You go ahead. I'll be here when you wake up."

Sammi felt the darkness closing in around her. A tremor of fear passed through her as she remembered the way it had swallowed her on Friday night as they'd beaten her unconscious.

I don't know what possessed you.

She feared that she knew exactly what had possessed Letty and the girls. The image of those black tendrils traced all across Letty's back loomed up in her mind again. Fueled by painkillers, her imagination made them slither under Letty's skin like snakes.

As Sammi let herself drift off, she prayed the drugs would keep nightmares at bay.

The nightmares came, just as she'd feared. Instead of keeping them away, the drugs only made them worse. By Monday afternoon, Sammi had taken to asking the doctor to decrease the pain medication, preferring the deep ache and sleep deprivation to the images that lurked in her subconscious, waiting for her to fall prey to sleep.

Visitors came and went. T.Q.'s mother was the first of her former friends' parents to come by. On Monday afternoon, she came in with a small mixed bouquet of flowers and stayed for less than fifteen minutes, made uncomfortable by the dreadfully awkward absence of her daughter. Caryn's parents sent flowers—and signed their daughter's name, which seemed almost obscene to Sammi, all things considered—but did not come by in person.

Adam did not send flowers. He did not call or come to visit. Sammi knew they had only met a couple of weeks earlier, but she had taken a fierce liking to the guy, and it hurt her that she hadn't heard from him. She asked for her cell phone, which she'd had in her pocket on Friday night when all hell broke loose. Maybe he'd left her a message. It could be that he didn't even know what had happened to her. But no one could locate her cell phone. In the midst of the chaos, it had been lost, and she did not have his number written down anywhere else.

Sammi asked her mother to try to track down a phone number for Adam, and she promised that she would. But as much as Sammi liked Adam, and as disappointed as she was, other things weighed more heavily on her mind.

Her father had visited for several hours on Sunday night and all of Monday morning. Sammi thought he seemed to want credit for missing work to visit her, then wondered if all of her thoughts about her father would be colored by such resentment from now on. Four or five times he stepped out of the room to answer his cell phone, and every time Sammi wished he wouldn't come back because she knew that her mother would stay gone until her father left.

She loved him, but for a while she planned to give herself the freedom to hate him. Her mother must have shared at least some of the blame, but Sammi didn't care. Her mother wasn't the one in the process of moving out.

Not once in his presence did she acknowledge that she was aware of her father's decision. If he wanted to talk to her about the fact that he planned to move out and separate from her mother—and eventually get divorced—he would have to muster up the guts to bring it up himself, to tell her to her face.

After he left, just after her lunch on Monday—soup and chocolate pudding—Sammi spent a few minutes just quietly crying.

On Tuesday, the police made their long-anticipated visit. Their questions seemed fairly routine. The doctor had already given Sammi an out, making it clear to her parents and the police that it was not uncommon for someone who'd been brutally beaten—and especially received head trauma—to have little or no memory of the incident. Sammi confirmed for the cops the first part of the story that Anna and Rachael Dubrowski and her cousin Zak had told them—that they had not seen the fight break out, but that Las Reinas had threatened violence against Letty and Caryn earlier in the week.

"Zak and Rachael had gone outside right before halftime—" she'd said.

"Why did they do that?" one of the cops had asked.

Sammi only smiled. "I'm guessing they wanted some-place to be alone for a few minutes."

After that, she lied to the police. She claimed not to re-member anything that happened after the first glimpse she got of the melee going on in the dark parking lot. The cops reminded her that Anna, Zak, and Rachael claimed it had been Sammi's own "friends" who had beaten her so badly, that Las Reinas had run off by then. Sammi had tried to shrug, but winced with the pain, hissing air in through her teeth.

"Are you sure you're not trying to cover for your

friends?" one of the cops—Ransom, she thought his name was—asked.

"What good would that do? You've got witnesses," she'd said.

But it was a good question. A better one would have been why? Why was she covering for her former friends? Sammi hadn't given it very much thought. She just knew that putting the girls in jail would not be the answer. Images of that tattoo creeping and spreading across Letty's back like poison ivy kept flashing in her mind.

Not poison ivy, she thought, as the cop droned on. *Poison ink.*

In her nightmares, she saw their faces again—T.Q., Katsuko, Caryn, and Letty, all grinning down at her with gleaming, dead eyes—and every time she woke from one of those dreams, her conviction became greater. Their behavior at school in the week leading up to the fight had made her suspicious, but that night she had become certain.

The girls she knew had not been an illusion. They had practically been her sisters. She had disappointed them, but not one of them would ever have willingly engaged in the kind of behavior she'd seen. And the violence . . . how could those four girls, none of them a fighter, none of them tough, take down six Reinas?

They couldn't.

Unless their behavior wasn't willing at all.

Sammi always stopped her mind from traveling any farther along the path of inquiry those thoughts would lead to. She couldn't think any more about it, couldn't dwell on it much. All her life she had loved mystery novels, and she'd haunted the shelves at Cruel and Unusual Books since she could read. Sherlock Holmes had always been a favorite, and while she knew her deductive powers were limited, one bit of advice Holmes had given in Arthur Conan Doyle's work had always stuck with her.

"When you have eliminated the impossible, whatever remains, however improbable, must be the truth."

But the great detective's reasoning had left one thing out, a question that Sammi had to deal with that Holmes never had. What if the only possible answer *was* the impossible one?

The police didn't stay long. Sammi learned from them that the girls were claiming that they were the victims, that any damage they inflicted upon Las Reinas was in self-defense, and that any injuries Sammi sustained had been caused by Marisol and the other Reinas. They were all going to court. They would probably get off with a slap on the wrist for the fight with Las Reinas, but for what they had done to Sammi, they might all spend some time in jail for assault.

Sammi said nothing. Part of her—the wounded heart of her—wanted to cheer and say the bitches deserved it. But another part of her could not get that tattoo, that poison ink, out of her mind, and she had to wonder if they had not all been victims after all.

Katsuko's parents visited on Wednesday. Like T.Q.'s mother, they did not stay long. But Sammi saw something

180

new and different in their eyes, and it chilled her to the bone. These proper Japanese parents had seen their perfect daughter transform into something crass and wild and brutal, and it terrified them. They were so frightened, and when they apologized to Sammi for the behavior of their daughter, they seemed to be searching not only for forgiveness but for some explanation.

Sammi had none to give.

Her mother stayed with her for stretches of four and five hours at a time, leaving only briefly when other visitors arrived, or for longer periods when Sammi's father lingered longer than she would have liked. Her mom had taken family leave from the bank and seemed anxious to get her back to her room and guitar, even though Sammi wouldn't be able to play the thing for a couple of weeks.

Zak came by with Rachael once, and Anna Dubrowski came by on her own twice, both times with a guilty look in her eyes, as though she blamed herself for some part of what had happened to Sammi. Nothing she could have done would have stopped the beating, but if Anna understood that, the fact seemed to comfort her not at all.

On Wednesday afternoon, while Anna was visiting, Sammi's mother went out to get a cup of coffee and a breath of fresh air. Anna seemed to have been waiting for a moment alone with her.

"Oh my God, I've got to talk to you."

"In secret? What's going on?"

Anna glanced around the room as though searching for the answer. "I don't know. Something's really wrong with those girls, Caryn and the others. I mean, duh, obviously they beat the shit out of you, so we know they're deranged. But everyone's talking about them at school, how weird they've gotten. They're totally spaced now, like they don't even remember things they've done from one minute to another.

"And they're creepy. I've heard them use the same phrases in the same tone of voice in the same day. Yeah, you spend serious time with the same group of girls and you're going to start to act alike, but this is way beyond that. Plus they're totally turning into party whores—"

Sammi scowled in disgust.

"I know!" Anna said, shuddering. "I mean, Simone Deveaux? But some of my friends were at a party on Sunday night they were all at and said they were getting high. Katsuko always came off as pretty conceited and uptight to me even before all this happened, but Jenny Carr walked in on her in a bedroom with Jeremy—they were naked and doing lines of coke off each other's stomachs."

The pain in Sammi's cheek and ribs had subsided a little each day. At that moment, she shifted on the hospital bed and they flared. She winced as she raised her head from the pillow to stare at Anna.

"Are you kidding me? Seriously?"

Anna nodded, regret filling her eyes. "I know I didn't see it myself, but I've been friends with Jenny since, like, second grade. She wouldn't make something like that up. Not about *anybody*."

Sammi felt like vomiting. "Oh my God."

"I know. Supposedly they all hooked up with people that night. Simone and Caryn totally made out, and everyone cheered them on until some guy from Methuen called them sluts. Simone threw him up against a wall—broke a mirror and everything. Jenny said he freaked and started calling her a crazy bitch and she just laughed."

Before Sammi could reply to that, her mother popped back into the room.

"Good news, sweetie! You're going home tomorrow!"

"That's great, Mom. I want to be in my own bed. Or, even better, on the couch with the remote. The TV selection here stinks."

Linda Holland glanced back and forth between the two girls as though sensing she had interrupted something. Sammi forced herself to smile. She and Anna exchanged a glance, but there seemed nothing more to be said. They were both horrified, but how could Sammi even begin to explain her suspicions to the other girl? She couldn't. Even with the way her former friends were behaving, Anna would never believe her.

I don't know what possessed you, her mother had said.

Sammi thought she knew, and it terrified her.

12

Sammi kept the window down, breathing in the fresh air of a warm September day. She'd been cooped up inside the hospital for nearly a week and freedom felt delicious. It made up—at least a little bit—for the agony of the car ride. Every time her mother went over a rut or bump in the road, it jarred her mending bones and she grunted softly. Her mom tried to avoid the worst potholes, but the ride still seemed to last an eternity.

It might not have been the bumps that made the trip home hard to endure. Somehow her parents had decided that it would be a good idea to pick up their daughter from the hospital together. So she sat in the backseat and tried to smile while they pretended that nothing at all had changed, making happy talk to Sammi and trying their best to conceal their spite toward each other.

"Phil, don't you have something for Sammi?" her mom asked as they rolled up to a red light a few miles from home.

"Oh, right!" her father said. Wearing that awkward, forced grin, he picked up a plastic bag from the floor of the front seat and took out a box, then handed it back to her.

Sammi stared at the picture on the box, which showed a razor-thin, cherry red cellular picture phone. A smile blossomed on her face, and her cheekbone hurt only a little as she tore the box open.

"So cool, Dad. Thank you."

"It's all charged and ready to go, honey," her father said.

The light turned green and her mother turned left onto a road that ran alongside the Merrimack River.

"In fact," her mom said, meeting Sammi's gaze in the rearview mirror, "there's already one number programmed in."

Sammi turned the phone on and it jingled its welcome tune. Curious, she waited for it to cycle through its setup, and then went to the menu page of programmed numbers. Only one name existed on the list: *Adam Levine*.

"You found him."

"Mrs. Parisi works at Kingston High School. She gave me his mother's name and I just looked them up in the phone book. That's the home number, though. Obviously I couldn't get his cell."

"No, this is great. Thanks." Sammi glanced at her father in the passenger seat. "Thank you both."

They were all smiles for a minute or so, but the

happiness was short-lived. Reality set in. Instead of awkwardness and resentment now, though, the atmosphere in the car became melancholy.

"So, how are you doing, Sam?" her father asked as they drew nearer to the house. "Healing up all right?"

"Pretty much. Percocet'll get me through the rest of the week. After that I've got to be really careful about my face and my ribs for a while. Dr. Morrissey said it would take six to eight weeks before they're totally healed, but as long as I take it easy, I should be okay. The fingers will take about the same, but with the cast I'm not worried about screwing them up. Mostly I plan to eat ice cream and watch movies. The hard part is not being able to play my guitar. But it's not forever."

"Ah, you'll be playing again in no time."

"Definitely. Meanwhile, I plan to milk my injuries for all they're worth."

Her mother laughed. "Your legs aren't broken, kid. You can get your own ice cream."

"Oh, you're nice," Sammi said. "I don't get even a few days of pampering?"

"Maybe a few days."

In the rearview mirror she saw her mother's eyes cloud and her smile slip away. Something troubled her, but Sammi didn't want to ask what it was. With her parents separated and divorce in the cards, she didn't want any serious discussion at all. Besides, she had a feeling she knew what had crossed her mother's mind. It had crossed hers as well. At some point she would be well enough to return to school.

Letty and the other girls would still be there, waiting.

Sammi said nothing, and in a few minutes they pulled into the driveway and all of her concerns evaporated. Just being home made her elated. Carefully she climbed from the car and hurried to the front door as her father grabbed her overnight bag.

Once the door had closed behind them and the three of them stood in the foyer, the awkwardness of the moment became too much for Sammi. As her father put her bag down, she clutched her new phone and faced them.

"If you guys don't mind, I want to lie down."

"Of course, Sammi. Go on up, honey. Do you need help?"

"No thanks. I'm good."

She started to walk gingerly up the stairs, wary of any sudden moves.

"I'll see you tomorrow, Sam," her father said.

She paused, a rush of sadness sweeping over her. Knowing that her parents were splitting had been one thing, but being here at home and having her dad say goodbye, going off to wherever he was staying now . . . it became all too real. As she turned, she could not hide her sadness, and when she spoke, she knew her bitterness would come out.

Instead, she forced herself to smile and just nodded. Her father was not fooled. In that moment she saw his own pain and regret but could not feel sympathy for him.

Sammi went up the stairs and down the hall to her bedroom. She heard her parents start speaking soft and low to one another. Her door hung open, and she stepped into her room. A wave of relief washed over her. Here she finally felt at home.

She bit her lower lip and shut the door behind her, staring at her bed, at her bookshelf piled with mysteries, and at her guitar sitting patiently on the stand in the corner.

She felt like crying but would not allow herself to do so. The emotion welling up within her came from entering her bedroom and realizing that until this very moment, she had felt endangered.

But here, she was *safe*.

It meant the world to her.

She tossed her new phone onto the bed and walked over to her guitar. Reaching out with her good hand, she ran her thumb over the strings. The sound that came from the instrument gave her even greater solace.

Sitting on the edge of her bed, she managed to get her shoes off and then lay back on a stack of three pillows. She usually slept on two, but her mother must have left her the third to prop her up. The remote control for the little TV in her room was on her nightstand but she ignored it. Instead, she picked up the cherry red phone and flipped it open.

The number was already programmed in. All she had to do was punch a couple of buttons. A glance at the clock told her it was after three o'clock. Adam ought to be home from school by now. She wondered if he had blown her off, or if he had left her messages on her lost cell phone and thought she had been ignoring him.

She called.

On the fourth ring, she almost hung up, unaccountably nervous. On the fifth ring, Adam answered.

"Hello?"

"Hi, stranger."

A pause. "Sammi?"

"Yeah. Hi."

His laugh was more like a snicker. "Damn, you're unbelievable. What the hell do you want?"

She froze. Of all the reactions he might have given, she would never have expected this one.

"I . . . I just hadn't talked to you and thought I should call. I didn't know if you knew I was in the hospital, and I lost my cell phone and—"

"You lost your cell, huh? Please. How stupid do you think I am? You act like a total bitch and a complete sleaze, you send me all those texts, tell me I'm a loser, and now, what? Did you change your mind? I'm not a loser anymore? You screwed every other guy in the Merrimack Valley and you're bored, so now you want to mess with me again? Well, no thanks, Sammi. Really, no thanks. Once was enough."

Her mind reeled, thoughts racing. What was he talking about? She hadn't sent him any text messages.

"I didn't . . . Adam, I was in the hospital."

"I hope it was a mental hospital. Their big mistake was letting you out."

189

Sammi flinched at his cruelty and sat up, her face and chest aching deeply. On the edge of the bed, she hung her head, pushing her fingers through her hair, trying to make sense of his words through their sting. If Sammi hadn't sent him those texts, then someone else had to have done it. And the last place she had her phone had been in the parking lot, when Katsuko, T.Q., Letty, and Caryn had been beating on her.

Oh, you incredible bitches, she thought, the realization stealing her breath away. She'd been telling herself that they were not in control of their actions, but at that moment she didn't care. Right then, she hated them.

"Adam, I swear, I didn't send those messages. It wasn't me. I've been in the hospital for like a week. I got in the middle of this fight Friday night and was in bad shape. One of those girls took my phone, and—"

"You expect me to believe that some girl stole your phone and sent all those texts just to screw with you?"

"Why would I make something like that up? Seriously, do you actually think . . ."

She let the words trail off. The phone line did not crackle. She did not hear Adam breathing, or any other noise. All she heard was a dreadful hollowness, and she knew that he had hung up.

Snapping the phone closed, she tossed it on the bed. She and Adam hadn't known each other long, but she had felt the electric charge of possibility between them. They might have become something. She had really liked him.

And now he hated her.

"Damn you," she whispered.

Her vision blurred and she let herself mope. But when she blinked and focused, she found herself staring at her bureau. On top of it was a small jewelry box, its lid not entirely closed. Sticking out from the opening was the edge of a folded sheet of paper.

Sammi knew instantly what it was.

She rose and went to the bureau, tugged the paper out of the jewelry box, and unfolded Dante's original design for the tattoo. The thick line of the circle still had the same drama, with the hole in its center, and the five waves still swept up from the outer circumference, representing the rolling ocean and five girls who had once been like sisters.

Unlike the tattoo on Letty's back, the design remained unchanged. No tendrils, no streamers of poison ink spreading across the page.

What Sammi had seen on Letty's back was impossible. But she had seen it, and felt sure it and the girls' behavior were connected.

In that moment, she knew she held the solution to her dilemma in her hands. The only way to figure out what was going on, the only hope she had of stopping it, was to go back to where it started.

She had to talk to Dante.

Her first opportunity came the following Wednesday. The bruising on her face had long since faded to an ugly yellow. Her ribs were still tender but only really pained her when she lay down in bed and tried to go to sleep. The doctor had warned her there would be weeks of such tenderness. Her cheek still ached and she had lost weight from eating only soft foods, but Sammi knew that overall she had been very fortunate.

On the Wednesday following her release from the hospital—the day before she planned to return to school—Sammi walked downtown and caught the bus to Vespucci Square. She went at lunchtime to avoid any possibility of running into Letty in the neighborhood, and wore jeans and dark shoes and a baggy New England Patriots sweatshirt, trying to be as inconspicuous as possible.

Despite the days and nights she'd had to consider what her first move would be, she had no plan. The only thing she could think to do was walk right into the tattoo parlor and confront Dante. All she really hoped to discover was whether he was aware of what his tattoos had caused, and what she could do to reverse their effects.

Because Sammi felt certain, now, that the tattoos were the problem. They had started everything.

But when she walked down Valencia Avenue on that early autumn day, the sun warm but the breeze cool, nothing happened the way she had imagined. The moment that she came in sight of that shop on the corner with its blacked-out windows—the neon Open sign glowing a dull blue even in the daytime—a chill went through her. Sammi remembered Dante's mesmerizing eyes and the raw sensuality that exuded from him. But in retrospect his charisma seemed more like manipulation, and his delight like cruel mischief.

Barely even aware of what she was doing, she backed

into a narrow path between a greasy pizza place and an empty storefront that had once been a dollar store. Goose pimples rose on her arms, and she felt her stomach tighten as she stared at the blacked-out door of the tattoo shop. The crack in her cheekbone might be healing, but it throbbed terribly.

Talking to Dante had seemed like the only option. And Sammi wanted another look inside the shop. Lately she had been thinking a great deal about the padlocked door at the back of the shop and wondering what Dante might have back there that he valued so highly. Not his equipment; that was all in the work area where he'd given the girls their tattoos.

He'd done something to them, that night. Something unnatural. Sammi had to find out what, but no way in hell was she going through that door while he was inside.

So she waited.

At first she worried that Dante might not even be inside. Letty had said that the rumors in the neighborhood claimed the shop was always open, that the blue neon always burned Open and Dante never left the place. But that was next to impossible. Even if the tattooist lived there, he'd have to go out and get food sometimes—unless he had someone bring it to him, but that seemed far-fetched.

Sammi laughed at the thought. Could anything be far-fetched where Dante was concerned?

She waited, and she watched the door. Cars pulled into parking spaces along the street. People ran errands or vanished along small side streets where crumbling duplexes awaited. A couple of vehicles never moved, owned either by people who worked in stores along that block or by neighborhood residents.

The black Harley in front of the tattoo shop never moved.

What are you thinking, Sammi? What, exactly, do you think you can do here?

Dusk found her still well hidden in that narrow alley. Sammi called her mother and said she was out with Anna Dubrowski and they were getting dinner, that she'd be home by nine o'clock. Her mother complained. After all, Sammi was supposed to start back to school the next day, but she relented. Her mother did not seem to have the spirit to argue with her since Sammi's father had left. Or maybe she didn't have the heart to deny her daughter anything, now, that might distract her from both physical and emotional pain. Sammi hated taking advantage of that, but her reluctance did not stop her. Had she asked to stay out any later, her mother might have fought her on it, but Sammi knew how far she could push.

After hanging up with her mother, she called Anna to make sure her alibi would hold up. Anna wanted to know what was going on, but Sammi told her only that she shouldn't worry, and promised to tell her the whole sordid tale later. A couple of little white lies. She had no intention of sharing her theories with Anna, or anyone else. Sammi had a hard enough time believing the impossible, and she had seen its effects with her own eyes.

What she needed was proof, and a plan. She hoped to get evidence tonight.

But the hours passed in utter boredom. When she had first slipped into the alley, her whole body had prickled with gooseflesh and her pulse had raced. By eight-thirty her legs ached horribly, her face hurt, and she felt more frustration than fear or anxiety. Dante hadn't left the tattoo shop. The blue Open sign glowed a ghostly blue in the dark.

Reluctantly, she left the alley and started back toward the bus stop in Vespucci Square. Sammi gave the black windows of the shop a final glance as she walked away and shuddered as she began to imagine them as dark eyes following her departure.

When she reached the square, the bus was already pulling up to the metal and Plexiglas shelter with its out-of-date movie posters. Sammi ran for precisely three steps before realizing what a mistake it was and clutching at her healing ribs. Pain radiated through her. She hurried as best she could, and the driver must have seen her in his mirror because he waited for her.

She held her breath against the stink of the exhaust fumes and climbed aboard, taking a seat halfway back. The engine rumbled and she kept her good hand pressed to her ribs as the bus jittered along the street. Slowly the anxiety that had built up in her began to ease, and she found herself quietly chuckling in relief and at her own foolishness.

What did you think you were going to do? Sammi rolled her eyes, amused at her own naïveté. Even if Dante had left, he would've locked the door.

The bus bumped through a pothole, and she hissed in pain. Her lingering injuries reminded her of the girls who

13

The tire iron came from her father's trunk and fit perfectly in her backpack. She stole it that Sunday when they went out to lunch and he tried to pretend nothing had changed. They had burgers at Memory Lane, and after he paid the bill her father had to use the bathroom. He tossed her the keys so she could wait in the car. Sammi opened the trunk, slid the tire iron into her backpack, and set it on the floor of the passenger side. It sat at her feet during the long ride home as they avoided discussion of separation and divorce. Sammi asked him where he'd be living, but he hadn't decided. The only certain thing, he said, was that he would be nearby. He promised he would never leave her.

Sammi couldn't keep the doubt from her face.

Her father's expression became pained. "I'm not going anywhere, Sam. I swear," he said, more engaged with her in that moment than he had been in years. Even Sunday-morning breakfast, she had come to realize, had been more about him than her.

"Don't you get it, Dad? You're already gone."

He flinched at the words, and it made Sammi happy. She felt no shame about twisting the knife. He'd earned it. No matter how many years passed, she would never believe he had put any real effort into working things out with her mother. He seemed relieved to be free and impatient to escape now from the daughter whose very existence was an uncomfortable reminder of his shortcomings as a father.

After he dropped her off, her mother came into her bedroom to talk to her. Sammi barely looked up from her guitar. With her unbroken left index finger, she'd been trying to play slide with the glass cylinder she'd bought at the music store. The cast was unwieldy, but it was nice to be able to wrest any music at all out of her guitar, and out of her heart.

"How'd it go?" her mother asked, innocently enough.

Sammi looked up and saw the worry in her eyes, the dark circles beneath them.

"Fine," she said. "It went fine, Mom."

Her mother seemed hesitant, eyes narrowing. Sammi forced a smile. "We'll be all right. He was never home much anyway. The only difference is going to be that we don't have to watch sports anymore. Just us girls, now."

A terrible sorrow passed over her mother's face and then lifted. She came into the room, smiling brightly, and kissed Sammi on the head. Linda Holland told her daughter that she loved her, and then left the room.

Sammi cried after she'd gone, but only for a few minutes.

Then she set aside her guitar and opened the backpack. The presence of the tire iron made her feel better. Her mother couldn't help her. Sammi would never add her own fears to what her mother was already enduring. But she had spent a couple of days back at school now and seen what had become of T.Q. and Letty, of Caryn and Katsuko. People moved out of their way in the corridors of Covington High and whispered venomous cruelties behind their backs. Most of which Sammi thought were probably true.

They were party girls, turning their lives into a wreckage of sex and drugs and violence. Lots of kids did the same—Sammi even knew some of them—but they didn't become that way overnight. The people her friends had once been had been completely eradicated.

Sammi had vowed to find out how it had been done.

Which was where the tire iron came in.

On a Thursday night, three weeks after she'd been released from the hospital, Sammi stood in the alley across from the tattoo shop and stared in astonishment as the blacked-out glass door swung inward and Dante emerged. For a few seconds she was so stunned that it did not occur to her to hide. He looked just the way she remembered, with his thick, wild hair and thin scruff of beard. She watched as he pulled out a jangling key ring and locked the door of the tattoo shop.

In the moment before he turned around, she realized

that she was not well hidden and plastered herself against the brick wall of the vacant dollar store. Nine o'clock had come and gone and the darkness cloaked her, but Sammi had staked out the place five times now—later on two occasions—and never seen him so much as set foot outside the building. Customers went in and came out, but Dante had never left.

Even now, as he made his way to the fat Harley-Davidson at the curb, the blue neon sign glowed Open against the night. Dante threw one leg over the motorcycle, pulled on a helmet, and kicked the Harley to life. The engine roared, then rumbled low like some ancient beast about to attack. It growled as Dante pulled away from the curb and Sammi stuck her head around the edge of the building just enough to watch him ride off.

"Holy shit," she whispered.

She turned to stare at the black window eyes of the tattoo shop. Adrenaline raced through her, her heart pounding. The moment the distant roar of the motorcycle vanished completely, she hurried across the street. Every instinct told her to run, to go as fast as she could before Dante had a chance to return. But if she ran, that would look suspicious, and anyone who'd noticed the girl in the baggy sweatshirt or the leather jacket hanging around the neighborhood might pay too much attention.

Dante had locked the door. That was good. Otherwise Sammi would have had to try the front entrance first to see if anyone was working there. But he wouldn't have locked the door with someone else inside, and she hadn't seen any customers enter since a heavyset bald guy had walked out just after seven.

Sammi walked around behind the building. A small alley ran behind that whole block, where blue trash Dumpsters overflowed with junk awaiting pickup. A single light burned in the dark alley, all the way down at the other end of the block. She found the back door of the tattoo shop easily. It was metal, and painted a dark color that might have been burgundy or brown; she couldn't tell without more light.

"You're not really doing this," she whispered to herself, flexing her good hand and taking a deep breath. But that was just fear talking. Sammi had not spent all this time waiting for Dante to leave to then ignore the opportunity.

Her world had been destroyed, her friends twisted, her life shattered. She wasn't walking away now.

Sammi set her backpack on the pavement just behind the door and glanced around to make sure she was unobserved. She listened a moment for the sound of a Harley-Davidson roar but heard only car engines going by on the street out front.

Unzipping the backpack, she took out a black leather glove and slipped it onto her right hand. Then she grabbed the tire iron. Its weight felt good in her hand. One end was tapered flat, intended to pry off hubcaps.

Her left hand would be useless except to help guide the tire iron into place. There were two locks on the door—one in the knob, and the other above it—but the keyhole in the knob looked rusted and ancient, as if it hadn't been used in a long time.

Sammi slipped the tire iron's flat end between the door and the frame. The door itself might have been metal, but the frame was wood. Carefully, she began to pry the bar into the space, wedging it in, trying to use it to pop the lock open, but with no luck. Sliding it beneath the lock, she pushed it deeper and rocked it back and forth, putting her weight behind it. When she had inserted it as far as it would go, she glanced around again. Then she pressed her cast against the bar, gripped it with her right hand, and shoved.

Something splintered in the frame.

Panic surged through her, and for a second she nearly bolted. The conscience she'd always had, the voice of the good girl she had always been happy to remain, urged her to stop. To run.

Screw that. She had to know.

Sammi shoved against the tire iron again and again. The door frame splintered, the lock tearing right through the old, damp wood. With a loud pop it gave way and the door swung open.

Breathing hard, her mostly healed ribs and face throbbing, she stopped to listen for Dante's motorcycle. Then she slid the tire iron back into her backpack, picked it up, and stepped into the darkness. Reaching out, she searched for a light switch on the wall just inside the door. When her gloved hand found it, she pulled the door closed behind her and turned the light on.

The illumination came from a single, dirty, overhead fixture and cast a yellow gloom on that room. A single glance made Sammi realize that she had broken into the area of Dante's shop that had been off limits when she and the girls had visited before. From inside the shop, the room was padlocked.

Now Sammi understood why.

A thin futon mattress lay in one corner with a tangle of sheets and blankets and a pile of pillows on top. A refrigerator hummed against the wall. Another narrow door hung open to show a dingy bathroom. Dante actually lived here after all. A shelf stocked with food and a microwave oven completed the picture.

But that was hardly all. Dante's living area comprised only about a quarter of the space in what had once surely been a storage room. A huge desk with a high-backed wooden chair had been set up in the middle of the room, not far from the door that led into the area where the tattooist did his work. Shelves lined the walls. There were a couple of floor lamps, but she didn't need the additional light to see the bizarre collection of items Dante kept in the confines of his sanctuary. Two tall shelves were full of books, mostly old, faded, leather volumes.

Conscious of the time, not knowing when Dante would return, Sammi hurried into the room. On other shelves she saw bottles and plastic jars of paints and dyes, as well as metal and bamboo spines that could only be the tools for the kind of slow, agonizing tattooing that some cultures thought of as an art and Dante claimed he did not do. One shelf had shoe boxes full of Polaroid pictures. She did not take off her gloves, but fished around in the top box. What she could see of the photographs made her stomach turn. The images were of grotesque body modifications, ritual scarring, strips of skin being torn off a woman's back and then painted, the ochre color mixing with her blood. There were piercings that made her feel sick to her stomach.

But the pictures revealed something even more unsettling. In many of the photographs, black and white and red candles burned in the background. Strange symbols were painted on the floor beneath a woman splayed out while her breasts were being linked together by a heavy chain connected to hooks that pierced her nipples.

In disgust, Sammi stepped away from the box. She turned to find herself face to face with a shelf covered with dried herbs unfamiliar to her, jars of strange-colored powders, and bottles full of cloudy liquid in which small objects floated. She couldn't tell what they were with the debris that drifted in that liquid, and did not want to know.

"What the hell is all this?" she asked the quiet of the room.

Hurrying now, her heart beating faster and a terrible dread twisting in her gut, she went to the bookshelves. Fumbling for the switch, she clicked on the floor lamp between them, illuminating that corner of the room. Most of the books were so old that their titles were obscured or to-tally faded. She could make out *Sons of Arkham* and *Mysteries of the Wurm* written in antique script. Others were in languages that might have been German and Latin, and one she recognized as French.

On more than one, she saw the word "grimoire."

She pulled one of those off the shelf and flipped it open. Inside were nonsense words and gibberish she didn't under-stand at all. There were inscriptions and pages of freaky symbols, and she shuddered. Her upper lip curling in dis-gust, she slid the book back into place and backed away.

Sammi looked around at the other shelves again. Some of it was just extreme tattoo and body modification stuff, but the rest . . .

"Magic." The word felt ridiculous on her lips. But hadn't she suspected as much all along? What other explanation could there have been? Evidence of a depraved mind filled the room, and the occult artifacts and grimoires were just a part of that. Dante was sick.

He'll know I've been here, she thought, and a fear unlike anything she'd ever felt went through her. In that moment, Sammi thought she understood what real fear was, the ter-ror of the unknown lurking in the dark that had plagued her ancestors in a time before civilization.

"Oh my God," she said. "He'll know."

No way could she fix the lock. Her only hope was that he would assume some thief had broken in.

Glancing around for something to steal, she saw

nothing of any value. No TV, no DVD player, no computer. Frantic, she hurried to his desk. On it were stacks of papers, a ragged leather book, and another shoe box full of Polaroids. Ignoring them, she started opening drawers but found only more papers. No cell phone. Nothing of value. To take anything worth real money, she'd have to get into the shop itself, and that would require breaking the padlock.

No way.

Just go, she told herself. *He can't know it's you.*

Unconvinced, she started to turn anyway, and the box of pictures caught her eye. On top was a Polaroid of a naked woman with long, red hair. An insidious certainty sent a chill down her spine even as her face flushed with the heat of embarrassment. Unable to stop herself, she picked up the box in her gloved hand.

T.Q. lay on a concrete floor in the midst of some kind of occult symbol drawn in chalk. Her body had been smeared with something that might be blood. She held a serpentine blade between her splayed legs in an obscene pose. Sammi refused to wonder where the blood had come from, if blood it truly was.

She dug through the box. There were other pictures, some playful, others far more obscene. Some had been taken on that same concrete floor, but many had been taken elsewhere, at Covington High or around town. All the girls were there—Caryn, Letty, and Katsuko—and none was spared. In one Polaroid, Letty was plunging a hypodermic needle into a vein between Caryn's toes. Caryn's eyes had rolled back to white and her mouth half opened in almost erotic pleasure.

Some were worse. Much worse.

At last, unable to look anymore, Sammi pushed the box away. She glanced down at the book that lay open on the desk. Its yellowed pages showed a number of strange designs, but unlike the occult symbols she'd seen, these were almost artful. She flipped a page and saw illustrations showing the very same antique tattooing equipment that sat on Dante's shelves, as well as what seemed to be directions for mixing different dyes and inks.

A photograph jutted from the top of the book like a bookmark.

Her mouth dry, feeling almost as though she were in a dream, Sammi opened the book to that page. The picture had been taken from a distance, its subject unaware.

The photograph was of Sammi. From the sweater she wore in the picture, one sleeve pulled down to cover most of her cast, she knew it had been taken the previous Tuesday in front of school, while she waited for her bus.

Her good hand came up to her mouth, and for a moment she thought she would throw up. But then she saw the illustration on the yellow page that the photograph had been marking. That thick, black circle with its hollow center, five waves sweeping up from its surface. The ocean, Dante had said. He had pretended to create the image on the spot, but here it was, in a book at least a century old.

The text seemed to be some kind of Nordic language. Whatever it was, she couldn't read it, but knew what it meant. Numb, forcing herself to breathe, she turned the page. There were other, similar designs, some with two, three, or four prongs, and some with more, all representing the number of people to be bound together by a symbol, by a ritual scarring.

By poison ink.

The girls hadn't been bound to each other by the tattoo. Somehow, they'd been bound to Dante. Like some kind of puppet master, he had to be manipulating their every move. And if the photograph of Sammi was any indication, he wouldn't be happy until the ritual was complete, until the spell that had been intended for five girls claimed the fifth.

Confusion filled her. If Dante wanted her under his control, why not just come for her? Why would he let the girls—or make the girls—beat her so badly? Letty and the others hadn't so much as spoken to Sammi since she had gone back to school.

An inkling of an answer came to her. They had all come here willingly, had offered themselves up to him. Sammi thought maybe that was the difference. Maybe whatever power Dante could put into that tattoo, it wouldn't work on her unless she asked for the tattoo—unless she wanted it. And there was no way in hell that would happen.

So why did the psycho have her picture?

Her thoughts were so busy with that question that she didn't notice the sound right away. But then the muffled growl of the motorcycle engine grew louder, and she cursed under her breath. Frantically she flipped pages to find the one the book had been open to. Hoping she'd remembered correctly, she crossed the room, snatched up her backpack, and eased the metal door open. Heart pounding in her ears, she reached out her cast and used it to switch off the dusty light fixture, casting the room into darkness.

The alley behind the shop remained mostly shadows, but none of them moved. There didn't seem to be anyone watching and she slipped out, ears attuned to hear any sound of Dante coming back into the shop from the front.

A frown creased her forehead. The growl of the motor-cycle engine had begun to diminish again. A wave of relief washed over her as she realized that, though it was as loud as Dante's Harley, this bike belonged to someone else. The noise of the motorcycle moved away.

Still, she owed its rider a debt. It must be at least ten o'clock by now, perhaps later. There was no telling when Dante might come back, but she had already risked too much.

Slipping the leather glove into her backpack, Sammi zipped it, then slung it across her shoulder and started walking. This time she headed along the narrow mainte-nance alley behind the row of shops toward the single light at the end of the block. Once there, she turned left and walked into a neighborhood of barking dogs and rusty swings. At the first cross street, she turned left again, and slowly made her way back to Vespucci Square.

The last bus came by at ten-twenty-five, according

14

The house seemed dark and silent when Sammi arrived home. Its stillness made it seem empty, almost abandoned, as she walked up to the front steps. Sammi frowned. Her mother had to be home. If she had gone anywhere she would have called. Sammi had her new cell phone in her pocket, set to vibrate.

She must be sleeping.

A layer of ice seemed to have formed on her skin. Sammi's insides felt brittle. Images swirled in her mind that she wished she could scour away forever. The photographs in Dante's sanctuary were things she could never unremember. But even worse than those Polaroids—than those images—were the epiphanies she had experienced.

She'd give anything to forget what she knew.

A snippet of an old song—one of her father's old

favorites—came whispering through her mind. *Wish I didn't know now what I didn't know then.* Truer words had never been spoken.

Once inside, she slipped her keys into her pocket. The tire iron felt heavy in her backpack as she closed and locked the door behind her. Dim illumination came from the back of the house. They had always kept the light over the kitchen sink on overnight, just in case anyone wanted to come down for a glass of water.

Sammi set her pack down quietly on the throw rug in the foyer and slipped off her shoes and jacket. She didn't turn on any more lights. A couple of windows had been left open a few inches in the living room, and she padded quietly over to the nearest and slid it closed and locked it.

"I guess it's your turn, huh?"

She spun, heart fluttering, and saw her mother curled on the sofa with her head on a burgundy cushion.

"Mom! Jeez, you scared the hell out of me!"

Sammi pressed her good hand to her chest and felt her heart beating wildly, a caged bird struggling to be free. She steadied her breathing and stared at her mother, frowning with the realization that her mom had been lying on the sofa in the dark without even the television on, and wondering how long she had been there.

"What's wrong, Mom? What do you mean, my turn?"

Her mother stared past her with glazed eyes. "What time is it, Samantha? After eleven, I think. You have school tomorrow. I expected you home two hours ago. Or did you just decide you don't give a shit anymore what I want or expect from you? That your mother's concern for you and the rules of this house weren't important?"

She shook her head. "It isn't like that. I told you I'd be late—"

"By ten, you said. And even then, I wanted to argue. I didn't, because I'm trying to give you some freedom. You need that right now. I understand. But this is too much."

Linda Holland sat up and pulled the cushion onto her lap, petting it like a lazy house cat. "Not that you'll listen. Or care."

Sammi stared. "Of course I care. I just . . . I screwed up tonight, okay? I lost track of time. I'm sorry. I am. But you're making way more of this than—"

"Than what?" At last her mother looked at her, eyes narrowed. But her gaze held pain instead of anger, and Sammi wished she hadn't looked up after all.

"You're sixteen, Samantha. In two years, you'll be gone, and I'll be on my own. I've been trying to prepare myself for that. What I didn't expect was that you'd leave sooner. College is almost two years away, but you're already gone. Just like your father. You'll do anything to avoid coming home, now. Just like him."

She spat the last word with such venom that Sammi winced, gnawing at her lower lip.

"Wait a second," Sammi said. "I come home late and you just assume the worst? I know things are pretty screwed up right now and you're having a hard time, and I'm sorry I haven't been around more, but I'm having a pretty shitty month, too, you know?"

213

She felt her composure cracking. "Never mind getting my ass kicked. I've lost a lot of things I thought I could count on. My best friends. This guy I thought might actually turn out not to be a total jerk. Not to mention my father—"

Her mother smiled without a trace of amusement. "You never had him, Sammi. Not really. Neither of us did. Counting on him was a mistake. The worst part is that the older I get, the more I realize that the only person you can ever count on is yourself. Your father's gone. I love you more than anything, but I'm not just upset with you for the way you've been vanishing lately. That's just helped me see the truth. You might as well already be gone. I've got to come to terms with the fact that I'm alone."

"That's not fair," Sammi protested.

Her mother shrugged. "What is? We live our lives. That's all we can do. Fairness is a myth, no different from Santa Claus or the Easter Bunny, but it's the one we hold on to the longest, right up until reality spoils it all."

Sammi tried to think of some way to explain why she'd kept her mother at such a distance the past couple of weeks. But just as her mother had been trying to hide the worst of her pain over her impending divorce, Sammi couldn't add to the burden her mother was already carrying.

"It isn't what you think, Mom. I've got a lot going on, that's all."

Linda stood. "Look, it's just life. I've got to figure out what mine is going to be now. In some ways you're doing me a favor, making me realize this sooner than if I'd waited for you to graduate high school."

"Mom—"

"I'm going to get a glass of water. Go up and get to bed. You've got school tomorrow."

Sammi felt a tightening inside her chest as she watched her mother turn her back. She didn't think her mom had ever done that before, and it hurt more than she ever would have guessed. She tried to think of something to say—something that would not require her to discuss the impossible turns her life had taken—but came up with nothing.

Under the weight of her regret, Sammi left the living room, picked up her backpack, and went up the stairs to her bedroom.

She peeled off her clothes and pulled on a T-shirt. Retrieving her cell phone from the pocket of her jeans, she flipped it open and scanned the menu of her programmed numbers. Adam Levine's home phone was still in there, listed as *Adam Levine*. She hadn't changed it to *Cute Adam*, as she'd listed him before. She couldn't bring herself to be that precious with him when he was so furious with her. When he hated her, which he surely must.

Maybe it was just a fantasy, but she thought she could have talked to Adam about all of this. Even if he hadn't understood what she was going through with her parents, and even if he didn't believe her about Dante, he had an openness that would have meant so much to her right then. She needed someone to talk to—someone to whom she could tell her plan.

But Sammi couldn't think of anyone who wouldn't think her crazy, and that was the last thing she needed right now.

With a sigh, she flicked her phone closed. Almost every day since she had first called him and discovered how the girls had destroyed any chance she had of having a relationship with the guy, she had sat and stared at his name programmed into her phone. Eventually she would call him again. Try to explain.

If she could just get him to listen long enough to tell him what Letty and the girls had done—how they had assaulted her, and that they'd stolen her cell phone and sent him those messages—perhaps they could start again. If she could just get him to believe her.

Sammi ran her thumb across the smooth shell of the phone. If she had his cell number, she could text him. That would be easier.

She frowned, realization making her feel absurd. Could it be that simple? With a shake of her head, she got up from the bed and went to her desk, took out a piece of paper, and started to write. Her mother knew the name of Adam's mother. With that, and the number, getting the street address would be simple. She would write a letter.

Tomorrow she would drop it in the mail.

By the time Adam received the letter, all of this would be over, one way or the other.

Friday morning Sammi came awake with a massive intake of breath, as though she'd forgotten how to breathe during the night. Her eyes went wide and then threatened to close again as the lure of sleep tempted her. But the sun streamed through her windows, which were partly open to allow the breeze to swirl around her bedroom. Sammi blinked against the daylight, reaching up to rub grit from her eyes.

With the early-morning sunshine, the events of the previous night seemed distant and even more impossible than they had before. But she knew they were possible, after all. More than possible. In all the films she had ever seen and stories she had read, the sunrise was supposed to chase away the shadows and the darkness. But Sammi did not feel safer now. In truth, she felt more exposed and vulnerable than ever.

Her cell had been charging all night. She disconnected it and glanced at the clock on her bedside table. Too early to call Zak. But if she wanted to make the morning bus, she'd have to hurry. Her mother hadn't bothered to wake her at the usual time, and Sammi tried not to read anything into that. Mom was just preoccupied these days, and understandably so.

When she had showered and dressed, she took the tire iron out of her backpack and hid it in her closet, underneath stacks of shoe boxes. The gloves went on the top shelf. Then she stuffed her books back into the bag, knowing of at least one homework assignment she hadn't gotten around to last night, and went downstairs.

Hurrying to the bus stop, she called Zak. His ringback tone was "Phantom Limb" by the Shins. Sammi rolled her eyes. Their earlier stuff had been much better.

Zak answered, his voice a rasp. "Better be good, cousin."

" 'Good' is not a word I'd use."

She could hear him grunting as he woke himself up more fully. "Sorry, Sammi. Just half asleep. I don't have a class until noon. How're you feeling?"

"Getting better. Wish I didn't have school today, but that's life."

"How's your mom?"

Sammi hesitated. Zak had been inquiring about her healing bones, but now he'd switched gears. The question about her mother wasn't idle curiosity.

"You heard?"

"Well, yeah. Of course. My dad is your father's big brother, Sam. Word gets around in families, y'know?"

"I know. It's not good, actually, if you want to know the truth. I don't know if it's ever going to get better. It's like a bomb went off, and we're all dealing with the fallout."

Zak sighed. "I'm really sorry, Sam. If there's anything I can do—"

"You know, there actually is."

"Name it," Zak said. It sounded like he wanted a task, some kind of challenge.

Sammi wondered if he was eager to do her favors to make up for not being able to help her the night she'd been beaten. She could have told him right then that what had happened to her hadn't been his fault. But if he felt guilty and that made him willing to help her, then absolving him of his guilt could wait a couple of days.

"What time does Rachael's shop stay open until tonight?"

"I think she closes at nine, why?"

"Do you guys have plans?"

"I don't think so. What's going on, Sammi?"

Zak had so much concern in his voice that she almost told him, right there on the phone. He was her cousin, after all. They were family, and she ought to be trying to hang on to the parts of her family that weren't falling apart. But she resisted the urge.

"Can you ask her if she'd be willing to meet me there at closing time? I really need help, from both of you."

"You've got it, Sam. You know that. I'm sure Rachael feels the same way."

Yeah, Sammi thought. *'Cause she was there that night, too, and couldn't stop the girls from kicking the shit out of me.* Nobody could have stopped them. But how to explain that?

"Now, are you going to tell me what's going on?" Zak asked.

"Tonight."

"Does this have to do with that tattoo those bitches wanted you to get?"

"Yeah. It does."

"You're not going through with it, are you? After what they did—"

"Zak," she interrupted. "Please. Just . . . I'll see you tonight, okay? And I'll explain it all."

By then she had arrived at the bus stop. She stood on the corner with Jimmy Paolini and Sara something, both freshmen. Most juniors wouldn't be caught dead riding the bus, out of sheer embarrassment. Sammi had never cared, but today she wished she had never left the house. Hell, she wished she could stay there forever, hiding in her room with her guitar.

"All right," Zak said, unsatisfied. "I'll see you tonight."

"Thanks. Later."

Sammi flipped the phone shut and slipped it into her pocket. Sometimes she socialized with the two freshmen, but this morning she said nothing to them, and they seemed to sense in her mood that she wanted to be left alone. She caught Jimmy staring at her cast a few times, but that was better than the way he usually stared at her breasts.

All day, Sammi avoided the girls. In class she kept her head down, eyes front, pretending that they didn't exist. At lunch she sat with Anna and laughed and smiled, as if this were just any other day. A few days earlier Marisol had come up to her in the hall and thanked her for trying to help Cori when Letty and the others were stomping on Las Reinas. If Sammi ever needed help with anything, she only had to tell Marisol and it would happen. A war simmered between the two factions, and so Sammi tried to avoid Las Reinas as well. She didn't want to light the fuse that would set off an explosion of new violence.

After school she went home and searched for ways to distract herself. Her teachers had gone easy on her after her release from the hospital, but Sammi still had some work to catch up on, so she busied herself with that. When her eyes hurt and her fingers were cramped from holding a pen, she got up and stretched, then fumbled with her guitar for a little while, still trying to get a clean sound playing with the glass slide on her left index finger. The cast got in the way. She wondered how long after it came off it would take before she got the dexterity back in her fingers—how long before she could make real music again.

When her mother came home from the bank, they made dinner together, a Parmesan-crusted chicken breast dish with risotto on the side. After dinner she offered to clean up, but her mother smiled tiredly.

"I'll take care of it. You can pay me back by taking me shopping tomorrow."

Sammi glanced at her in surprise. "Girls' day?"

Doubt touched her mother's eyes. "If you want to."

After the harsh words of the night before, her mom was reaching out to her. Sammi felt a bittersweet happiness welling up inside her. She'd been trying to keep it in, but her mother had hurt her deeply last night.

"I'll even take you out to lunch."

"I'd like that," her mom said. "Do you have plans tonight?"

Sammi nodded. "I'm going to go get ice cream with Zak and Rachael."

She hated how smoothly the lie came out.

"Ooh, bring some back for me?"

"If we don't go anywhere after, for sure," Sammi said. "And if we do, I'll find some Ben & Jerry's somewhere."

"Ah, yes, Ben and Jerry. Friends to lonely women everywhere."

The joke had the sting of truth, but mother and daughter both chose to laugh and ignore it. They were done talking about anything serious for a little while.

Sammi went upstairs. Nervous, she paced back and forth across her bedroom a couple of times, then stopped to stare out the window. It was after seven, and the long afternoon shadows were coalescing into evening.

Taking a deep breath, she fished her cell phone from her pocket and flipped it open, then dialed a number she knew by heart. None of the girls had her new cell number, so they wouldn't have it programmed in. No one would know it was she calling. Sammi tried Katsuko first, but when she got no answer she hung up without leaving a message.

Next she tried T.Q. and listened to her ringback tone, a metallic sound that simulated the way phones had rung in times gone by.

"Hello?"

Sammi couldn't breathe a word.

"Hello?" T.Q. said, an edge to her voice, maybe wondering if the call had been dropped, or thinking someone was screwing with her.

"T.Q. It's me. Don't hang up."

The soft laugh that came over the phone sent a chill

through her. "Sammi. Now, this is interesting. What, you want another ass-kicking?"

"I'll pass, thanks. What I want is the tattoo."

Silence fell on the phone line, lingering long enough that Sammi wondered if the call had been cut off. Then T.Q. asked her the question she'd been dreading.

"Why? You wouldn't do it before. Scared your uptight parents would crush you under the weight of their disappointment. So why now?"

"I know what I did to you all, how much it must've hurt. I turned my back on you. I'm not gonna lie, T.Q. What you all did to me, I'd like a little payback for that. It wasn't right. But some of it, maybe I had coming. As for my parents, forget them. They're getting a divorce. My father moved out. Whatever I thought I had here that I wanted to protect, obviously it was an illusion. And besides . . ."

Sammi swallowed hard.

"I miss you guys."

God, those words hurt to say. The lies were easy. But the truth broke her heart.

T.Q. must have heard the pain in her voice.

"Could be we went too far with you that night," she said. "But you know how it is. You're with us, or you're against us."

"I want to be with you again."

"You still have the original design?" T.Q. asked.

"Yeah."

"When do you want to do this?"

"Tonight. I'm going down to Rachael Dubrowski's shop on Whittier Street. They close at nine, but she said if I came by around nine-thirty she'd do it for me without my parents' permission."

"She goes out with your cousin, right?"

"Yeah, Zak," Sammi said. "Rachael did that airbrush one for me. But I told her I want the real thing now."

"Why not go to Dante's?" T.Q. asked.

"Does it matter? My mother knows I'm going out with Zak and Rachael tonight. She's been looking over my shoulder constantly since my father moved out. I can't get away with anything. Besides, isn't the design what matters? It's supposed to connect me to you guys, right? As long as I follow Dante's design exactly—"

She almost said, *The spell will still work*, but cut herself off. For long seconds, T.Q. was silent, and Sammi began to worry. She wasn't some kind of witch or whatever. If Dante needed to paint the tattoo on by himself, her plan wouldn't work at all.

"You want us to meet you there?" T.Q. asked.

Sammi steadied her breathing, feeling her face flush with heat. This would be where things got risky.

"Just you."

"What?"

"It's just, I always felt closest to you, T.Q. And when everyone found out I'd done the airbrush thing, you never seemed as totally furious as Letty and Caryn and Katsuko. I would've just surprised all four of you, but I need a witness. No secrets this time.

"Will you do it? Meet me downtown at nine-thirty and be my witness, so when I show the other girls, there isn't any doubt about the tattoo?"

"Yeah. I'll meet you there," T.Q. said.

"Excellent."

"And Sammi?"

Sammi paused, thinking of a thousand ways T.Q. could screw up her plans. "Yeah?"

"Welcome back."

15

Rachael's tattoo shop embodied everything that Dante's did not. Whittier Street had a frame shop and a dry cleaner's, a bagel shop and a candle store. There had been a funky little shop that sold the kinds of cloaks and gowns, swords and leathers popular at Renaissance fairs and fantasy conventions, but it had lasted less than a year. A sign in the window advertised a comic book shop opening soon, but for now that storefront stood vacant.

A light still burned in the bagel shop, but as Sammi walked along Whittier Street, the rest of the windows were dark. Only the restaurants stayed open this late in Covington. Last time she'd glanced at her cell phone, it had been about ten past nine. She picked up the pace as she hurried toward the purple awning in front of Skin Colors. A lantern hung by the door. The drapes had been drawn across the large window in front, but the little sign—Body Art by Rachael—was illuminated by the lantern light.

The Closed sign had been turned around.

Sammi rapped softly on the door. As she waited, she reached down and felt the little plastic bottle in the pocket of her leather jacket. Impatient, she glanced around for any sign that T.Q. had already arrived, but the only other person on the street was a young guy in a business suit walking up to the front door of one of the old factory buildings that had been converted into condos. A little Kia drove by, and she raised her hand to knock again.

Before her knuckles could hit the door, she heard someone fiddling with the lock. The door swung inward and Zak stood on the other side of the threshold. Normally he would have been smiling, but not tonight. Whatever would go down here, he knew there was more to it than Sammi had let on.

"Hey," he said, backing up so she could enter.

"Hey." She swept past him.

Zak closed the door behind her, and she heard the lock tumble back into place. "So, you going to tell me what this is all about?"

Sammi smiled. "Where's Rachael?"

The shop couldn't have been more different from Dante's. Yes, the equipment was there, but it was all elegance and art, tapestries and candles, almost a Victorian feel. Heavy curtains hung at the rear of the front room, closing off an area for more intimate procedures. That was where Rachael had given Sammi the airbrush tattoo she'd used to try to deceive the girls.

"Washing up. She'll be out in a minute."

He still wore that expectant look, waiting for her to start talking.

"I just need to use the bathroom real quick. T.Q.'s going to be here in a minute. Hopefully alone. Please let her in. She's my witness."

Zak flinched. "Sam. You're really doing this? This girl helped put you in the friggin' hospital."

"Trust me."

She went through the curtains and then through the door that led into the storage area at the back of the shop. Rachael glanced up from a shelf of plastic ink containers she'd been rearranging. There were a couple of empty boxes at her feet.

"Hey!" she said. "Great to see you. Anna said you were doing well. You look amazing."

Sammi smiled. *Amazing for a girl who got stomped a few weeks ago*, she thought. But she didn't say it. Rachael was being nice.

"Thanks. Listen, I really appreciate you doing this. You have no idea how much I owe you."

Rachael rolled her eyes. "Please. When you really needed help, I couldn't do anything. You don't owe me anything."

"Good. Then I'm going to ask you one more small favor."

Something that might have been suspicion but was at least curiosity crossed Rachael's face. "Name it."

"When my friend gets here, I'm going to act like I want you to get started. Instead, I want you to stall. Clean the needle. Pretend it's jammed. Something. Just for a little while. Twenty minutes, tops. Make conversation, whatever."

Rachael crossed her arms. "I can do that, Sammi. But I'd kind of like to know why."

"I swear I'll tell you. Right after that."

After a moment's hesitation, Rachael shrugged. "All right."

"Great!" Sammi hugged her, the cast only getting in the way a little. "Hey, do you have anything to drink?"

Rachael smiled. "You know I keep the fridge stocked. What do you want? Soda, iced tea, lemonade, or water. It's all there. Help yourself."

The last time Sammi had been here, Rachael had served her the greatest iced tea. She'd hoped to find that option again tonight. Iced tea was T.Q.'s favorite. "I'm just going to pee, and then I'll bring drinks out for everyone."

"Ooh, service," Rachael said. "I could get used to that."

Sammi went into the bathroom. She had genuinely needed to go, but now her nerves had driven the urge away. Instead, she waited a minute until she heard the door close, indicating that Rachael had gone back into the front of the shop. Then she flushed the toilet and washed her hands.

Peeking out of the bathroom, she made sure she was

alone. The refrigerator stood near the back door of the storage room, humming softly. From a cabinet she took down four glasses. She filled two with lemonade and one with root beer—which she knew Zak would enjoy—and poured iced tea into the last one.

The plastic bottle in her jacket pocket held the remainder of the Percocet she'd been prescribed upon her discharge from the hospital.

On a counter near the fridge, Sammi found a plastic tray for the drinks. She carried them from the back room into the curtained-off privacy area at the rear of Rachael's studio. She heard T.Q.'s voice out in front and paused to take a deep breath and plaster on a fake smile. Then she stepped out through the parting of the curtains.

T.Q. had never looked more beautiful. Her red hair glinted gold in the studio lights, and she wore a bone white top over black jeans and shoes. When she smiled at Sammi, it looked almost genuine. She stood between Zak and Rachael, who both looked supremely uncomfortable, and they all glanced up at Sammi as she entered.

"Hey," T.Q. said.

Then she shifted slightly, and Sammi saw that she hadn't come alone. Behind her, Katsuko stood in shadow, clad all in black, her hair cut into a severe bob that made her look even more petite. When Katsuko looked up, her smile had an edge to it—a predator's smile.

Sammi couldn't keep herself from flinching. "Hey," she said.

"I know you wanted me to come alone, but Kat and I were out and about tonight. And two witnesses are better than one, right?"

Kat? Sammi thought. Katsuko hated that nickname.

Or at least, the real Katsuko did.

"Yeah," Sammi said with a nervous laugh. "You don't even need a camera this way."

The tension in the studio continued to build. They were waiting for her to let them know how this was all supposed to go. But Sammi didn't know anymore. Her pulse sped up as she tried to work the angles in her mind. The plan she'd come up with wasn't much of a plan, really. Desperation had driven her to it. But it was all she had, and the only choice now was to go forward.

"I brought out some drinks," she said, stating the obvious. "I didn't realize Katsuko would be here, so I'll get another."

Barely able to breathe, she offered the tray to Zak first, praying that she knew these people well enough to have predicted correctly. When he took the root beer from the tray she felt herself exhale a little and then turned to T.Q., who studied the three remaining drinks too long for Sammi's liking. She resisted the urge to try to influence the girl's decision.

T.Q. took the iced tea. She sipped it immediately, then tipped the glass back and drained a quarter of it, ice clinking.

As Sammi offered the tray to Rachael, who took a lemonade, Katsuko stepped up and took the other from the tray, leaving Sammi without a drink.

She glanced at T.Q., then at Rachael. "Let me just grab another lemonade."

"There's a ton of sugar in this," T.Q. said.

Rachael frowned. "Sorry, I didn't realize—"

"You never do," Sammi interrupted. "Rachael always overdoes the sugar. I kind of like it that way, though."

T.Q. said nothing, but took another sip. "You didn't drag us down here for nothing, right? You're really going to do this?"

Sammi's stomach twisted with nausea, but she smiled. "I said I would."

Katsuko sniffed. "You've said it before."

"I know." Sammi glanced away, hiding her anger and anxiety, knowing they would think she wouldn't meet their eyes out of guilt. "But there's no turning back this time."

"No," T.Q. said. "There isn't."

Her tone frosted the room. Unnerved, Sammi glanced at Rachael. "You all set?"

Rachael blinked, as if only just remembering what they were all doing here in her shop. She shot a look at Zak. "Almost. Sorry. Give me just a few minutes."

She stepped through the curtains into the privacy area at the back of the shop. For a second it looked as though Zak intended to follow her, but he must have caught the flash of panic on Sammi's face because he stayed.

"So," he said, looking from Katsuko to T.Q. "Can I see this infamous tattoo?"

Brow furrowed, T.Q. stared at him. "No. It's personal.

Sammi has the design if you want to see what it's going to look like."

Of course you won't let him see it, Sammi thought. *It doesn't look anything like the design anymore, does it?*

T.Q. drank the rest of her iced tea, swishing the ice around and drinking the last bit of melt at the bottom, even crunching on a piece of ice. If she wrinkled her nose at any bitterness in the dregs of her tea, it didn't seem to trouble her.

That's right. Every last drop.

"I hope you don't think this makes up for anything," Katsuko said, glaring at Sammi.

"It's a start, isn't it?" she asked, then had to bite her tongue to keep from asking how they planned to make up for her broken fingers, for putting her in the hospital, for casting her out.

What good would it do? The girl in all black with the severe haircut wasn't even really Katsuko to begin with. Katsuko had been trapped somewhere deep inside.

"A start," she relented. "But not much of one." Katsuko glanced at T.Q. "Should've done this at Dante's. What's the point, otherwise?"

Zak threw up his hands. "Hey, Rachael knows what she's doing. She'll ink it in exactly the way it's drawn in the design. Personally, I don't know why the hell Sammi's even bothering trying to placate you crazy bitches, but whatever."

T.Q. and Katsuko did not even flinch. They gave him

blank looks, then turned to Sammi with Cheshire cat smiles.

"She misses us," T.Q. said, reaching out to stroke Sammi's hair. "We've been waiting for her to realize just how much."

Sammi shivered. Gooseflesh formed on her arms, but she managed to smile in return.

Katsuko took a sip of her lemonade, then set it down. She slipped off her long black coat and looked around until she found the rack of coat hooks on the wall, then hung it there.

"Your girlfriend's taking her sweet time," she said.

Zak scowled at her. "Whatever."

He looked at Sammi then with such disappointment in his eyes that she had to look away. Soon he would understand. When he did, he might be even more disappointed. For now, she had to just endure his anger and be grateful that he stayed with her, that he didn't try to call the whole thing off right now. Rachael would be breaking the law by giving her a tattoo without parental consent. She and Zak were going out on a limb for Sammi, and she hadn't even told them why, yet.

Tense minutes passed. They heard Rachael moving around behind the privacy curtain. A metal pan rattled. The tattoo machine purred to life for a few seconds and then shut off again. The door into the storage room opened and closed more than once.

Katsuko and T.Q. had been impatient from the

moment they entered the shop. As Rachael stalled, they became increasingly more so, until at last Katsuko walked to the privacy curtain and yanked it open.

"What the hell?" Zak snapped.

But Rachael wasn't there. Katsuko went to the door of the storage area and swung it open without knocking.

"What's the holdup?" she demanded.

Rachael came out immediately, glaring at her, carrying a small container of black ink. She set it on the counter that ran along the back of the privacy area.

"No holdup. I don't rush my work and I don't take shortcuts when it comes to art, or to the health of my clients. You've got a problem with that, no one's keeping you here."

Katsuko didn't get out of her way.

Sammi held her breath, wondering how far the girls would allow themselves to be pushed before they pushed back.

"You and your boyfriend ought to watch your mouths," Katsuko said, glaring. As petite as Katsuko was, she had a few inches on Rachael.

T.Q. stepped up beside Sammi and whispered in her ear. "You need a better class of friends."

Both Rachael and Zak were staring at Sammi unhappily now, waiting for some sign of what she planned to do next. Sammi felt her throat go dry. Nothing had gone as she had hoped. She glanced over at T.Q., who cocked her head and stared back, perfectly alert.

Stomach knotted with dread, she looked at Rachael and forced herself to breathe. "Ready to go?"

Rachael hesitated a second. Sammi had told her to stall, and she was prepared to do that. But now Sammi gave her a slight nod, hoping she would understand.

Arching an eyebrow, Rachael gestured to the privacy area. "Whenever you are."

Sammi uttered a nervous laugh. *That's all right. It's normal to be nervous*, she told herself. *Don't try to hide it*. That would only make them more suspicious. She gave T.Q. and Katsuko a sheepish grin.

"Were you guys this nervous?"

T.Q. crossed her arms. "We were all in it together, that night."

"Or we thought we were," Katsuko said.

Sammi swallowed, her throat constricted. "So, after tonight, you'll stop twisting the knife on that, right?"

Neither of them replied. Sammi looked at Zak and Rachael and hated the disapproval she saw there. But neither of them seemed like they were going to pull the plug, which was good. Vital.

She drew Dante's design out of her back pocket, unfolded it, and handed it to Rachael. "Here you go."

Rachael studied it. "Simple enough. Where do you want it?"

Sammi had never intended things to go this far. She glanced at T.Q. Had her eyelids just fluttered a little? She did look tired, but had she looked that way when she'd first come in? Sammi didn't know.

"Um, I was thinking right here," she said, pointing to the same place on her lower abdomen where Rachael had originally put her fake tattoo.

"You sure?"

Sammi thought about it. Whatever Rachael did to her now would be permanent. She'd never intended for the tattoo to be finished—she feared what that would mean. Originally she had wondered if it would give Dante power over her even if he hadn't been the one to mark her, but T.Q. and Katsuko were going through with it, so she guessed she knew the answer to that.

No way could she allow Rachael to give her the whole tattoo. But she needed more time. Another glance at T.Q., and she thought the girl's eyelids looked heavy. T.Q. stretched, as though exhaustion was setting in.

Sammi had to have Rachael start somewhere it wouldn't show later, but she needed to be able to keep an eye on the girls as well.

"Yeah. I'm sure."

"Pants off, then," Rachael said.

T.Q. laughed softly at that. Zak cursed quietly and looked away as Sammi unzipped her pants. Katsuko applauded slowly, watching in almost salacious admiration as Sammi took off her shoes and then slid out of her jeans.

"Up here," Rachael said, patting a padded table much like the one in Dante's studio.

The drapes at the front of the shop were drawn so no one could see through the front windows. The privacy curtains were left wide open as she hopped up onto the table in only her shirt, socks, and a pair of blue panties.

"Zak, it's fine," Sammi said. "It's not like I'm naked. Just pretend we're at the beach."

He surveyed the room for a moment before meeting her gaze. His eyes were dark and grim, but he didn't look away again. Instead, he searched her face. Sammi knew he was looking for some sign as to what would come next, but she dared not try to give him any warning.

Rachael cleaned the area where the tattoo would go with an antibacterial gel, then put down paper around it as though Sammi were about to have surgery. The young tattooist was meticulous.

The tattoo machine whirred to life.

T.Q. and Katsuko stood at either end of the table, watching as Rachael picked up the tattoo needle, tested it, then returned it to its slot. She went to the counter where she'd left the black ink she had brought from the storage room and started to open it.

"This will hurt, Sammi, but not very much. It stings, but you'll get used to it as I go along."

With the ink open, Rachael reached for the tattoo needle again.

"Wait," Katsuko said. The word had been a command.

They all looked at her. She moved back across the shop, fished in the pocket of her long, black coat, and retrieved a small, sealed plastic container similar to the one that Rachael had just opened.

"We'll use Dante's ink."

Rachael stared at her, but instead of anger, Sammi saw suspicion in her eyes. "Why would I do that? I have no idea what's in that."

T.Q. bent over the table and looked down at Sammi. "The whole idea was for the five of us to be bound together by this thing, right, Sammi? I mean, it's like a ritual. If we're supposed to be sisters, if this design marks us forever and ties us to each other, then the tattoos should be exactly the same. That means the same ink."

Only fear kept Sammi's face blank. She felt herself go pale, and a chill spread all over her body. They had planned this all along.

"When did you get that?" she asked.

Katsuko cocked her head. "T.Q. picked it up before we came here. Look, if you don't want to go through with it, that's fine. But this is the last time we let you waste our time. We've already been looking for a fifth girl to replace you."

T.Q. flinched and shot Katsuko a dark look.

"Fifth girl?" Zak asked. "You're, what, auditioning for a new friend? Why would you need to do that?"

Katsuko stabbed a finger at the design that Rachael had hung from a clip above the table as reference. "Five waves on the ocean. Five spokes on the wheel of life. Five girls."

Once more they all looked at Sammi. She steadied her breathing, covering up a fear unlike anything she had ever experienced. It glistened like tears at the corners of her eyes and trembled on her lips like a scream unvoiced.

Forcing herself to be numb, she looked at Rachael. "Go ahead."

Rachael didn't like it. Sammi could see that. But it no longer mattered. She felt herself inside a strange bubble, separated both from her friends and from the monsters the girls had become. Of the five of them gathered in the shop, only she knew what was really unfolding here.

It made her alone.

Just as with her parents—her absent father and her confused, withdrawn mother—she was alone.

Rachael took the ink from Katsuko and set it on a tray beside her. She opened the container and put the fresh ink into the proper slot in the tattoo machine.

The machine whirred. Rachael picked up the tattoo needle again, lifting it to make sure the cord was clear of any obstruction. She gave Sammi a glance that said, *This is your last chance to back out.* Sammi wanted to hug her for it. Instead, she just nodded, urging Rachael to get started.

Rachael glanced again at the design. Sammi did not. She never wanted to see it again. She wondered how much of the ink would have to be in her skin before it tainted her. Surely the whole design would be necessary to control her, but how much ink to scar her forever?

Just a dot, she felt certain.

The needle touched her, and she flinched.

"Don't move," Rachael said.

It stung, just as she had promised. But Sammi clenched her jaw and watched as the artist began to do her work. As Dante had, she began with the central circle, the hollow at the core of the world. Her hand was sure and careful. When she had airbrushed the same design onto Sammi's skin,

Rachael had not taken it completely seriously. It was temporary, after all. But Sammi could see that this time, she was far more careful.

Sammi laid her head back. As Rachael worked, she watched the others watching her. Zak looked full of regret, maybe wishing he had never gone along with this. Katsuko wore a sneer. T.Q. had a kind of lazy smile on her face that made Sammi think she might succumb at any moment to the pills that had been powdered and mixed with too much sugar in her iced tea.

But T.Q. only watched.

Long minutes passed. Before Sammi knew it, she glanced down and saw that Rachael had done the outline of the outer circle and begun to fill in the heavy black between inner and outer. Another ten minutes and she would begin the waves that swept up from the circle, from the wheel.

And then what? Sammi asked herself.

A terrible understanding settled upon her heart. *This isn't going to work.* She would have to call a halt to it. The girls would know she had lied to them. Then they would be lost to her forever. Dante would continue to destroy their lives, to tear them apart, to be master of their souls. And there was no telling what they might do to her this time.

Almost in the same moment as this realization, Sammi glanced over at T.Q. and saw the redhead's eyelids flutter. She swayed a bit.

Then T.Q.'s knees buckled and she went down hard, reaching out to try to catch herself but instead crashing into Zak before collapsing in a sprawl of long limbs on the floor.

Zak swore, backing away from her. Rachael started to stand, holding the tattoo needle up as she turned to stare.

"T.Q.!" Katsuko called, and dropped to her knees beside the muttering, disoriented girl.

Sammi started to sit up.

Katsuko whipped around to stare at her, sudden understanding etched upon her face with an ugly hatred.

"You—" she started.

Sammi grabbed the metal tray Rachael had been using, knocking its contents to the floor, and swung it as hard as she could. Katsuko tried to turn and managed to get an arm up in time to partially deflect the blow. The tray struck her in the head.

Sammi fell on her then, driving her to the floor on her side. She swung the tray a second time, and a third, and this time Katsuko couldn't reach to interfere.

The metal thudded against her skull.

16

Something had snapped inside Sammi. She screamed a torrent of verbal abuse at Katsuko as she hit her. The girl tried to buck her off. Sammi hit her in the face with the metal tray. Katsuko twisted under her, throwing her off balance, and struck her across the temple with a backhand.

"Sammi, stop!" Zak shouted.

Rachael tried to pull her off Katsuko, but Sammi shook free and tried to hit her again with the tray. Her plan would be ruined if Katsuko left right now, if she knew what Sammi had done to T.Q.

Zak grabbed Sammi's wrists, and Rachael tugged the tray out of her hands. Panic shot through her.

"No!"

"Bitch! I'll kill you!" Katsuko screamed, and again she bucked.

Sammi spilled off her, dull pain flaring in her ribs.

Scrambling, she got to her feet, but by then Katsuko had risen. Zak reached for her, trying to prevent the vengeance that burned in her eyes. Katsuko went to kick him in the balls. When he twisted to avoid the attack, she grabbed his hair in one hand and scratched his face with the other, drawing blood. Zak roared with pain and lashed out, knocking her away.

But Katsuko had wanted that.

She spun toward Sammi.

"Quit it! Just stop! You guys are insane!" Rachael screamed.

Katsuko lunged at Sammi, slammed into her, and took her to the ground. Her nose bled from the blow Sammi had delivered to her face with the metal tray. A small rivulet of blood dripped from her upper lip, and a drop fell onto Sammi's cheek.

She tried to stop the descending fist. Katsuko aimed for her face, where her cracked cheekbone was still healing. Sammi twisted, and the blow struck the other side of her face. Pain flared in her ribs. She tried to buck Katsuko off her, but though she must have weighed thirty pounds more, the petite girl was much stronger.

Sammi punched her in the face with the cast on her left hand. She struck Katsuko's already bleeding nose. Still Katsuko wouldn't let go. With a powerful hand she gripped Sammi's throat and began to squeeze, cutting off her air.

"Get off of her, you crazy bitch!" Zak snarled.

He picked Katsuko up with both hands. When the girl tried to attack him again, he threw her across the room.

Katsuko pinwheeled her arms but couldn't keep herself from crashing into the wall. A whole shelf of knickknacks and a small painting fell to the floor with a crash.

Sammi spared one glance toward T.Q., who tried to rise from the floor, eyes heavily lidded, but collapsed as though she'd had far too much to drink.

"Stay there!" Zak screamed at Katsuko, pointing down at where she crouched on the floor amid the rubble of knickknacks. Then he spun on Sammi. "Have you totally lost your mind?"

Sammi saw Katsuko move. "Zak, watch her!"

Zak started to turn. He would have been too late if Rachael hadn't been there. She grabbed Katsuko's arm, yanking her back. Katsuko pulled herself free, but by then Zak was ready. He grabbed her by the wrists, tripped her, and drove her down to the wood floor, sitting astride her to pin her in place.

"Just stop!" he shouted.

Sammi started toward them and Zak whirled around. "Goddamn it, Samantha, you too! Just stay right there."

Katsuko writhed beneath him, snarling and panting like an animal, her eyes beginning to roll up in her head.

"What the hell is wrong with you?" Zak screamed into her face.

But Rachael's expression had gone slack and pale. She stared at Katsuko, and as Sammi moved a little nearer, she saw what had captivated Rachael's attention. The girl's shirt had ridden up, exposing her belly.

"Zak," Rachael almost whispered.

A wave of icy cold swept through the tattoo shop. Zak looked at Rachael, saw her expression, then looked down at Katsuko's bared stomach. Neither of them would have seen anything like it before, but Sammi had. Once.

The black tendrils of ink that made up the spreading poison of her tattoo covered her belly like intricate calligraphy. But as they all stared, and as Katsuko spat at Zak, the tattoo vines were moving beneath her skin, slowly twisting like a basket of vipers.

"Holy shit!" Zak shouted, and he started to get up.

"Don't let her go!" Rachael snapped.

Zak looked at her and nodded, gone quite pale himself. Both of them turned to look at Sammi.

"You better tell us what's going on here now, Sam. Don't leave anything out. And you better start with what the hell you did to the redhead over there," Zak said, nodding toward the unconscious T.Q.

Sammi took a breath, forcing herself not to think about the setbacks she might have suffered because of her struggle with Katsuko. As unnerving as it was to see the tattoos moving and to see Katsuko go almost mindlessly feral, it had given her the opening she needed.

This could still work.

"I drugged her. I powdered four of the painkillers I had left over from the hospital."

"Oh my God," Rachael whispered.

"I had to," Sammi said, staring at her. "And I'll tell you the story, starting right now. But while we're talking, there's something you've got to do."

"What's that?" Zak asked, incredulous.

"Rachael needs to destroy their tattoos. Katsuko's first, then T.Q.'s."

"Why?"

"Are you blind?" Sammi asked. She pointed at Katsuko's exposed stomach. "Have a look. Use that ink. The stuff that they brought with them. If I'm right, that'll work better. Go to the center of the tattoo, the original tattoo, before it started to grow. Fill in the hollow. Color in around it, where the waves were—where those lines start. I don't care if it's just a blotch or a square or whatever. Just do it. You've got to ruin the original design."

Zak and Rachael stared at her.

Katsuko had begun to hyperventilate and to make a low keening noise with every swift breath. Her eyes were focused now, though, and she glared at Sammi with a hatred that made her recoil. Being looked at that way made her feel hideous, but one look at the twisted ugliness that Katsuko's face had become also served to remind her why she had done all of this.

"Why?" Rachael repeated. "You want me to do this, Sammi, you have to tell me why."

Sammi pointed at Katsuko's belly. The black vines of the tattoo had almost completely stopped writhing. It might have just been ink on the skin now. But it was impossible to miss that those lines were not entirely still. One would shift, just slightly, and then another, as though they were attempting to go unnoticed.

"That's why."

"Sammi—" Zak started.

"Listen to me. There's this guy, Dante. You heard them talk about him. That's his ink. He's the one who did the tattoos. He's done something to them, don't you get it? With the tattoos. He's controlling them. Maybe you think that sounds crazy, but your own eyes aren't lying to you. I'm not asking you to kill her or even hurt her. Just blot out that tattoo, using that ink—I think that's important, because if they brought it for you to use on me, it's got to be a part of the . . ."

"The what?" Rachael asked.

"The spell," Zak said.

Frowning, Rachael turned to look at him. Sammi stared.

"Not you too," Rachael said.

Zak took a breath and let it out. "I read about something like this. I did this paper on African tribal magic. Tattoos were a part of it."

"So what did you learn?"

He laughed. "Not a lot. I got a C. But there was something about ritual tattoos. And Sammi's right. Whatever this is, the ink on this chick is severely not normal."

Rachael looked from one to the other, over at T.Q., then back at Zak. "I am so going to jail."

Sammi started toward her. "Rachael—"

But the diminutive tattooist held up a hand. "Just get her on the table, the two of you. And try not to trash any more of my place than you already have."

Rachael shot a dark look at Sammi. "And you. Talk."

So Sammi talked. She and Rachael stripped off Katsuko's pants and Sammi lay across her legs while Zak pinned her shoulders. And Sammi talked. She told them the story from beginning to end, and from time to time she glanced up and saw the horror in their eyes. If they hadn't seen evidence for themselves, she knew they would never have believed her, even having been witness to the way Letty, Caryn, T.Q., and Katsuko had beaten Las Reinas in a fight and then stomped the crap out of Sammi.

But they'd seen it. They could never unsee it. They had to believe her.

"Rachael?" Zak said when Sammi had finished.

But his girlfriend didn't raise her head from her work. She had started, as Sammi suggested, by filling in the hole at the center of the tattoo—the hollow in the world, Dante had called it, though surely it served some other purpose. Then Rachael had moved out from there, using that ink to broaden the central circle, working out toward what would have been the edges of the original tattoo.

"I can't—" Rachael said.

"Can't what?" Zak asked.

"I can't think about it."

She lifted the needle from Katsuko's skin. Half the time they'd had to wait for pauses in her cursing and spitting and bucking for Sammi to continue her story and for Rachael to continue eradicating Dante's original design. The work went slowly and the tattoo needle moved a lot. The work Rachael had been doing would not be pretty. There were lines where the ink had striped Katsuko's skin when she had tried to twist away.

"What do you mean?" Sammi asked.

Rachael looked up at Zak. "I'm afraid. I don't want to think about it. I just want to get it done. Mostly, I'm afraid it won't work, because then . . . what happens to us? What's this guy going to do?"

She shook her head and looked over at where T.Q. lay mumbling blearily on the floor, disoriented but no longer unconscious. Sammi had planned for her to be the first to have the tattoo destroyed, and that would have been so much easier. But Katsuko hadn't left her any choice.

Rachael glanced at Sammi. "I mean, what even makes you think this will work? We don't have enough ink to cover her whole body, and if the tattoos are spreading . . ." She shrugged. "You don't know anything. You're totally guessing. Why didn't you take that book from this Dante guy's place, figure out what the hell he did to them?"

"Do I look like some kind of witch to you? What the hell do I know about this stuff? I had to get out of there, and I didn't want him to know it was me. That grimoire or whatever wasn't even in English."

"So this is all just a guess!" Rachael said.

"What do you want from me?" Sammi cried. "I'm sorry I got you into this, but I didn't know what else to do. You saw what he did to them. You saw what *they* did to *me*."

Zak lifted one arm to reach for Rachael and Katsuko grunted, tried to get up. He forced her back down, cursing at her. Then he glanced at Rachael.

"Just get it done. I get what Sammi's saying and I know you do, too. If the design's the thing, if it's such a part of this guy's magic, then screwing it up is the only thing I can think of. If you've got a better idea, Rach, I'd love to hear it."

Rachael's hand shook as she lowered the needle again.

A few minutes later, Sammi noticed that the twisted black lines on Katsuko's body had stopped moving entirely. She frowned, staring at them, waiting for movement, but there was none.

Then she saw the tears sliding from the corners of Katsuko's eyes and the wretched humiliation on her face.

"Oh my God," Sammi whispered.

Rachael set down the needle. Zak stepped back and Rachael got up, sliding into his arms. They stared at the girl on the table, holding each other. Rachael shook a bit, fear and relief and this final bit of evidence overwhelming her.

"It's all true," she said.

Zak said nothing, but Sammi saw the terrible truth of those words settle on him. They had been frantic before. Now the reality had created a new fear in them.

"Katsuko," Sammi said. She sat on the edge of the table.

Katsuko pulled her legs up into an almost fetal position, lying on her side. She began to sob softly and Sammi lay across her, putting her arms around the girl.

"I'm sorry. I'm so sorry," Katsuko whispered.

Sammi's heart broke for her, the horror of it coming to her all at once. What must it have been like to be a passenger in her own body, able to see out through her own eyes,

251

aware of the things that her puppeteer had done to her body?

"You'll be all right," Sammi said. "We'll all be okay, now."

"You don't know what I did. What I did, Sammi," Katsuko whispered.

She opened her eyes, gaze full of anguish, and Sammi shook with relief to see the real Katsuko in those eyes. People always said that eyes were windows to the soul. Sammi held Katsuko close again.

"It doesn't matter. We'll help the other girls now. Then we'll all be together again."

"And we'll make the son of a bitch pay?" Katsuko asked, her voice thick with emotion.

Sammi scowled in disgust. "Oh yeah. Yes we will."

Somewhere inside Skin Colors a clock ticked the seconds away. Sammi let the sound become white noise, focusing instead on the softer, more intimate whispers and moans that came from deep inside Katsuko. She cradled the girl in her arms, sitting on the floor of the tattoo shop, just holding Katsuko against her. The ugly behavior Sammi had seen had been only a fraction of the horrors the girl had performed with Dante pulling her strings, and more of those came out with every passing moment, as though Sammi had become her confessor. Katsuko and the others had caught up to girls in dark alleys and beaten and violated them. They had made whores of themselves for Dante's amusement, debased themselves in ways that made

Sammi physically ill, and descended into a maelstrom of drug use that would have intimidated the biggest coke fiend at Covington High.

All Sammi could do was hold Katsuko and tell her none of it had been her fault, that she had to treat it like a nightmare from which she'd awoken.

But the nightmare had not really ended. All through the long minutes when Sammi held the traumatized Katsuko, Rachael worked to eradicate the tattoo on the back of T.Q.'s neck. Zak had lifted the tall redhead from the floor. Already she had started to awaken, but she remained too disoriented and unable to function to fight him.

Sammi heard the hushed mutterings of Rachael and Zak. T.Q.'s tattoo had spread its poison vines in whorls and swirls down the girl's back and over her collarbones and down onto her chest as well. The dark lines etched upon Katsuko's skin had begun to fade, and Sammi expected that T.Q.'s would do the same, once the tattoo had been blotted out.

"I'm so sorry," Katsuko said.

Sammi pulled back from their embrace and held her shoulders. Katsuko's dark eyes were wide. Despite the sorrow in those eyes, Sammi felt so much hope at seeing them.

"You keep saying that. You don't need to. Please."

Katsuko took a breath and nodded. She seemed to be coming out of her shock somewhat as she glanced around the shop, ending on the table where Rachael continued working with the tattoo needle on the back of T.Q.'s neck. The machine whirred.

"What about the others?" Katsuko asked.

"What?" Zak asked, turning toward her.

But Katsuko wasn't ready to talk to him. She turned to Sammi. "Letty and Caryn. What about them? How are we going to save them?"

"The same way," Sammi said, smiling. "There'll be five of us, now. We'll get them down here together and we'll hold them down if we have to."

Katsuko nodded thoughtfully. She winced and reached up to touch her swollen, blood-encrusted nose.

"Sorry about that," Sammi said.

"I had it coming."

Sammi smiled at her, and Katsuko managed a thin, tired smile in return.

"What's she saying?" Zak asked.

At first Sammi thought he meant Katsuko, but when she glanced up she saw Zak staring at T.Q. The redhead had her face down on the padded table and mumbled something muffled by the padding.

Rachael paused and pulled back the tattoo needle. T.Q. felt the release of pressure and her head lolled to one side. Her bleary gaze locked on Sammi immediately. Though she spoke as though in a trance, those eyes never wavered.

"Coming," she said. "He's coming. Riding fast."

Sammi froze, staring at her. Abruptly she rose, pulling Katsuko to her feet and glancing quickly at the front door of the shop.

"Are you almost done?" she asked Rachael.

The diminutive artist shrugged. "Kind of hard to tell, but I think so."

"Hurry."

Zak raised both hands. "Um, hello? What was that? She's totally whacked on painkillers. It's gibberish—"

"No," Katsuko said. "I don't think so."

"Neither do I." Sammi rushed to the heavy drapes that hung across the front windows and peeked outside. A car passed, headlights washing over the shadowed pavement, but it did not even pause.

"What are you saying?" Rachael asked.

"I'm saying I think maybe when you cut the strings, the guy working the puppets is gonna notice," Sammi said. Then she lowered her voice to a whisper. "I think he felt it."

Zak swore, then tapped the table next to T.Q. "Rach, hurry up, honey."

Rachael nodded. The tattoo needle whirred softly as she got back to work. A terrible quiet descended upon them. Zak and Sammi and Katsuko glanced back and forth at one another and at the front of the shop. Sammi opened the door into the storage room so she had a clear view of the back door.

"Maybe you should make sure it's locked," Katsuko said.

"I'll check the front," Zak said.

Sammi went into the storage room and tried the back door. The knob had a lock and there was a deadbolt as well. She tested it and found it secure. As she turned, her eye caught something in the corner next to a metal shelf full of art books and inkpots. Rachael kept shovels here for the wintertime. On the ground in front of the shovels was a gigantic bucket of ice melt. One shovel was for snow, but the other was a long garden tool with a square metal blade. Sammi figured Rachael must have used it for chopping ice.

When she went back into the studio, she had the shovel in hand. Rachael didn't even look up from working on destroying T.Q.'s tattoo, but Zak's eyes widened. Katsuko gave a small nod.

"Sammi?" a soft voice said.

The whir of the tattoo needle stopped. Rachael pulled back and they all looked at T.Q. Again she let her head loll to one side, but this time her expression had changed. Her eyes were slitted and her face contorted with such wretched sadness that for the first time, she looked ugly.

"T.Q.? Is that you?" Sammi asked.

"Oh my God," the girl mumbled, her words slurred. "Oh my God."

She managed to bring one hand up to cover her face. Katsuko went and sat beside her, talking softly and stroking her hair. Rachael paused for a moment and then set down the tattoo needle.

Sammi would have spoken, would have offered gratitude and apologies to Zak and Rachael and comfort to T.Q. But before she could utter a word, the whole shop trembled with the rising thunder of a passing motorcycle. Its engine roared, revving, and then it quieted to an idle for a moment before cutting out.

Katsuko and Sammi exchanged a glance.

"Is that him?" Zak asked.

Sammi looked at Rachael. "Call the police."

She didn't hesitate. Running to the small reception desk at the front, she picked up the phone and dialed. As frightened as she was, Rachael didn't so much as tremble. None of this had anything to do with her. Not once had she tried to blame Sammi for dragging her into it. Now Sammi wished she could have gotten Rachael and Zak out of here before trouble arrived, but fate had not worked out that way. Desperation had driven her, and now it was too late to make other plans.

"Hello?" Rachael said, voice full of hope. Then she frowned. "Hello?" She dropped the phone into the cradle and turned to stare at Zak, only at Zak. For the first time, Sammi really saw the love between them—in their fear for one another.

"The line went dead," Rachael said.

Sammi pulled out her cell phone and flipped it open. "I've got no service."

"What, he cut the line?" Zak asked.

"And blocked the cell signal? I don't think so," Katsuko said, voice full of loathing. "It's nothing like that."

"Magic," T.Q. muttered from the table. "It's magic."

The shop seemed to shrink around them. Sammi felt as if the air had been sucked out of the place. They all stared at each other, trying to figure out what to do next.

"We should get the hell out of here," Zak said, crossing to Rachael and taking her hand.

Sammi shook her head. "It's too late for that."

Zak spun on her. "He's just one guy!"

"He won't be alone," Katsuko said.

Dread scurried like spiders down Sammi's spine. No, Dante wouldn't be alone. But what kind of magic might he really be capable of? So far it had all had to do with the tattoos, with symbols. Even in the Polaroids she'd seen at his studio, his dabbling in the occult all seemed to revolve around designs or runes or whatever the hell they were. He wasn't some immortal sorcerer, just a sick bastard with a fetish for humiliating teenage girls. If Sammi had to bet on it—and she did—she'd be willing to wager that Dante could bleed.

Gripping the shovel, she turned to Zak.

"Okay, you're right. Let's go. If we have to fight, better off in the street. Someone will hear. A car will go by. Someone will call the cops."

Katsuko went to the padded table. She shook T.Q., whose eyes opened blearily.

"Hey. We've got to move, T. Can you get up?"

T.Q. took a deep breath. "I don't know."

Katsuko whispered, "Dante's here."

The words made T.Q. flinch, but the redhead started trying to push herself up into a sitting position. Katsuko helped her.

"I just want to go back," T.Q. mumbled. "Back to before."

We all do, Sammi thought. *We all do.*

T.Q. started to slump against Katsuko, who gave her a

sharp slap to her face. For a few seconds, T.Q.'s gaze became perfectly clear. She slid off the table. Katsuko shot Sammi an expectant look.

Taking the cue, Sammi started for the front door.

Then faltered.

She'd heard a noise, a kind of squeak against the plate-glass window at the front of the shop. The heavy drapes hid the window from them, but the sound continued, increasing in volume and speed. Something dragged wetly on the glass, as though someone were cleaning it.

"He's just a guy," Katsuko spat. "Just a guy with a few nasty tricks. He's not some friggin' master sorcerer. He's a sleazy son of a bitch who found a new way to get what he wanted."

But they all stared at the drapes, listening to that scraping, squeaking noise, and no one took another step.

The tattoo machine died. The lightbulb in an antique lamp popped, startling them all. One by one, the lights went out, all except for the crystal fixture hanging from the ceiling, throwing its shadows around. When Sammi spun to look at Rachael and Zak, she thought what she saw on Rachael's face was just another shadow.

She wished it were shadow.

Blood dripped from Rachael's nostrils. As Sammi stared at her, and as Rachael reached up to touch the warm red on her lips, blood began to slip from the corners of her eyes like scarlet tears.

Rachael screamed.

"Rach!" Zak yelled. "Oh my God, Rach!"

But even as Zak reached for her, he froze, then touched one hand to his right ear, fingers coming away covered in his own blood. Sammi watched as streaks of blood began to run from his eyes and nostrils as well. She glanced over at Katsuko and T.Q. and they were bleeding, too, faces striped crimson.

Then Sammi tasted the copper tang of blood on her own lips.

"What's he doing to us?" Rachael cried.

T.Q. slid to the floor. Katsuko shouted in pain and reached up to clutch both sides of her head. Sammi felt it a moment later, a skull-crushing migraine that staggered her and made her drop the shovel to the floor with a clang. Rachael and Zak leaned on one another.

"We've gotta get out of here!" Zak groaned, fighting the pain that afflicted them all.

But Katsuko tried to pull T.Q. up and could not, bent over with pain herself. Rachael began to wipe her hands all over her clothes, smearing her own blood on her shirt and pants, whispering what might have been prayers.

The squeaking against the glass continued.

Sammi knew she would collapse in a moment. With the strength going out of her legs, she staggered to the front of the shop and managed to bunch up the drapes in her fists.

She threw the drapes open.

Dante stood grinning at her on the other side of the plate-glass window. With his bare hands, he continued painting an intricate design on the window with numbers and arcane symbols surrounding it.

His palms were bleeding. He drew the hex upon the glass in his own blood.

Behind him, on the sidewalk, Letty and Caryn stood with lifeless, doll faces and dull, blank eyes, each with a long carving knife in one hand. The blades glinted in the light from the lantern in front of the shop.

Sammi fell to her knees in front of the window, stomach convulsing, and threw up blood.

Dante could not control her.

So he was killing her.

17

Sammi clutched her hands to the sides of her head, wishing she could alleviate the pressure. She choked on the blood running down the back of her throat. *Is that from my brain? Is it bleeding?* Her nostrils were flooded with blood, making it harder to breathe. She drew her sleeve across her nose, soaking the fabric red.

She blinked, blood sticking to her eyelashes, gumming them up, covering her eyes with a scarlet webbing. Sammi peered at the window, where Dante traced a labyrinthine circle in his own blood. A dabbler. He couldn't shoot fire out of his hands or anything like that. He wasn't Merlin. Those symbols—they were his magic. That and more. But he could be fought. He could bleed.

If she could ever get to him. The hex he'd put on them with the blood on the window would kill her before she got the chance. Unless she did something about it.

Katsuko cried out and fell to the floor, curled into a fetal ball. Zak railed against Dante, fury and pain merging on his face, trying to get up and stagger to the window—to attack him—only to fall again with a new burst of pain that sent blood spurting from his nose. T.Q. lay on her side on the padded table, bleeding and moaning. Rachael sat on the floor wiping at the blood on her face over and over and screaming.

Only Sammi was close enough.

She let the pain take her down to the floor, tumbling backward and turning onto her side. The pressure radiated down her shoulders now, and when she looked at her hands through the veil of blood over her eyes, she saw that fresh crimson had begun to leak out from beneath her fingernails. They couldn't be losing this much blood. But magic thrived on the impossible.

With a shout of pain she thrust out her right arm and grabbed the shovel she had dropped. Dragging it toward her, she drove herself along the floor, sliding on the wood, until she bumped against the wall underneath the plate-glass window.

Seething with pain, breath coming in ragged gasps, she forced herself to stand. A fresh burst of agony struck her, clamping around her skull and squeezing. Sammi screamed.

She cocked the shovel back awkwardly, the unbroken fingers of her left hand barely able to grip the wood, and swung it as hard as she could.

At the last instant, Dante's eyes widened.

The glass shattered, tiny shards raining down and enormous guillotines collapsing out onto the sidewalk.

The pain ceased. Rage burned its way up through Sammi, and she wiped as much of the blood from her eyes as she could. Behind her she heard Katsuko and Rachael muttering their relief. Zak choked a moment, spat a huge clot of blood onto the floor, and started for the window, staring at Dante.

"You're dead, asshole."

Dante had never stopped smiling. "Letty. Caryn. Kill them."

"No!" Sammi shouted.

She cocked the shovel back again, ready to cave in Dante's face. But Letty and Caryn were fast. Brandishing those gleaming kitchen knives, they rushed past the tattooist and leaped in through the shattered window. One hanging, jagged triangle of glass raked Letty's shoulder and she didn't even flinch. Whatever kind of awareness they'd had while they were on Dante's leash, it had been taken away. He was in complete control now.

Grinning, Letty ran at Zak. He lunged for her at the same time. She swung the knife, slashing his left hand, but he grabbed her around the throat and they went down in a tangle on the floor, and Sammi saw no more. All of that she had caught in only a glimpse.

Caryn came at her. Sammi stood her ground, shovel in both hands. Instead of swinging it, she drove the handle into Caryn's gut. The attack staggered the girl and Caryn slipped in the blood that coated the floor—Sammi's blood—and went down.

"I'm sorry," Sammi said, only loud enough to hear it herself.

Behind her, Rachael screamed, but Sammi couldn't afford any distraction. Katsuko and Zak were there. They would have to fend for themselves.

She brought the shovel down on Caryn's wrist. With a grunt, she dropped the knife. Sammi let the shovel fall, dived for the knife, and scrambled onto Caryn's back.

Caryn tried to escape her, tried to throw her off just as Katsuko had done. But Sammi knew that the cost of losing this fight would be her own life, as well as the lives of all of her friends. If Sammi let Caryn win, it would kill them both.

She slammed Caryn's face against the bloody floor, dazing her. Gripping the knife, she slit the back of Caryn's shirt and tore it open. The black tendrils of the tattoo writhed and twisted on the girl's deep brown skin. Like the others, they had no substance. The tattoos did not come off Caryn's body or even seem to be moving beneath her skin, but instead glided over her flesh in almost hallucinatory fashion.

Sammi pushed the tip of the knife into the skin of Caryn's shoulder blade. Blood welled up and ran down the center of her back. Entranced by Dante's control, Caryn did not even cry out. Sammi bent the knife and began to slice.

Dante screamed a torrent of filth at her, but Sammi

didn't even look at him. She worked fast, slicing into Caryn's skin as though she were peeling an apple. When the girl bucked, Sammi pressed her cast against the back of her head and slammed her skull against the floor again. With the working fingers of her left hand she pulled up the flap of skin she'd already sliced off, then slid the knife through and cut the original tattoo away completely.

Only then did Caryn scream in pain. Blood flowed, but she was free. Sammi scrambled back away from her, knife in hand, and Caryn rose, sobbing in anguish, saying over and over that she was sorry.

"Zak!" Rachael cried.

From the corner of her eye, Sammi saw that Dante had not moved. Then she turned with Caryn—whose shirt hung in rags from one shoulder—and they both saw Rachael leap up onto Letty's back.

Zak lay at Letty's feet clutching a stab wound in his abdomen. His hands were bloody, but there was no telling whose blood it was and how much came from him.

"Letty, stop!" Katsuko shouted. "It's him, not you! Think! I know you're in there!"

As Rachael choked her, Letty seemed about to reach back with the knife and stab her. Katsuko tried to rush at Letty then, but she slashed the blade through the air, keeping Katsuko back, then let Rachael drag her backward until she crashed into the wall, slamming Rachael into the wood and forcing her to let go.

Rachael fell in a sprawl on the floor.

"Samantha Holland," Dante called from beyond that shattered window, his voice low and insinuating.

Letty went after T.Q. The redhead had managed to get to her feet, leaning against the padded table, but still in the depths of her Percocet stupor, she would have no chance to defend herself. Just staying conscious was effort enough.

Katsuko grabbed Letty's wrist and they struggled, keeping the knife away from T.Q.

Caryn moved silently, adrenaline and fury canceling out the pain of the wound Sammi had sliced into her back. She slammed into Letty, knocking Katsuko aside and driving Letty right over the top of the padded table. In a twist of limbs they spilled over the table and onto the ground on the other side.

"Sammi," Dante said.

And only then did Sammi wonder if anyone else could hear him. She turned and looked at the tattooist, at the son of a bitch who had torn her life apart, and still he wore that smile.

"You ruined all my fun," Dante said. "I'll go soon. But not until you've suffered enough."

He produced a piece of blue chalk and then dropped out of sight. She could hear the sound of the chalk on the sidewalk, and knew he had begun some new magic, some hex that would cost them all even more blood and pain and other precious things.

Sammi tossed her sweaty, blood-streaked hair from her eyes. "I haven't suffered enough?"

Something snapped inside her. She moved with a swiftness she had never known she possessed, dropping down to pick up the long garden shovel. Dante barely had time to look up from his blue-chalk scrawl before she swung the shovel. The square metal blade hit him in the side of the head with a crack that only made her want to hurt him more. Whatever pain her fractured ribs and cheek might cause her, she could feel none of it now, taken over by terror and rage.

Scrambling away, he tried to rise.

Sammi stepped out through the window and swung the shovel again. Dante turned and took the blow against his back, but he reached out and grasped the base of the handle, and with a sneer he tore the shovel from her hands.

"You hurt me!"

He jumped on her, drove her down to the sidewalk with the wooden handle across her throat. Sammi hit her head on the concrete. The wood pressed down on her, and she had to use both good hand and cast to keep him from crushing her windpipe with it. But Dante had weight and muscle on her.

He would kill her.

"That's not the way it works," he whispered, lowering his head so he could whisper in her ear. He pulled back and looked into her eyes. "I'm the one who does the hurting. It's my show. All the girls perform for me, Samantha."

She spat in his face.

He reared back and slapped her, then grabbed the

shovel again before she could try to get up. Dante came in close again and whispered in revolting intimacy.

"Show some respect, bitch, or I'll change my mind. I won't kill you. And trust me, for an uptight little thing like you, living would be much worse. You'd be just as much a slut as the rest of them. Peel back the layers on you girls and that's what you find inside, the sweet candy surprise underneath the good girl—"

Sammi drove her head up, slamming her forehead into his nose.

Dante went off balance, and she pushed the shovel handle away with both hands, driving him back. He sat too far forward on her torso, which left her legs free. She threw both legs up, wrapped them around his head, and pulled him off her. Using that momentum, she scrambled to get on top of him.

He punched her in the chest. A spike of pain shot through her from her fractured ribs.

Sammi grabbed him by the throat, dug in her fingernails, and ripped furrows in his flesh. If she could have torn his throat out with her bare hands, she would have. Dante screamed like a little girl, and Sammi liked that sound very much. He deserved that kind of pain, and far worse.

Another scream rose above his, a keening wail of total anguish and horror that made Sammi freeze with dread. A terrible certainty struck her, but she would not acknowledge it.

She sprang off Dante, picked up the shovel, and swung

it at his head again. The edge of the blade tore his cheek, and he slumped to the pavement.

Sammi stepped back into the shop.

The scene she found there made her knees weaken. She began to shake her head slowly back and forth, and for a moment her mind would not function, her lips could not speak words. Dante had destroyed her life, but she had meant to take it back, to rebuild it and to save the girls—these girls she loved—from the abhorrent things he had done to them. Sammi had told herself that she could undo the damage.

No more.

At the back of the shop, Letty stood behind Caryn with the bloody knife in her hand. The blade was slick with blood. Caryn's head lolled back, revealing a wide, grinning slash in her throat. Blood streamed down her chest.

Katsuko stood half a dozen feet away, one hand clamped over a hideous gash on her chest. Her face had gone slack and tears streaked the blood on her face.

Zak lay on the floor near the reception desk, Rachael pressing both hands to a stab wound in his stomach. Both of them stared in shock at Letty, even as Caryn slid to the ground, dying in front of their eyes.

Propped on the floor, disoriented and swaying, T.Q. stared at them, murmuring, "No, no, no" over and over.

Dante's voice carried through the room, a gleeful whisper.

"Well done, Letty," the magician said. "Now it's time for the knife to find your heart."

Sammi spun to see him standing silhouetted against the lantern light out on the street, framed in the jagged jaws of the broken window. His face had become a mask of blood.

Then the words sank in.

"No!" Sammi shouted, running toward Letty.

Katsuko moved quicker. She grabbed hold of Letty's arm, but the petite girl did not have the strength to stop her. Letty plunged the knife into her own chest, pulled it out and tried again to stab it into her heart. Sammi reached her, then, and as Letty fell to the floor, she and Katsuko wrested the knife away from her.

"Oh no," T.Q. said, sobbing. "Oh no, Letty. Caryn. No, no."

Sammi stared at Caryn's dull, lifeless eyes. Her cheek lay in a widening pool of blood that soaked and matted her hair.

Katsuko bent over Letty's twitching body, weeping from somewhere deep in her soul, and pressed both hands against the wound in her chest. Sammi pulled Letty's head into her lap and stroked her face.

She glanced toward the window, but Dante had vanished.

Outside, a motorcycle engine roared to life, then began to diminish into the distance.

Sammi slipped her cell phone from her pocket. This time, when she flipped it open, she had service again. She dialed 911, and as she lifted the phone to her ear, she began to shake uncontrollably. The stink of blood filled the shop, and somehow she knew it would linger always in her mind.

EPILOGUE

It rained on the day they buried Caryn Adams. A tent had been placed over the gravesite and mourners gathered beneath it. The floral arrangements gathered around the casket produced a sickly sweet aroma that seemed to saturate each drop of moisture in the air. Sammi could taste it on her tears. She wept silently as the priest read over Caryn's grave.

Mr. and Mrs. Adams had framed several of their daughter's most beautiful dress designs and they stood—along with an enlarged photograph of their smiling daughter, her eyes sparkling—on easels around the edges of the tent. They wanted everyone to know that their loss had also been the world's loss. Sammi agreed.

Caryn would never drag her into another art studio down on Washington Street, but she had a feeling that she would find herself wandering into them on her own. She would stare too long at antique paintings and little artifacts handmade by local artists, and now and again when she had money, perhaps she would buy one.

At the wake, the casket had been closed.

Sammi stood just beneath the tent, barely out of the rain. It pelted the canvas so loudly that she could hardly make out the priest's words. Not that it mattered. A hollow ache filled her and she wouldn't have been able to really listen. Her ribs had been injured all over again and she'd set back the healing of her fingers a couple of weeks. Other than that, physically she would be fine. But the numbness of her spirit would take longer to heal.

Her mother and father were both in the gathering, sharing a black umbrella out in the rain at the edge of the crowd. Sammi did not bother looking around for them. They would be waiting when this all came to an end, and then they could all stop pretending to still be a family.

Sammi felt a hand touch her own, fingers twining in hers, and she looked up at T.Q. She'd tied her red hair back into a ponytail, perhaps thinking even that bit of brightness too much for such a black day. From the other side, Katsuko slid her arm around Sammi's waist. She laid her head on Sammi's shoulder. They cried together, the three of them.

Conspirators.

As they embraced, Sammi could not help feeling the new bond that they shared, a bond manufactured from lies. That terrifying night, amid the stink of the blood-soaked abattoir that Rachael's shop had become, they had waited for the police and ambulances to arrive, and Katsuko and Sammi had kept looking at one another.

"What if he knows she's still alive?" Katsuko had said, her voice a rasp, even as she put pressure on Letty's wounds to keep her from bleeding to death.

Sammi had said nothing. They all knew what had to be done. With Dante gone, the power worked fine. She had taken up the tattoo needle and the small plastic pot of that black ink, and she'd gone to work on Letty's tattoo. Rachael had shouted at her, but she refused to leave Zak's side and so could not stop them. Not that she would have tried. They were risking Letty's life by turning her on her side, even as Katsuko kept pressure on that wound. And Sammi did a terrible job with the needle. If she lived, Letty would have scars and a hideous blotch of a tattoo. But if the ambulance took her away and Dante still controlled her, could still make her his puppet, she might as well have been dead already.

Letty survived.

It had been a near thing, touch and go for the first forty-eight hours. The knife had missed her heart, but only barely. Had Katsuko not grabbed her arm, she would probably have been dead. Zak had also not yet been released from the hospital. The abdominal wound he'd received had led to a section of his intestine being removed, but he would survive.

Katsuko, Rachael, and Sammi had all been treated and released, but had remained in the hospital all that first night waiting for word about Letty and Zak. During that time, the police had questioned them all, and each of them—Rachael included—had stuck to the story. A madman named Dante had broken into the shop while Zak and his cousin, Sammi Holland, and her friends had been waiting for Rachael to close up so they could all go and get ice cream. Dante must have been on some kind of drugs because his speed and strength were shocking. He stabbed Zak first, taking out the one person who might have been able to stop him easily. He had two kitchen knives and he went crazy, stabbing Letty and slitting Caryn's throat.

The police believed it all, but Sammi thought they believed it mostly because there were so many other things they didn't understand. Why had they all started bleeding from their noses and eyes and ears? None of them knew.

But they found Dante's blood all over the broken shards of Rachael's plate-glass window, and when they went to the address the girls gave them, the police had found it burning. Sammi felt sure he would have taken his grimoires with him when he left, but she hoped that the Polaroids were all part of the scorched ruins.

A chilly wind blew across the cemetery, making the tent billow and flap and driving the rain sideways for a moment. November would not arrive for another week, but already Sammi could feel winter coming on. Autumn could be beautiful, but it was the season of the dead. Today she truly understood that for the first time.

With her left hand still in the cast, she reached up and used her unbroken fingers to wipe tears from her cheeks. Her eyes burned and her body felt heavy with exhaustion.

All through the wake and through the funeral and now here, awaiting Caryn's burial, she found herself staring again and again at the casket and wondering when it would be her time to lie within, to be lowered into the ground.

Sammi let out a sob and turned to bury her face in the crook of T.Q.'s shoulder. Katsuko rubbed her back, and the three of them embraced, taking strength from each other. They cried not just for the loss of Caryn, but for the loss of everything they had once meant to each other. Discussion of such truths had been taboo, but Sammi knew they all sensed it. T.Q., Katsuko, and Letty each had black blotches where those tattoos had been, and Sammi had a small circle with a hole in the center—a hole like the one in her heart. They had been branded, marked forever by the atrocities they had endured. The tattoos had bonded them, but not in the way they had hoped.

And Letty—the one they had all loved—would never recover from the knowledge of what she had done. Dante had murdered Caryn using Letty as his weapon, but Letty's hand had still held the knife. The secret would haunt them all.

The priest completed his words, and the mourners began to file past the casket. Following the example of so many others, Sammi plucked a single flower from the arrangements around the grave and dropped it on the casket as she passed. She touched the cold surface and whispered her final goodbye through a veil of tears.

She walked from beneath the tent with T.Q. and Katsuko, letting the rain mix with her tears, though already they had begun to subside. Anna Dubrowski spotted her in the departing crowd. She had come with a group of other students from Covington. Sammi nodded to her and forced a thin smile. Rachael Dubrowski had not attended the funeral. With Zak still in the hospital, her shop wrecked, and the police investigating whether she had been illegally tattooing minors, she had chosen to stay away. Sammi would go and talk to her, eventually, to see if Rachael could forgive her for Sammi's dragging her into the midst of such horror.

If not, Sammi would survive. She could survive almost anything, she had learned. One day soon, in a few weeks' time, she would be playing guitar again, and all of her sorrow could be expressed in music. Until then, she would carry it with her and keep it close.

"Your parents . . . ," T.Q. said.

Sammi looked up and saw them, standing together under that black umbrella, rain spilling off the edges.

"Nothing's changed. They're getting the divorce."

"Sorry," Katsuko said.

"Me too."

The three girls said their goodbyes and promised to call each other later. And they would, this time. But Sammi knew the time would come when such promises would not be kept. It was inevitable now. Blood and sorrow were what they shared now, and who wanted to be reminded of that?

Sammi went to her parents. They stood together, but would be leaving in separate cars. She kissed her father on the cheek.

"I love you, Dad. Thanks for coming."

He mumbled something in return, but Sammi wasn't listening. She kept walking, let her mother catch up to her, and they climbed into the car.

Linda Holland drove home in silence. Sammi knew her mother was giving her space, and she appreciated it. When she felt like talking, her mom would be there for her. Someday she might even tell her mother the story and explain the half-finished tattoo on her lower abdomen. Linda had been so terrified by coming so close to losing her daughter that she had not uttered a single word about the tattoo upon first seeing it. Sammi had told her they'd talk about it, soon, but she had a feeling her mother didn't really want to know.

As they turned up Washington Street, Sammi reached into the glove compartment for her cell phone. She'd left it in the car. Now she turned it on, and a soft jingle played.

She had a text message.

For a trembling moment, she feared that, somehow, it would be from Dante.

The text had come from Adam.

Saw the news, it said. *I should've listened to u. So sorry. Can we talk sometime?*

Sammi hesitated a moment, then deleted it.

Sometime, Sammi thought. *But not today. Maybe not ever.* Being with Adam would only remind her of all of this. If she was with him, she'd never forget it, just as with her friendship with the girls. She and Katsuko and T.Q. wouldn't stay close for very long. It hurt too much. They would drift apart now. Dante's poison had tainted everything, spread much further than even he could ever have known.

Dante was still out there, somewhere, hurt but alive. She wished she had finished the job she had started with him, ended it once and for all. What troubled her most was the fear that he would feel the same, that he would be back someday.

The shushing of the windshield wipers was broken by the distant, guttural roar of a motorcycle engine. The sound had come as though summoned by her thoughts, and she flinched. Sammi peered out the windows, searching the streets for the source of that familiar roar, but saw nothing.

Only the rain.

Christopher Golden is the award-winning, bestselling author of many novels for teens and young adults, including the thriller series Body of Evidence, honored by the New York Public Library and chosen as an ALA-YALSA Best Book for Young Adults, and the horror quartet Prowlers. His novels for adults include *The Myth Hunters*, *Wildwood Road*, and *The Boys Are Back in Town*. Golden cowrote the lavishly illustrated novel *Baltimore, or, The Steadfast Tin Soldier and the Vampire* with Mike Mignola. With Thomas E. Sniegoski, he is the coauthor of the dark fantasy series The Menagerie, as well as the young readers fantasy series OutCast and the comic-book miniseries Talent, both of which were recently acquired by Universal Pictures.

Golden was born and raised in Massachusetts, where he still lives with his family. There are more than eight million copies of his books in print. Please visit him at www.christophergolden .com.